BURDEKIN HEARTBEATS

Genre: Historical Fiction /Romance/Adventure

Cover design created by Cat Petersen

Cover photo - The Burdekin River – by Jan Callow

i

BURDEKIN HEARTBEATS

Published at Ingram Spark
by Elizabeth Rimmington. 2020.
Queensland
Australia

Copyright 2020 © Elizabeth Rimmington
National Library of Australia
State Library of Queensland

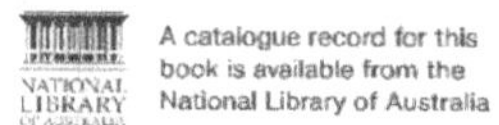
A catalogue record for this book is available from the National Library of Australia

ISBN
978-0-6485257-5-2 (Print)
978-0-6485257-6-9 (Epub)

Disclaimer

This novel is a work of fiction and the property, Emerald Flats, is a fictional block of land on the banks of the Burdekin River. While some of the names, characters and business places mentioned may have existed, their interaction with the story characters is pure fiction. All incidents are either the products of the author's imagination or have been used in a fictitious manner. The opinions expressed or beliefs held are those of the characters and should not be assumed to be the opinions or beliefs of the author.

BURDEKIN HEARTBEATS

Written by Elizabeth Rimmington.

Previous novels by Elizabeth Rimmington.

Shadow of the Northern Orchid   2019

Shadows on the Goldfield Track   2020

Elizabeth Rimmington

From a childhood in the Burdekin River District of North Queensland to a nursing career followed by a stint as a taxi driver, author of two previous novels, "Shadow of the Northern Orchid" and "Shadows on the Goldfield Track", Elizabeth Rimmington, delights her readers with a third novel, "Burdekin Heartbeats".

Now living in rural South East Queensland, Elizabeth continues to explore her fertile imagination to deliver further stories with which to thrill her audience.

Visit the author at www.elizabethrimmington.com.

Join the mailing list.

DEDICATION

To all the immigrants who, through determination, hard work and strength of character have built this country into one to be proud of.

While this novel is a work of fiction, many incidents within the story evolved from tales my forebears, pioneers of the times, related to the family.

APPRECIATION

To Caroline, Margaret and Natalie, all with the eyes of a hawk.

To Tom and Jan for their invaluable assistance.

To Anne for her assistance with research.

To the fellowship and support of good friends within the local writing groups.

To the staff at the Gympie Library for their support.

List of the main characters:

Michael Doolan: Uncle to the Doolan family and owner of Emerald Flats.
Shamus Doolan: Nephew of Michael Doolan. Husband to Mary and
                 father to Shauna and Lindsay.
Mary Doolan: Wife of Shamus Doolan. Mother to Shauna and Lindsay.
Shauna Doolan: Adult daughter of Shamus and Mary. Sister to Lindsay.
Lindsay Doolan: Youngest child of Shamus and Mary. Brother to Shauna.
Patrick McIntyre: Paddymac: Rescued by Michael Doolan. Wife, Thelma.
Mark McIvor: Irish immigrant along with brothers. Husband of Shauna.
James McIvor: Irish immigrant with brothers William and Mark.
William McIvor: Irish immigrant with brothers Mark and James.
THE WONG FAMILY:
Old Mr. & Mrs. Wong: Met Michael Doolan at Gulgong goldfields 1871.
Déhuã Wong: Son of the Old Wongs: Wife, Ching Lan – 4 children
                 including the boy Anguó
Chang Wong: Son of the Old Wongs: Wife, Lee Wong – 2 children.
Déshi Wong: Son of the Old Wongs: Wife, An Wong – twin boys.
Babygirl Wong: Daughter of Old Wongs. In Townsville with 3 children.
THE BOBANGLE FAMILY:
Harry Bobangle: Husband of Mabel. A kanaka - remained in Australia.
Mabel Bobangle: Wife of Harry. Of the Bindal aboriginal family.
Gabby Bobangle: Son of Harry and Mabel. With wife, Sophie have 4
                 children including sons Akama and Sabbo.
Sophie Bobangle: Wife of Gabby Bobangle. Aboriginal/Melanesian.
Haddie Bobangle: Son of Harry and Mabel. With wife, Rosie have 4
                 children including Cabri.
Rosie Bobangle: Wife of Haddie Bobangle. Aboriginal/Melanesian.
Milly Bobangle: (E'Mia) Daughter of Harry and Mabel Bobangle.
Tilly Bobangle: (Fadia) Daughter of Harry and Mabel Bobangle.
LITTLEWOOD FAMILY: from Leaning Rock Station, Charters Towers.
Matthew Littlewood and Mrs. Littlewood parents of:
Bella Littlewood: The eldest daughter
Maryann and Thomas the Littlewood twins.

Chapter One

Romance at Sea

A long low gasp escaped his lips. He felt his heart had stopped beating. He knew he had stopped breathing. It seemed like hours until he sucked in a ragged breath. Inside his chest, his heart now pounded like a steam train. On the deck outside the lounge room, James stood transfixed staring at the vision through the partly open doorway. Auburn hair hung in soft waves past her shoulders. Her skin, white against the blue of her evening frock. A sea breeze ruffled James's sandy curls as he rested his tall frame against the ship's rail. In the night's shadows, he knew he could not be seen by those inside the lantern-lit room. This was truly a sight to be savoured. Soft music flowed from a portable gramophone. Someone or something, out of James McIvor's line of sight, had captured the beauty's interest. Who or what he wondered?

Pain ripped through his chest. In disbelief, he watched his older brother Mark, approach the girl. The angel in blue extended her hands. Mark held her fingers. The burning gaze between the pair spoke volumes.

James groaned. "Look at him, dressed up in his Sunday best. What's he doing with this beauty?"

A quiet voice spoke beside James. "Holy cow! Is that our brother? No surprise then why he's been so elusive this trip. Who would have thought there could be anything to tempt Mark into spending a night with the old folk in the music room?" William, almost a copy of his older brother James, tall, slim, brown hair, arrived on silent feet. "Didn't take him long to forget Theresa Donnelly. No doubt this one will become just another triumph in Mark's long list of conquests."

Nearly knocking his brother over in his rush, James turned. He spoke gruffly.

"Yeah, come on, William, we might as well get back to the Pitch and Toss game. I'm sure Mark won't want to join us. He appears otherwise occupied."

They made their way to the lower deck where the Pitch and Toss game had gathered quite a crowd. The caller struggled to make his voice heard above the din. The game held no interest for James. It was not too long before the brothers decided to call it an early night.

The cabin did not have a lot of room to spare with two double bunks and minimum cupboard space. Being boys, tidiness was not high on their list of priorities, despite the strict upbringing of their childhood in Ireland. Still, they were lucky it was only the three of them. The door slammed shut behind them as the younger man threw himself on a bottom bunk.

"What do you think Mark's up to?" William paused in thought. "He seemed pretty taken with that redhead. I wouldn't like to be in his shoes if Theresa Donnelly hears he has eyes for another woman. She made it very clear Mark was her property and she intended wedding bells to ring. Come to think of it, Mark was very lucky to slip out of her clutches and join us on this trip to Australia."

From the top bunk, James frowned at the memories. Mark seemed to have spent his life trying to disentangle himself from the plans of one woman or another.

"When he comes back you can ask him yourself," he replied.

William was not silly. He knew better than to poke his nose into Mark's business. Mark's short temper was well known within the family. At twenty-two years of age, Mark was the eldest of the three brothers. He always seemed more aloof. William knew from experience Mark would not tolerate too much interference. Being the youngest at eighteen years of age, William was grateful Mark showed more patience with him than he did with twenty-year-old, James.

Inside the music room, Shauna Doolan was having trouble with her erratic heartbeats as she gazed into the blue eyes of Mark McIvor. She felt the rush of blood to her face. She felt the sharp eyes of her mother on her back. No doubt, later, her mother would scold her for appearing too forward with this young man whom she had only met on board ship. Shauna knew she would rather chop off her hands than reclaim them from his gentle grasp. At five foot three inches tall, in stockinged feet, her alabaster neck stretched back to search his face, eleven inches above her own. His dear face, with those piercing eyes, neatly trimmed moustache and curly brown hair. A shadow flickered in the depths of her green eyes. She knew so little about the handsome man other than he was here with his younger brothers. They were on an adventure to explore the opportunities available to them in Australia.

Shauna loved the evening walks along the upper deck with her parents. Vibrations from the engine below were felt in the timbers beneath their feet. Smoke from the funnel drifted like a pennant over the stern.   Tonight, a large moon rose high in a cloudless sky bewitched with stars. A cool breeze laden with the salt air rippled along the deck. This evening, as they returned to their cabins, the group was rather quiet.

Shauna's thoughts were filled with this wonderful new man in her life. After the death of Kevin, her fiancé, two years previously, life had lost all meaning. Mam had said repeatedly, 'Time will heal a broken heart.' Shauna had not believed such a thing possible. Now, perhaps, Mam may be proved to have been correct.

Shauna entered the cabin, which she shared with Lindsay, her eight-year-old brother. She stood for a moment thinking it was rather a cosy cabin. Not a lot of room perhaps but quite adequate for the travellers. It had taken a couple of nights to get used to the strange bunks on either side of the room but she admitted they were quite comfortable. Nothing like the cottage they had lived in on the family farm in Ireland.

Her face softened as she watched the sleeping Lindsay. A wave of nostalgia flowed through her body like a flash flood in a mountain stream. She was going to miss home and the small school where she had taught the local children. Unconsciously, her body straightened and her shoulders lifted. Her family was together and they planned to make a new home in the country called Australia.

In the cabin of Shauna's parents, Mary struggled in her mind with how best to remind her daughter the forward behaviour, displayed this evening with young Mark McIvor, could very well put a young woman's reputation at risk. The last thing she wanted was to get Shauna's back up. Shauna could be a very determined young lady. On the other hand, Mary was pleased to see her take an interest in life again. Since Kevin drowned, there had been few signs of the old fun-loving, care-free, impetuous, young woman Mary loved so much. She worried when her daughter showed little interest in life. It was grand to see the girl smiling again.

Shamus, Shauna's father, replayed in his mind the conversation he had with Mr. Ronald Cartwright; a gentleman whom he had come to know quite well during this ocean voyage. Both their families had ties to relatives in the low lands of Scotland. Both were from farming stock, although Ronald had gone on to be a solicitor in Glasgow. Ronald was a well-mannered gentleman who had recently lost his wife. This had been a very distressing time for him and this move to Australia was to make a new beginning. The man had requested Shamus's permission to court Shauna. He felt she would make a good wife for a successful solicitor. Shamus agreed although he held some reservation as to Ronald's age. At forty, the man was twenty-one years older than Shauna, closer to his own age of forty-eight years. Shamus explained how he wished to talk things over with his wife before he would make a final decision.

Mary was the wise one in the family. He was just the farmer, the third son of a landholder in Ireland. His older brothers and their families lived on and ran the family farm. Until they had decided to emigrate, Shamus, Mary, their daughter Shauna along with their son, Lindsay had occupied one of the farm cottages. The fortuitous arrival of a letter from his Uncle Michael's solicitor in Australia set their plans in motion. An aging Michael wished to sign his property, in North Queensland, over to his nephew, Shamus. The household had been in an uproar as they searched for the family's atlas. Where on earth was this place called North Queensland? Shamus brought his thoughts back to the ship's cabin. He smiled at Mary as she prepared to retire.

"What brought the smile on husband, dear?"

But Shamus sat quietly with the wobbly smile on his lips and admiration lapping at his thoughts. How many other wives would have been willing to leave their modest luxuries behind and come on a journey to the other side of the world? She was a true gem.

Shamus moved to hold his still-beautiful wife, closely.

"Oh, Mary, my sweet muirnīn, this trip has been a great experience but I'll be glad when we dock in Townsville." His rough finger threaded through her once-glorious auburn hair now speckled with grey. He smiled as he remembered it when even more impressive than Shauna's. The wobbly smile turned into a crooked grin. Like her daughter, Mary stood a little over five feet tall but when she chose to present her impervious side, the vision was terrifying. He took a deep breath and decided to wade in.

"Now, my girl, there's something I need to discuss with you. I'd like to hear your opinion," he said. Gently he took the book from Mary's hand and placed it on the small locker.

"You intrigue me," replied Mary. She looked more closely at Shamus. "You've been very quiet this evening. What's on your mind?" Mary stretched out and turned the lantern low.

"I had Mr. Cartwright speak to me today. He wants to seek the hand of our Shauna. He asked my permission to court her."

A frown flashed across Mary's forehead. It disappeared as quickly as it had appeared. Mary's heart rolled over. Heaven's above. She felt sure this was not the news Shauna wanted to hear. Her daughter had deep feelings for Mark McIvor. *Oh please, God, don't let her be disappointed again.*

"What did you tell him, Shamus?" Trepidation filled her voice. Shamus was a wonderful husband, father and provider but he could be as stubborn as an old mule if approached in the wrong way.

"Oh, I said I'd talk it over with you before I gave any permission."

"What are your thoughts on the idea?" Mary swallowed.

"He's a solicitor and has good prospects. His wife died last year and he's never settled since. He'll need someone by his side when beginning again in Australia. He seems very well off and appears a gentleman. He said he was a Protestant."

"Yes, that's all fine. It's a shame he's so old. You've always wanted Shauna to learn to make a go of life, learn by the knocks and setbacks. Remember our discussions when she wanted to become engaged to Kevin? It takes strength and courage for a young couple to build their lives from scratch. Mr. Cartwright could give her almost everything she wanted. I'm not saying this is a bad thing but I had agreed with you before. I hoped she'd gain the mental strength needed by doing without at times."

"Then, should I refuse my permission, do you think?"

"No, my dear husband. I think this is something we have to discuss with Shauna. She's nineteen years of age. She has her certificate as a teacher. She has done a wonderful job organizing help for the local community back home. I think she's earned her right to make this decision." Mary stopped talking to take a breath. She bit her tongue trying not to say too much. "What do you think?"

Shamus sat pensively for some time before speaking. He rubbed his greying head. Shamus believed women of the family should be consulted on things regarding their destiny but he did find it tried his patience at times. He was concerned Shauna was too young to make such a momentous decision. Eventually, he spoke.

"As usual you're probably right, my dear. I have to admit some concern myself at Ronald's age, although many a satisfactory marriage came from the union of a young woman and an older man. It may be a comfort knowing Shauna would be secure and not want for anything. Do you think we could talk privately with her tomorrow? Maybe while Lindsay plays the French cricket or is doing his gymnastics which he loves so much?" He smiled as his son filled his thoughts.

In the McIvor's cabin, James swung his pillow down to disturb William who was dozing on the lower bunk.

"Look alive. I think Mark's at the door now."

Mark attempted to slip quietly into the darkened cabin but as usual, there was plenty to fall over. Tonight, it was someone's boots.

"Damnation!" he swore.

"How was your night, Mark?" asked William.

"Sorry, did I wake you? I tried not to make a noise but this cabin is life-threatening. I had a pleasant evening. What did you and James get up to?"

"Oh, we spent a bit of time at the Pitch and Toss game. It's really taken on and became quite crowded." William paused for a moment as he pondered the wisdom of saying more. He decided to tempt the devil. "We did come looking for you to see if you wanted to join us. When we saw you were occupied with the red-headed beauty in the music room, we left you to it." If the light had been brighter, Mark would have seen the twinkle in William's eyes.

"Yes, well thanks," Mark replied shortly.

When nothing more was forthcoming, William decided it might be prudent to ask no more questions. He settled back to sleep. Mark would tell them what he thought they should know when he was good and ready. On the top bunk, James sighed and rolled over to wrap his mind around his earlier vision.

Once undressed, Mark lay back on the bunk, his hands intertwined at the back of his head. An unseen grin filled the dark cabin. He had spent the last two or three years of his life avoiding the issue of marriage but here he was making the plans himself. Tomorrow he would ask Shauna to be his wife. What if he stood there all tongue-tied? She'd think him a complete idiot. A girl like that could have anyone she wanted. When he thought about it, why would she be interested in him? An ex-farmer, with no settled roots? He figured he was not too bad to look at and he was financially independent thanks to a doting Grandfather and the shipping side of the family business. His thoughts continued to spin. Shauna did seem to like him. His recollection of her smile set his stomach swirling. What about her parents; would they approve? According to Shauna, they were on their way to Australia to take up a farm owned by an uncle. What would they think of my joining them there with Shauna as my bride? Australia was still a very young country. It would need a lot of taming. I'm healthy and strong. I could make a worthwhile contribution. Mr. Doolan might appreciate a set of young shoulders to help him. At this point, Mark began to doze. Suddenly he sat upright as another thought burst within his head. *I don't think I'd like her family to be too much underfoot. She'll be busy looking after me and then our children. I could buy land nearby. Shauna could visit her parents occasionally.* Sleep eluded Mark as his mind roamed.

Mary also lay awake with her thoughts. She planned the confrontation yet to come with Shauna. She replayed her talk with Shamus. A hint of a smile curved her lips when she remembered Shamus had at least agreed to discuss Mr. Cartwright's proposal with Shauna. Now, would Shauna contain her temper and listen to her father or jump the gun and refuse outright. I'll endeavour to talk to her quietly first, and the two of us can plan a strategy. *Good Heavens, what am I thinking! Have I already decided I wish her to marry her Mr. McIvor?*

Shamus's gentle snoring lulled her to sleep.

In the next cabin, excitement barrelled through Shauna's veins. Butterflies fluttered within her stomach as she sensed again the feel of his touch on her fingers. Was Mark ever going to ask her to marry him? What would she answer? Was she ready to think of marriage again, after Kevin? A vision of her previous, now dead, fiancé filled her head. They'd been so young. Her deep sigh filled the cabin. Kevin's face disappeared behind the image of Mark. What would her parents think? Where would they live? What would they do? A few children with Mark's sparkling eyes appealed. A dreamy smile played on her lips. Her thoughts churned. The voice of her Granny echoed in her head. 'Don't put the cart before the horse.' Shauna wished her Granny was still alive. Granny always knew the right things to say and she knew how to keep her feet planted firmly on the ground.

The early morning sun found Shauna on deck supervising young Lindsay as he performed his daily exercises with a group of other children. She smiled as she recalled their conversation before they left the cabin. This was after the routine argument about a face and hand wash.

"I'm going to be a world champion like the 'Blue Streak,'" Lindsay had stated.

"Who on earth is the Blue Streak?"

"You know the tall black-haired kid I do gymnastics with? He reckons an Australian fellow won a big race in South Africa a couple of years ago. He set a world record. His name's Jack Donaldson. He always wears a blue singlet and blue shorts and that's why they call him the 'Blue Streak'".

"The sun cannot compete with your lovely smile, Miss Doolan," the now familiar voice spoke beside her.

Her heart raced within her chest. The smile on her lips outshone the sun above.

"Thank you, Mr. McIvor. Did you have a nice evening?"

"Wonderful, thanks to the pleasant company," Mark stated.

Shauna felt her face blush red hot.

"Miss Doolan, Shauna, I wish to ask you something very special and I know this isn't exactly the time to do so but it's the only time of the day we have to ourselves, well almost to ourselves." Wearing a wry grin, Mark looked around the deck towards the boys hard at their exercises. He reached down and gathered Shauna's hands in his own.

The couple cast guilty glances around the upper deck where several other early risers were out to welcome the new day. They drew in closer to where several barrels were secured against the bulwarks. Smoke spewed from the ship's funnel to drift across the portside-stern.

"Please go on, Mr. McIvor, Mark," Shauna whispered. She could hardly breathe.

"I … well … er … I … I'm from a respectable family and have had a Christian upbringing." Mark felt his face redden. His tongue filled his dry mouth. What an idiotic thing to say. Where were all the terrific phrases, he'd practiced most of the night? He almost wished he could sink through the deck. He tried again. "I've a modest income … er … would you mind … not be angry … if I asked your father for your hand in marriage. I adore you. I … I more than adore you, I worship you, Shauna. I promise I'll look after you so carefully." Mark sucked in a big breath then held it. Sun sparkled on her hair as it lifted on the breeze. It waved behind her beautiful head. An emerald scarf around her neck matched her twinkling eyes.

Shauna's face lit up. After only a short time to consider, she replied.

"Mark, sweet acushla, I would love very much to be your wife. I find myself looking forward to seeing your dear face every day. The thought of never seeing you again after this journey's end fills me with fear."

"Oh, Shauna, Shauna, my sweet colleen," was all Mark could say. His knees trembled. He wanted so much to enfold her in his arms but the call from Lindsay at their side left Mark only the chance to grip her pale hands tighter.

"Excuse me. What's happening? You've silly grins on your faces and you both look as if you're sunburnt." Before either the stunned Shauna or Mark could make a reply, Lindsay continued, "I'm starving, are we going to go get ready for breakfast?"

While Shauna and Lindsay moved off to prepare themselves for breakfast, Mark stood transfixed. Shauna turned back with a coy smile. She lifted her parasol a fraction. Mark was sure she gave a slow wink before dropping her eyes again demurely and moving on. His insides somersaulted and he knew it was not due to any seasickness. Strong arms wrapped his waist to hold himself together. Were his feet floating above the deck? Ten minutes passed before Mark was able to move off to his cabin and prepare for breakfast himself.

James and William were ready to exit as Mark entered the cabin.

"Hello, big brother, you look like the Scotsman who dropped a penny and found a pound," piped up William. "I do hope you've not been doing anything you shouldn't. Bloody Hell! You haven't, have you?"

"No, I have not," replied Mark with a scowl. "Our Ma wouldn't be best pleased with that language. You'd be eating your meals standing up for at least a week if she or Pa heard you." A grin returned to his face. "Remember lad, curiosity killed the cat."

James, all the while, sat silently on the bunk, bent over re-tying his shoes. A lead weight filled his stomach. Dread draped his body. The thought of food sickened him; maybe he was coming down with something. If Ma were here, he'd get a dose of cod liver oil.

Mark grabbed his jacket and moved out of the cabin before William could interrogate him further.

"See you at breakfast," he called.

"You were a lot of help," William turned to the unusually quiet James. "Did you see that? Oh boy, I bet the grin on his face has something to do with the redhead he was talking to last night. What do you make of it?"

"None of our business," replied James shortly. "You'd better get a move on or you'll miss breakfast and it's a long time until lunch."

As they made their way out of the cabin, James felt more like jumping off the ship than eating breakfast. What was the matter with him?

"Lindsay, go clean yourself up and dress for breakfast. I'm going to say good morning to Mam and Pa. Meet me at their cabin," Shauna called. When she knocked on her parent's cabin door, she found only her mother pinning up her hair.

"Where's Pa?" she asked.

"Impatient, as usual. He'll meet us in the dining room," was Mary's reply. "Where's young Lindsay?"

"Hopefully, having a wash and getting dressed."

"Shauna, while we've a moment alone, I want to talk to you about something your father brought to my attention yesterday. You've met your father's friend, Mr. Cartwright, haven't you?"

"Yes, I've spoken to him on occasion, I think. Nice old man, like Pa, a little rotund with a receding hairline. A bit of a bore at times though."

Mary realized this was going to be harder than she thought; particularly as she agreed wholeheartedly with her daughter.

"Yes, well, your father and I aren't so old yet, you know. Mr. Cartwright spoke to your father yesterday requesting his permission to court you." A loud silence filled every nook and cranny in the cabin. Mary went on hurriedly. "I know you still pine for Kevin but life does go on you'll find. One day you'll want to marry and have children. Mr. Cartwright is a man of considerable means and his wife would have a very comfortable life." Mary spoke persuasively but quailed inside herself at the stillness of Shauna. "I'm sure Pa wouldn't force you into a marriage that was abhorrent to you but this gentleman has considerable merits. Your Pa would like you to think about it."

It was some moments before Shauna found her voice.

"Oh, Mam. I know Pa wants the best for me but I don't love Mr. Cartwright. I barely care for him at all. I may feel a little empathy for him at the loss of his first wife but that's it. Should one marry a man for pity? You know I care deeply for Mr. McIvor. He's asked if I'd mind his requesting Pa for permission to marry me."

Mary's heart sank. She had not realized things between her daughter and Mr. McIvor had gone so far. Both ladies sat in deep thought for some moments. It was Mary who broke the silence.

"Shauna, I can't say I'm totally surprised but I do wish you'd think more about this. You've only known Mr. McIvor for several weeks. It may only be a shipboard romance. What do you know of him? Remember Granny's old saying, 'Marry in haste and repent at leisure.'"

In a more patient tone than she thought she was capable of, Shauna spoke. "Mam, we've only known Mr. Cartwright since boarding the ship also and we only know what he has told us about himself. I do know I look forward to seeing Mark every day but I'm not sorry if weeks go by and I've not seen sight nor sound of Mr. Cartwright. Doesn't this say something?"

"Yes, my dear, you're correct. You'd better prepare your arguments for your father. Remember, he doesn't like to be told what to do by his offspring so a little tact will go a long way. Oh, Heaven's above, he'll be in a fine to-do when Mr. McIvor speaks to him also." She hid the secret smile as it exploded upon her face.

A knock on the door heralded Lindsay's arrival.

"Hi, Mam, I'm so hungry I could eat a horse and chase the rider."

Mary smiled at the exuberance of her son. "Where did you learn that saying my lad and look at you growing so fast. You're at least two inches taller and the seams of all your clothes are bursting. We'll need to buy some material at Townsville when we make port. I think we can presume material will be available there. I understand it's a large town." Mary turned towards the thoughtful Shauna. "Come on, Shauna, we'd better not keep this starving waif away from his food."

In the dining room, Lindsay drifted off to the large table by itself at which most of the children ate their meals. Shauna and her parents dined at a quiet table by a port-side window. Shamus greeted the ladies.

"Good morning, Shauna. Hello, my dearest," he directed to his wife. The trio was mostly quiet during the meal, taken as they were with their thoughts. When they sipped their tea, Shamus asked, "Shauna, my dear, has your mother spoken to you of my conversation with Mr. Cartwright yesterday?"

"Yes, Pa, we spoke earlier," replied Shauna, determined not to say too much or speak too soon.

"What are your thoughts on his request?"

"Pa, Mr. Cartwright appears to be a very respectable gentleman."

"Do I detect a 'but' there somewhere?" Shamus asked.

"Yes, Pa. I've known what it is to love someone very deeply; with Kevin. I wouldn't like to accept anything less. The last thing I wish to do is appear uncooperative or to go against your wishes but I ask you to consider how this may feel." Shauna's green eyes never left the blue eyes of her father. "Mr. Cartwright is rather old. It would feel like being married to a father figure. That can't be a good thing, can it? I prefer to deny this request if you're agreeable."

"If that's what you think, Shauna, I'll respect your wishes. By the way, would that young McIvor lad have anything to do with your decision?" Shamus did not miss the sudden guilty alertness in both women drinking their tea at his table. He smiled softly. "Your mother thinks I miss most of what's going on but I have eyes in my head," Shamus said. His smile widened at the look of astonishment on the faces of both ladies.

He watched the blushing Shauna. His thoughts were confirmed. *So that's the way the land lies.* He was taken with young McIvor himself although he felt the boy's eyes were too close together. His Ma always said she would never trust anyone with their eyes too close together. He shrugged his shoulders; *superstitions*, he thought. No, he was not unduly upset by this turn of events. Shamus was pleased to see his Mary remained quiet but her eyes sparkled.

Lindsay joined them, a little reluctantly, as they made their way outside. He was to spend the next two hours at his school lessons under Shauna's tuition.

When Mr. Cartwright approached, Shamus was sitting in a quiet spot on the upper deck reading an old paper he had found in the lounge.

"Excuse me, Mr. Doolan. May I ask if you have come to a decision regarding the request, I made of you yesterday."

"Er ... yes, yes. I've spoken to my wife and our daughter. With all due respect, Mr. Cartwright, Shauna appreciates, but must deny your kind offer."

"You mean to say, you've let your daughter make such an important decision. Do you think that's wise?" The man drew himself to his full height of five foot eight inches and began breathing in and out noisily. His eyes widened until the whites were visible around the irises. "It's not passed my attention how forward she is when talking to that McIvor chap. Not behaviour I'd wish for in a wife at all. It seems I've made a lucky escape." He stomped off in high dudgeon.

"Yes, and I think our Shauna may have made a lucky escape also – pompous ass," mumbled Shamus quietly to himself.

No sooner had Shamus returned to a very interesting article in his paper about a rail bridge being built over the river in the district to where they were heading, when another voice interrupted his concentration. *Bother*! Shamus had to bite his tongue.

"Mr. Doolan, Sir, please excuse me."

On looking up, Shamus found the eldest McIvor lad standing with a deep frown on his face.

"Yes, young man, what can I do for you?"

"Sir ... Sir, I wish to speak to you on a very personal matter."

Shamus sighed. "Yes, of course, Mr. McIvor, go ahead."

"It's about your daughter, Shauna, Sir."

Shamus's eyes opened wide. "Good Heavens! What's happened to our Shauna?"

"Nothing, Sir. It's just ... well, Sir, I've had a Protestant upbringing, and I've had good schooling and I've an independent income and I ..."

"Well lad, get on with it, what are you trying to say? I'm not interviewing a hopeful employee, am I?"

"No, Sir. You're not interviewing a hopeful employee, only a hopeful son-in-law," replied Mark. "I wish to ask for Shauna's hand in marriage and I'm requesting your permission to do so."

Shamus's mouth dropped open. "What on earth is going on around here today? This is getting as busy as the main street in Belfast." He sat thinking for some time.

In front of Shamus, Mark stood with his hands twisting behind his back. He was barely able to control his impatience as he watched the different emotions pass across the older man's face. He couldn't decide whether they boded good or bad.

The sound of a prolonged scream tore across the ship's decks. Both men forgot their contemplations. Shamus bounded out of his chair but Mark was already hurtling towards the starboard side of the vessel. Shamus rounded the wheel-house to see Mark unhitch a lifebelt from the rail and leap up onto the top of the bulwark timbers. With the briefest of pauses, the young man threw himself out into the sea with the lifebelt flapping against his right arm.

"What's going on, Pa." His daughter's voice sounded at his shoulder. "Where's Mark?"

He drew the girl into the curve of his arm. Relief washed over him when his Mary moved up to her other side. It was Mary who reported the gossip from the onlookers.

"It's the McIvor boy. He's jumped in to rescue a youngster who fell overboard." The vibration of the engines beneath their feet ceased. The sudden stoppage almost caused the trio to lose their balance. The captain's voice was heard shouting a volley of orders. Crew members ran towards the lifeboats.

Shauna's face drained of colour. Her hearing was acute.

"Which McIvor boy, Mam, which one?"

Mary hugged her daughter close.

"It's Mark, my dear."

The sea captain's soft voice of two years before now screamed inside Shauna's head. 'He's dead, Shauna, your fiancé has been drowned at sea.' Was life to repeat itself?

"No, no, don't say that. I can't lose another man to the sea, Mam. I just can't."

They pressed their way forward through the gathering crowd to the rail.

"Look, there!" Mary's shaking hand pointed towards James and William McIvor who were all for diving overboard to join their brother while three deck-hands struggled to hold them back. "They're Mark's brothers, aren't they?"

"Yes, that's James and William." Shauna gulped as the tears began to fall. She strained to see the two figures with the lifebuoy disappearing into the distance behind the ship's stern.

When Mark had rounded the cabins on the deck, a group of boys hung over the ship's side, screaming. Out in the ocean, pale short arms flailed in the water. The child attempted to call but each time he did so the water rushed into his mouth. Without hesitation, Mark kicked off his shoes, grabbed at the closest life-buoy and jumped. Before he hit the water, he pinpointed, in his mind, the exact location of the youngster. The water was colder than he expected and the saltwater stung his eyes. With the help of the buoy, he powered his legs towards the surface. The vessel had passed their position by the time Mark surfaced and swam towards the weakening boy's side. As he attached the lad to the lifesaving device, he took in his surroundings including the disappearing ship. His heart quailed.

"Well, lad, it looks like we're in for a swim. One arm reached out and dragged at the sea. "You can kick your legs if you feel like it. We may make it to the boat before teatime." He hoped the youngster didn't hear his misgivings as they shook his voice. It was such a wide-open stark sea in which to find two small bodies. Mark positioned himself to protect his floating companion from the small wavelets as they crashed over their heads. "What's your name, son?"

"Jack, mister, Jack Evans."

The sun was well past the zenith when voices stirred the somnolent Mark. His body shivered in the cold waters. Determination alone forced his legs to push them in the direction of the sound. He struggled to tear the shirt from his back. He shook the small sun-reddened body resting on the buoy. "Listen, Jack, can you hear anything?"

The wet eyelashes opened slowly but the child was unable to answer.

Mark struggled to clear his salt-burned throat and yelled. "Over here." He waved the shirt vigorously.

Voices called back from the rescue boat. Mark again flapped his shirt furiously. A groundswell of relief as big as any of the ocean's waves, rolled over him when he felt the strong arms reach under his shoulders. Other arms lifted Jack with the buoy secured to his body.

It seemed everyone on board the ship had gathered on deck to welcome the hero's return. His brothers berated Mark even as they shook his hands and patted his back. Wide smiles chased the anxious frowns from their faces. The red-haired beauty pushed through the crowd in a most unladylike manner before throwing herself at the shirtless man dripping with saltwater. Tears streamed down her cheeks as she crushed him in her grasp. Manly tears were seen on the brink of his reddened eyes. He clasped her close. On the edge of the gathering, both Shamus and Mary shed a few tears of their own. James McIvor eased out of the crowd and slipped away.

When Mary returned to their cabin late that night having seen Shauna settled next door, Shamus held her gently in his arms.

"Mary, Mary, my head is swirling like a whirlpool. With the rescue dramas, I haven't had the chance to tell you all that has happened this morning." Shamus's fingers threaded through her hair. "Mark McIvor had just requested our permission to ask for Shauna's hand in marriage when the young lad fell overboard." Shamus moved over to stretch out on the bunk with his arms under his head. "What do you think of that? I might add it happened only a few minutes after Mr. Cartwright walked off in a huff when told of Shauna's rejection."

A smile filled Mary's face. "Is that so?" she replied.

"You know something I don't? What have you and Shauna been hatching up?" asked Shamus perplexed.

"No, my dear husband, we've not been hatching anything up, but I'm happy. I think mostly because I know Shauna will be happy".

"Women!" was all Shamus could say. He rolled over.

It wasn't until the next morning, when Mark was released from the sick-bay, the conversation with Shamus continued.

The older man was first to speak after he had shaken Mark's hand for much longer than was usual.

"Shauna's nineteen years of age. About two years ago she lost her, then, fiancé in a shipping accident. It left her devastated. We were afraid she was going to lose a loved one again."

Mark opened his mouth as if to speak but Shamus went on.

"That girl has been a wonderful daughter and a great companion to her mother and to me, I may add. What sort of life can you offer her? Where would you live?"

Mark went to speak again but his voice failed him.

"I understand you and your brothers are planning adventures in the goldfields and mining districts. I don't think those places suitable to take a wife, particularly a daughter of mine. We planned on Shauna's help during our transition to living and working on an Australian block of land."

Despite his throat still raw from the salt, a determined Mark spoke, his voice husky.

"I respect your concern, Sir. I've asked myself these questions. I wouldn't take her to an area unsuitable for a woman. I understand you're joining your uncle on his farm south of Townsville. You may need young shoulders to assist you, particularly if your uncle is getting on in age. He may not be able to do too much of the heavy work required."

Shamus looked more closely at the young man standing in front of him. His thoughts scurried around his mind. *My goodness, this man and Shauna have spoken quite a lot together. I wonder what that monkey has been saying?*

"If Shauna agrees to marry me and if you saw fit, we could live on your farm. I'd be happy to work shoulder to shoulder with you. This would enable us to get to know each other better. Eventually, I'd like to buy a farm of my own or maybe a trading store, within the district. In the meantime, I could be learning the local farming methods."

Shamus chewed at his lip. "You've it all thought out, haven't you, young fellow? What does Shauna think of all this?"

"Sir, I haven't discussed this with her as yet. I thought it preferable to have your permission first."

"Mr. McIvor, Mark, isn't it?"

"Yes, Sir."

Having a fair idea of how the land lay with Shauna and her feelings for this man, Shamus said, "I'll have to discuss your offer with my wife. If she thinks you'd be suitable for our daughter, I'll give you my permission to talk to Shauna and to ask for her hand in marriage. You'll take Shauna's decision as final. I don't want to hear you've pressured her in any way. If Shauna does give her acceptance then you'd better make sure you look after her with your life. That girl is the apple of my eye. Woe betides anyone who hurts a hair on her head or brings a tear to her eye. And for Heaven's sake stop saying, Sir, and Mr. Doolan, my name is Shamus."

"Yes, Sir, … er … Shamus."

"Seek me out later this afternoon. I should have an answer for you then."

When Mary was informed of the latest interview with Mark McIvor, her eyes shone.

"Oh, Shamus, how wonderful. I'll speak to Shauna about her plans. Where will she want the wedding to be? We're going to a new district with limited resources. Maybe not even a church or minister. Perhaps she may choose to be married on the ship before we land."

"Now, wait one minute. I've just agreed, I think, to allowing her to be married but not so fast. They should get to know each other; for at least five years, I'd think. Churches and things will be built by then," Shamus blustered.

"Would you have waited five years for me?" Mary asked with a coy smile.

"Yes, well, this is different somehow."

Mary continued to smile.

Eventually, Mark found Shauna reading at a quiet secluded table in the lounge room.

"Hello, beautiful lady," he greeted her, "May I join you?"

"Yes, of course, Mark. I'm just correcting Lindsay's school work from this morning and setting work for him tomorrow," replied Shauna.

"Would you mind if I interrupted?" he asked.

"I'll enjoy the change."

"I spoke to your father this morning."

Knowing, or at least hoping for what might be to come, Shauna blushed. It was a relatively private corner in which they sat. No prying eyes noticed when he took her hand in his. Mark slipped down onto his bended knee.

"Shauna Doolan, will you do me the honour of becoming my wife?" He held his breath, waiting. He had done it. It had not been as hard as he thought it would be, assuming she had not changed her mind. Women did that a lot, he'd been told.

Shauna surprised herself at how quickly her reply came out.

"Yes, Mark. Oh, yes. I'll be proud to be your wife."

Mark lent forward and kissed her softly on the lips.

"If my throat wasn't still so sore, I think I'd rush outside and shout until my voice bounced back off the nearest mainland," he laughed.

Shauna smiled. They sat quietly for a long time, happy to enjoy the pleasure of their own company. Sometimes words can ruin the moment.

Mark broke the silence. "When do we set a date? Where do you want to be married?"

Shauna thought for some time.

"I think we've three options: one is to be married on board the ship before landing or we could be married onshore, in Townsville, when we do land in about a week or so. If you prefer, we could wait until after we've settled on the farm. What do you think, Mark?"

"My choice would be to marry on board this ship. Rather suitable, don't you think? After all, this is where we met and fell in love."

Shauna was pleasantly surprised to find Mark seemed quite the romantic.

"I agree, as long as it doesn't appear to be too hurried. The Methodist minister, Mr. Cameron, who holds the Sunday services on board the ship, wouldn't mind marrying a pair of Presbyterians, I'm sure. Should we ask him?"

"Sounds grand, my lady. Before we do anything though, we'd best go and tell your family. After we do that, will you come with me to advise my brothers about our plans?"

Chapter Two

Michael and Paddymac's Story

Sweat poured from his body as he thrashed in agony. The coarse grey blanket upon which he lay was saturated as was the horse-hair mattress it covered. Michael Doolan groaned feebly as the pain in his joints reached new heights. His friends, Paddy McIntyre (Paddymac, Michael called him) and Harry Bobangle, the Kanaka, stood with worried frowns on their faces. Mabel, Harry's wife, endeavoured to cool Michael's body by sponging him with a cloth, wet with river water from the bucket near the bed. She encouraged Michael to sip fluid from a chipped pannikin. The past twenty-four hours had been spent in a state of semi-consciousness which did not appear to be abating. Semi-conscious was preferable to being fully aware of the screaming pain in his head and his limbs.

Michael heard Paddymac's voice as if from a great distance, asking Harry to send his son Gabby, to fetch Old Mister Wong at the market garden.

"He knows lots of things about herbal medicine. He may be able to help Mister Michael. He's helped before when anyone of us has been ill."

The market garden, run by Old Mister Wong, and his family, was nearly a mile or so from this small farm hut.

Old Mister Wong and his wife had several children, the names of which Michael could never fathom. He mostly referred to them as the young Wong boy or girl. Now, to make it even more difficult there was another generation. They were good workers, all of them, right from an early age, growing their vegetables, fruit and herbs. He had first met Mister Wong on his arrival in Australia at the Gulgong goldfields in 1871 – forty-two years ago. Who would believe so much time had passed by? They had then met again in 1873 on the goldfields of Charters Towers. Two years after Michael acquired this property on the Burdekin River in 1893, Old Mister Wong brought his family here to begin a market garden on land leased from Michael. Since last year, 1912, when work began on the new rail bridge spanning the Burdekin River and on the Inkerman mill on the south side, the Wong boys made trips to the workers' campsites selling their produce.

Harry, who had been a stalwart friend to Michael and Paddymac, was one of the Kanakas the Government had brought out to work on the sugar-cane farms in the districts south of here. Now married to Mabel, an aboriginal woman, he lived in a hut near the river-bank with his family.

A blackness drifted over Michael like a moonless night. The voices of his friends faded away altogether. When once more consciousness eased into his mind, his thoughts remained in the early days when Paddymac, Harry and himself had built this hut from split timber and corrugated iron. A hallway separated two small rooms, running from a front veranda to a small back veranda where a set of stairs led down into a separate kitchen. Each room had large push out timber and corrugated iron windows. These allowed any small breath of air to flow through the hut. Usually, it was quite effective. This was a big step up from the paper-bark humpy Michael and Paddymac had shared for the first few years on the property. When the hut was completed, he and Paddymac had shared a nip of rum under the new roof. Michael, in a moment of nostalgia, named the place Emerald Flats.

The fever continued unabated. Michael's mind meandered through the meadows of his home in Ireland. The rolling fields and the green – the beautiful green. 'Forty shades of green,' Granny said every morning as she looked out from her kitchen window.

Inside his head, the boy once more lay on the bank of the brook with his fishing line, hoping for a bite. While watching the cork at the end of his line, he listened to the music of the water as it ran through the fallen tree branches. The boy, Michael, offered up all sorts of prayers to God, promising anything if He would organize a nice fat fish to take his bait. God must have been busy most of his fishing days. More likely, He did not believe Michael's promises. It was not too often his mother got to cook his catch for tea. Not on THE DAY though. He did not want a fish to disturb the line on THE DAY. He had prayed no fish would snavel the bait that day.

On the far bank, Lord Vickers' three children, two boys and a girl, had come to play with a bat and ball. They were supervised by a snooty looking lady, probably the Governess. Young Michael knew he would be in trouble if he was seen fishing here. He slowly withdrew into the shade of the branches drooping from the enormous willow trees. With great care, he began to wind in his line on the end of which was a cork above a bent pin hook with the piece of potato cake still attached. He endeavoured not to cause movement on the surface of the water or he would be spotted for sure. Once he retrieved the line and was safely hidden behind the tree trunk and other bushes, he took more notice of the playing children. The young girl was a corker with long black plaits hanging down her back and a cheeky crooked grin. She looked about one or two years younger than him. A baby really, compared to his esteemed age of ten years. Oh, but she could hit that ball – better than her older brothers. One of whom must have been about ten also, while the elder was about twelve or maybe thirteen. She whacked the ball repeatedly. The boys ran great distances to fetch it.

"Jessica! It is not ladylike to hit the ball with such force. A lady should just give a gentle bat to the ball," called the Governess.

"You hear that, Jessica? You are not to hit the ball so hard," whined the younger of the brothers. "Miss Cowan, could we have a rest now?" he asked. "Miss Cowan, will you be coming to London with Papa and Mother next week?"

"Yes, Geoffrey. Even though you and your brother David will be going to boarding school there, Jessica will need to be given her tuition."

"How long before we come back to the Manor?" young Jessica asked wistfully.

"That will depend on your father's responsibilities in the House of Lords, I presume," Miss Cowan replied. "Now, gather up the bat and ball it is time we returned to prepare for tea. Jessica, I wish you would wear your hat properly. A young lady does not want to have freckles on her face. Now, let us be going."

Disgruntled, Michael waited for some time before he moved out of his secure position. So much for his fishing expedition. It had been such a pest them coming down to the brook and spoiling his fun. Now, he needed to be slippery or his Pa would be on his tail for not bringing the cows up for the milking. Little did he appreciate then the massive impact her cheeky grin would have on his life in the years ahead.

Vaguely, Michael heard Paddymac, Harry and Mabel talking quietly in the background. Then Old Mister Wong asked Paddymac to lift Michael's shoulders. A foul-smelling liquid, with a taste to match, ran down his gullet. His head felt as if it was going to split open. Maybe it had and that was where all the memories were coming from.

Let me sink back into oblivion, let me die in peace, he thought as the shadows began to float before his eyes.

It was four or five years later before the boy, Michael, saw Jessica again. He was just getting settled at the brook with his line in the water and a book in one hand when a young lady of about twelve or thirteen sat on the bank on the far side of the stream. She also held a book in her hands. He had not recognized this girl until she looked over and smiled. Should he flee or stay?

"Do not let my father catch you with that line in the water. He thinks he owns everything in sight. You are the boy who was here fishing some years ago when my brothers and I came down to play bat and ball, were you not?"

Out came that wonderful crooked grin. Her hair was still in long plaits and her hat sat only partially upon her head. She was growing into quite a beauty.

"Yes, I'm he," replied Michael. "I didn't realize you'd spotted me. I'm sorry; I'll bring the line in now."

"I do not mind if you fish. I am sure we could spare a few fish. Are you able to catch many?"

"No, I don't catch a lot but I do enjoy the peace and tranquillity and the time to read my books," Michael responded.

After that day, he couldn't recall how many times he went to the brook with his line in one hand, a book in the other, and wild hope in his heart. Occasionally their visits coordinated but not often. They did find they had much in common and enjoyed similar books. Jessica raided her brothers' rooms or her father's library to indulge herself in more exciting and interesting books other than those prescribed by the Governess. If the book she was reading was 'unsuitable for a lady' she would hide it in the rug spread on the grass to protect her clothes. He noticed she always chose a place to sit amongst the shady trees so as not to be seen from the manor.

The pounding in his chest, as his mind recalled the past, added to the uneven flutter of his feverish heart in the bush hut, on the other side of the world, so many years later. The joy he felt when she made her way over the little bridge to join him on his side of the creek. The feel of her hand in his which had lasted forever. The first time she gently pressed her lips to his, still sweet upon his mouth. Oh, and the roar of Lord Vickers' voice from the other side of the creek.

"Jessica! Come home, AT ONCE!" The look of devastation on both their faces as they realized, they would most likely, never see each other again.

Harry and Mabel slept on a blanket in the corner of the small room. They had looked exhausted when they eventually settled down about an hour ago. Paddymac looked over at them with a fondness in his eye. No wonder they were worn out. Harry, with the sprinkling of grey throughout his thick hair, must be nearly seventy years old. He was older than Mister Michael who was much older than Paddymac. Mister Michael said Paddymac was five when they first met in Gulgong so that now makes him forty-seven-year-old. Harry's wife, Mabel, did not seem to have changed from the day they had met twenty years ago.

As Paddymac sat on the floor by the bed, his thoughts wandered. A straight back leant against the old ship's trunk Michael had carried from the goldfields. Inside were the two books with which Paddymac first began to learn his letters. There were many other books in there now. Mister Michael loved to read. He had books on adventures, how to do things such as building, breeding cattle and the newest was on sugar-cane growing. Thanks to Mister Michael's help, Paddymac now owned a block of land recently won in a land ballot allocated for cane farming. It was not too far distance from the east boundary of Emerald Flats; downstream and closer to where they were building the Inkerman Sugar Mill. After they had the timber cutters in, Gabby Bobangle, Harry's son, spent much of his time working with Paddymac clearing some of the smaller stumps using mattocks, shovels and axes. This work had brought out the sweat and blisters. Paddymac smiled at the memory. Old Mister Wong prepared an herb mixture to be rubbed on the wounds at night. It did take the pain away and hastened the healing. Last autumn they planted sugar-cane by hand on the cleared area – again, using the mattocks and shovels. They planted around the larger tree stumps still left in the paddock. Mister Michael said he would show Paddymac how to blow them out with gelignite one day.

Paddymac's eyes roamed about the room which held, besides the trunk, a bush-made chair now supporting Michael's saddle gear, a cupboard of sorts made of kerosene tins belted into submission and the bed upon which Michael now lay. Paddymac felt sick in his stomach. What if Mister Michael should die? Mister Michael had protected him since he had been belted senseless by his father in Gulgong. He had never seen his guardian as ill as this. What would become of him, without Mister Michael's guidance? At that moment, Paddymac jumped to his feet. The ill man, who had settled since drinking the herb brew earlier, now began to twitch and groan again. Paddymac wiped the sweat-covered body with the wet cloth to no avail.

"Oh, what should I do?" He whispered.

He remembered the instructions Mister Michael had given him on many occasions.

"If anything happens to me, let young Mister Wong know first. After I'm buried, you're to go to Mister Chiswell, the Solicitor in Townsville, and let him know. He'll help you. Now, Paddymac, you do remember where to find Mister Chiswell in Flinders Street, don't you?" He'd been to the big city with Mister Michael about twice a year, every year since they'd arrived on the Burdekin nearly twenty years ago. Mister Michael had shown him where he kept his money belt and instructed Paddymac to take it with him to pay for the trip. Paddymac was good with money. He'd learnt a lot in Mister Michael's store at Charters Towers. Not so good with other things. Mister Michael said it was because of brain damage when he was very young.

Paddymac nearly cried at the thought these actions may be needed. He pulled at his brown straggly hair incessantly. When he was younger, Mister Michael had taught him about the bible and God and how to pray, so that was what he began to do now as he watched his tormented friend.

In his fever, Michael's mind stirred. He had seen the sadness and compassion in his mother's eyes while his father read out the letter written by Lord Vickers. His groundsman had delivered it to their door the same evening.

"What were you thinking, lad? You know us farmers can't mix with the gentry. They'll have none of it. Lord Vickers has promised his daughter to a Lord in England. What could you offer her to compare? She's never done a lick of work in her life. Having servants throughout the house, she wouldn't know how, let alone be able, to keep going all day as your poor mother does. You must see reason and wish her well. Lord Vickers says, in this letter, he'll be removing his daughter to London as soon as possible."

Michael still recalled the paralysing numbness creeping through his body like the finger of the devil. He remembered his older brother, George's, quiet hand of support on his shoulder.

After this dreadful evening, he had thought his father was punishing him for causing such an uproar in the area. His mother assured Michael; work was the only way his father knew for getting over a disappointment. Work! Michael found work did indeed occupy his body but at night, Jessica filled his thoughts, keeping sleep at bay.

Within weeks he was on a ship bound for Australia. He carried very little baggage which included two of his and Jessica's favourite books. It was 1871 and he was twenty-one years of age. Oh, the pain. He could still feel it in his head and joints, in fact, in his whole body.

Paddymac kept his vigil. Mister Michael had looked after him for many years. It was Mister Michael who stood up to his father when in his drunken rages. Mister Michael never became impatient with Paddymac, even though he was slow to learn things. It was Mister Michael who had taught him to read and write.

Old Molly, at the hotel in Gulgong, said she had known Paddy since he was a mite and there was nothing wrong with his learning ability in those very early years.

"It was the savage beatings around the head by your drunken father that caused brain damage." Old Molly had gone on to say, "Your father was an angry man since your mother died giving birth to you, Paddy. I think he blamed you, which of course ain't right. It's one of the many things we just have to live with."

The heat, overwhelming heat! Now, Michael felt that unbearable heat again. Hotter even than he had felt every day when he made his beginning on the Gulgong goldfields shortly after he arrived in Australia. What a shock this new country had been for him. But there was no going back so he had to adapt, and adapt he did. Strange friendships began. It was thanks to the guidance of Old Molly and her husband at the local hotel, he had waded through the Government bureaucracy enabling him to purchase his claim. It was thanks to the help of a young Chinese fellow on an adjacent claim, Mister Wong, who taught him the intricacies in the art of gold-digging and panning. He did reasonably well at the claim near the Black Valley. It was probably good luck rather than good management. Mister Wong and he spent many Sunday afternoons discussing a wide range of issues: different country cultures and politics, the gold prices and who was honest and who might not be so. Michael sometimes talked of his home in Ireland but he was mostly reticent on his past life.

The fellow working the claim on his other side was hardly ever seen but he was heard a lot. He was a drunken lout with a small boy, of about five or six years of age, in tow. They lived on the claim in a hovel worse than any of the other campsites. Often the fellow could be heard yelling and cursing the lad. As far as Michael could tell, the lad was a good worker and was doing far more than he should or could do. On several occasions, Michael intervened. He could not stand by and watch the fellow use the child as a punching bag. The vision filled his head of the little fellow as he struggled to carry a kerosene tin of water to camp. The tin was almost bigger than the child. The drunk punched him around the head repeatedly while the little fellow tried to protect himself yet hold the water-tin upright. Michael had known it was not his place to interfere with a man bringing up his son, but enough was enough.

"Why don't you pick on someone your own size?" He called. "If you want to use someone as a punching bag you can try your fists out on me." The man never said a word, just went into his tent.

Michael's fevered brain took him to another incident in the town when, from the other side of the street, he had seen the child struggling to pull a cart laden with supplies. The drunk laid into him again with his fists, telling him to get the load home and have his tea ready when he came in later. The fellow had then stumbled back into the hotel. Michael went over and gave the kid a hand. In fact, he dragged the cart home with the young fellow sitting on top of the load. The smile on the little one's face was a sight to behold. Michael was appalled at the living conditions of the child who quickly put the stores away and began to fetch wood to start the fire.

"I have to get a Johnny-cake cooked for my Da's tea. Thank you for the ride, Mister."

It was one of those quiet Sunday mornings. He was returning from Mister Wong's claim when he noticed the young lad lying on the ground out in the burning hot sun. There was no movement in the twisted body. He ran over and found the lad unconscious. His head and limbs were black and blue. The small left arm looked as if it was probably broken. The child's entire visible skin was burnt red. Gently, he raised the lad and carried him back to his tent where he laid him on the bunk. When he pulled aside the tattered shirt, he found the boy's trunk also covered in bruises at all stages of progression. Michael cleaned the child up as best he could and was able to splint the arm as he had seen his mother do for the small animals at home. Gently he attempted to spoon water into the boy's mouth. Most of it ran down his chin but the lad was making small attempts to swallow, which was encouraging. Late in the afternoon, Mister Wong called in on his way back from the town. He was full of news.

"Have you heard about your drunk from next claim? Last night he in a fight. He get himself killed."

Michael was not at all surprised.

"Well, I've a surprise for you, too. You may be able to help with one of your herb brews."

Mister Wong was as dismayed as Michael had been at the evidence of beatings this young body had endured. Mister Wong examined Michael's attempt at the arm splint and seemed to think it was very good.

"I back soon with mixture for boy to reduce fever and lessen pain. What you do now he got no father? Who knows where his mother is?"

Michael did not reply. He would worry about that later. Firstly, he had to get the child back on to his feet.

It was several days before the lad could move about the campsite. He told Michael his name was Paddy McIntyre and he was five years of age.   It was not long before Michael had nicknamed him Paddymac. Paddymac became his shadow and was still with him over forty years later or was it a bit more? It must have been about that anyway. Michael's head hurt so much he could not remember clearly.

Harry and Mabel worked downstairs in the kitchen. Old Missus Wong had sent over a chicken soup having killed, plucked and cleaned the chook before daylight.

"Harry, go help Paddymac feed Mister Michael. Missus Wong say he must swallow more fluids if we are to make him better," Mabel handed her husband the tin plate and bent spoon.

As he lay exhausted on the bed, Michael felt his friends raise his head and spoon the soup into his mouth. At least it tasted better than Mister Wong's brew. The resulting coughing fit was not pleasant on top of his aching limbs and splitting headache though. He welcomed the darkness as it enfolded his mind and relieved his body of pain.

The look on young Paddymac's face when he had his first sight of Sydney set Michael laughing so much, he thought he would choke just like he was doing now. The boy's eyes looked ready to pop out of his head. When they boarded the ship on which they were to sail to Townsville, in North Queensland, the youngster's eyes filled his face.

During the trip, Michael started teaching the child to count and to read his alphabet. The lad was slow to learn but if things were explained to him clearly, he seemed to understand all right.

This time it was the heat of the Charters Towers' goldfields which tormented his ailing body. The unrelenting sun burnt on the way down to the land from where it bounced back and burnt you again. Oh, so much heat. It was 1873. Young Paddymac helped him as he worked his claim at Charters Towers. They made a good team. The lad never stopped smiling. He was keen to help. Unintentionally, Michael hurt the boy's feelings when he declared a job too much for one so young. Paddymac was game; that was for sure. Michael's lips twitched when, in his dreams, he smiled at the sight of the stray mongrel pup which had followed Paddymac back to their humpy. Paddymac hid the small pup in his bed not sure how Michael might react. The child needed something to call his own so the pup became the boy's constant companion. Heaven help anyone who might even look sideways at the lad. The dog set up such a show of bare teeth and rumbling growls which ended in outbursts of sharp barking. It looked as if the dog was going to tear a leg off – probably would, if let go.

Over time, Michael realized the only guaranteed returns on a goldfield were in merchandise supplies. After a particularly spectacular month's work, he decided to sell his claim and venture into the business. He bought six horses and a large wagon. With Paddymac as his offsider, he made regular trips to Townsville where he bought food and equipment such as shovels, panning dishes, separation cradles, tents and other supplies. These he sold quickly to hopeful gold fossickers, miners and prospectors. Each round trip took almost two weeks. Paddymac would have been about ten years of age by then. The boy had a magic way with those horses. They stood like angels when he hobbled them at night and in the morning, they returned to camp at the sound of his voice; happy to receive the little titbits hidden in the pockets of his pants.

The business had done so well, Michael bought a store in Charters Towers. He hired a fellow called Peter Coghlan to take the wagon to Townsville and return with the supplies. Young Paddymac went with him on each trip. Peter was good with the lad and never raised his voice. They kept that up until the railway line was built in 1882. Paddymac and Michael continued in the store for many years. There was much jubilation when Mister Wong, their neighbour from Gulgong, with his wife, two small boys and a baby girl walked through the door. Michael shut up shop and spent the afternoon catching up with his friend.

Rivulets of sweat tickled on their way down his face and into his hair. He struggled to scratch at other rivers of sweat running over his body. It seemed as if he floated above the room. His thoughts returned to sweet Jessica. Fresh pain knifed through his heart as he read, in his mind, word for word, the letter his brother George sent five years ago. Jessica had been killed in a riding accident when hunting with the hounds. Maybe she was here with him now. Perhaps he should join her. It would be so easy just to slip away.

Paddymac brought out his button accordion and began to play some of the tunes he had taught himself. Mister Michael always said it made enough noise to wake the dead. Maybe this is what he should do to ensure his friend stayed alive. While his fingers roamed the buttons on the musical instrument his thoughts roamed the pathways of his mind. Harry and Mabel had gone to carry out the routine farm chores. Three cows needed to be milked before being put out to feed. One of the female goats had a new kid yesterday and Mabel wanted to check they and the other few goats were safe and put out to pasture also. The few goats and sheep were all locked up in the small paddock near the house at night where the farm dogs kept away any prowling dingoes. Chooks, ducks and geese all waited to be fed. In a couple of days, Mabel would be looking for the fattest to kill and cook for Christmas. Before he had left the sick-room, Harry said he planned to saddle a horse and check the cattle.

Paddymac was glad they had moved from Charters Towers to this farm on the Burdekin River. Mister Michael and he had first explored the area on horseback. They travelled along the Burdekin River during the months of winter speaking to farmers who were already growing cane on the north side of the river. Here, with the animals, was better than the stark lands of the goldfields. On Emerald Flats, they ran over three hundred head of cattle including several grumpy old bulls, breeding cows, and bullocks. He was in charge of the horses. These were used for riding, pulling the sulky and several draught-horses pulled the wagon and dray. He had already begun training four of his favourites to pull the new plough when it arrived on the goods train.

In only a week, Mister Michael's nephew and family were due to arrive from overseas. Mister Michael said they would help with the workload, now he and Harry were growing old. Very fast, it seemed at times. Will they be nice people? Mister Michael says so.

"Please, God, make Mister Michael better."

On the rumpled bed, confusion filled Michael's mind. An explosion of his head felt imminent. It took some time to fathom the cause, then, "Paddymac! I told you that thing would wake the dead! What are you doing?"

No answer. Paddymac ceased playing immediately he heard Mister Michael's voice. He sat quietly and watched as his best friend blinked his eyes open and shut. Michael rubbed his eyes and face.

"What day is it, lad? How long have I been lying about? Shouldn't you be out working? What've you done to my head? It feels like I've been hit with a sledgehammer?"

A smile split Paddymac's face. Tears formed rivulets in the dirt on his cheeks. Mister Michael was awake and already starting to issue instructions.

"Harry and his boys are going out to check the cattle after they milk the cows. Can I get you something to eat and drink?"

"The first thing I want is a bath. I smell like a pig in a pen," said Michael. He hung his legs over the side of the bed and sat up. His hands flew to his head. "Ouch, this room is spinning. I feel as weak as a kitten."

Paddymac assisted Michael upright. With shuffling footsteps, they made their way down the stairs and over to the shower, under the tank-stand beside the windmill. They made an odd pair. Paddymac stood tall and stringy, clean-shaven with thinning salt and pepper coloured hair. Michael was at least three inches shorter with a head of thick fluffy snow-white hair and a full white beard. By the time they arrived, Michael sank gratefully to the stump where they usually put the towels. The large metal blades of the windmill screeched with every rotation. The rods rattled as they moved up and down delivering clear cool water from deep underground to splash cheerfully into the high tank.

"I'm sorry but the fire hasn't been lit under the hot-water drum for a couple of days so it'll probably be a cold shower," said Paddymac.

The large hot-water drum rested in a hollow dug out of the ground. Ant bed had been packed around the sides and a bed of coals lay under the base. A system of pipes channelled the water as the temperature rose when the fire was lit under the drum. This piped the hot water to the shower.

"That's the least of my worries at the moment," replied Michael. "Now leave the towel, I'll manage."

Worried at Mister Michael's pallor, Paddymac moved away a short distance. Mabel could be heard over in the kitchen cooking the porridge and boiling the billy on the woodstove.

Wearing a clean pair of trousers and a grey flannel singlet, Michael sat in the kitchen at the large table built out of split timber by Paddymac. In front of him rested a pannikin of strong tea.

"What day is it?" Michael asked for the second time this morning.

"Friday, the nineteenth of December, 1913." Paddymac referred to the calendar hanging lopsided from the rusty nail on the wall. "Your nephew, Shamus, and his family should have arrived in Townsville two days ago."

"Is it Friday already? What happened to the last three days?" Michael did not wait for an answer. "Right, now let's see. Mister Chiswell was going to meet Shamus and his family at the Townsville landing and deliver them to the Queen's Hotel. They'll stay there until next Tuesday when they're to catch the morning train to Home Hill. He should've seen them at his office yesterday to sign the necessary papers. What do you think, Paddymac? I do hope I've done the right thing by making Shamus partner in the property. My brother, George, always said in his letters how Shamus was the spitting image of me in all ways. I hope it'll be a good thing."

"If he's like you, he'll be a good man," replied Paddymac. "And if things don't work out as you planned, I've my own farm to live on now, Mister Michael."

Michael sat quietly remembering his family left in Ireland. It all seemed so far away and long ago. Eventually, he shook himself and spoke again to Paddymac.

"I doubt I'll be up to going into town in the wagon next week to collect them and their luggage from the train. You'll need to do it on my behalf, Paddymac. You might ask one of Harry's lads to take the horse and sulky to town as well. Come to think of it, you'd best take Haddi with you. Gabby can get on with the work at your place. If you left Haddi there on his own, with no one to supervise him, not a lick of work would be done. With two ladies arriving who knows how much luggage there might be. Shamus's wife and daughter might not take kindly to sitting on top of the load. With Christmas next week, we'll need room in the wagon for supplies from Coutt's store as well as all their gear."

Paddymac's left hand pulled at his hair while the other twiddled with the button on his shirt. He nodded. A raging bull might be easier to face than these strangers. But, for Mister Michael, he'd go willingly. He changed the subject.

"I'd better go saddle Bessie and get back to my place. The man should be arriving any day to inspect the site for the new pump. Tomorrow I can check the wagon, sulky, and harnesses to make sure they'll be ready for early Tuesday morning. Will I help you back upstairs before I go?"

"Yes, please. I'll rest in the squatter's chair on the front verandah for a while. If you see either Harry or Mabel ask if one of the family could help with the cleaning up before Shamus arrives."

After Paddymac left, Michael thought about all the jobs needing to be done. He was going to move into the workers' barracks. This was a large wood and corrugated iron, one-room building, on the other side of the house yard. There were several bunks with mattresses to choose from. On those nights when Paddymac slept at Emerald Flats and not in his humpy at his farm, he would join Michael there. Usually, any workers, such as the timber cutters, stayed there and made use of the general kitchen beside this hut. The builders, who had made a start on reconstructing the house Michael had bought-for-removal when last in Charters Towers, also slept in the workers' barracks. They weren't here at the moment having returned to Townsville for the Christmas break. It would've been much simpler if the dismantled building had arrived earlier as planned. It might've been completed if that were the case. Shamus and his family could have moved into it on their arrival. No good worrying about things that can't be changed. Bent fingers stroked the white beard.

On his last trip to Townsville some months ago, Michael brought back two large beds with mattresses, linen, blankets, pillows, and mosquito nets. Once the hut has been cleaned out, these beds were to be set up in each room. The single bed was to go on the verandah for the boy to sleep in. Lindsay was the lad's name.

"I hope that damn carpet snake doesn't make an appearance for a while. I don't want the family scared out of their wits with the thing slithering around the rafters chasing rats and birds. At least not until they've had a chance to settle in." Michael spoke to the old mongrel dog lying at his feet. The animal's ears flicked. The tail thumped on the wooden floor. "How long is it since I needed a daytime nap, dog?" asked Michael. "I feel quite sleepy." His eyes drooped and the dreams of the past continued.

When they first arrived at Emerald Flats, Harry and Mabel Bobangle were living with their family in a humpy on the river-bank. What would he have done without them? It was a good-sized block of land running beside the river. The property was mostly flat country with occasional small elevated areas. It was on one of these he had chosen for the house site. A large lagoon almost in the middle of the block of land linked via a channel to the river. When the tick fever decimated the northern cattle in the eighteen-nineties, they had lost quite a number of their stock. Paddymac struggled during that time. He hated to see the animals suffer. After the first dozen or so died, Paddymac fretted for days, cursing. As the numbers rose, he just stood over each dead body; his face closed. Only his clenched jaws reflected the turmoil inside. When they noticed how the surviving cattle seemed resistant to the tick fever and later discovered the progeny of those cattle appeared to have a resistance to the fever, they altered their breeding program. The losses were now minimal each year. Re-building the herd had been a slow and arduous process.

Shovels and crowbars were the prime tools when they first commenced fencing. Years later, Michael purchased a used hand-operated post-hole digger. There were many times when he grumbled bitterly telling anyone who listened, "Turning the damn thing around in the ground was no easier than using a shovel". Usually, he was a patient man but many a time he'd thrown the contrary thing to billyo while shouting loud curses after it. Scars still patterned his hands and arms where the barbed wire had torn the skin to shreds.

The other big job had been splitting the timber to build the cattle yards. They had persevered and built the yards large with several pens. Now a milking shed stood beside one of the yards. It was in this shed they milked the few cows each morning. Here, the saddlery gear was stored and lovingly preserved with lambs' fat by Paddymac.

An equipment shed stood in the north-west corner of the house yard and the house under construction awaited completion in the north-east corner. Harry's Camp and the Wong's lease lay near the river-bank.

Giggling awoke Michael from his slumbers. Millie and Tilly, Harry and Mabel's two youngest daughters stood at the top of the steps.

"Hey! You getting an old man, Mister Michael? How come you sleep in the middle of the day? Mum sent us to clean the place."

"Thanks, girls, and enough of the cheek. I'm not so old yet." Millie was usually the shy one while Tilly, her younger sister, was quite bold. Put them together and all they could do was giggle. They were married now and living with their families on the other side of the river, at Ayr. Michael explained to them what he wanted before dozing off again, leaving them to it. He knew everything would be ready for the family's arrival next week.

Chapter Three

Arrival in Australia

Mary stood at the ship's rail watching the hustle and bustle on the Townsville wharf. Her raised parasol did little to protect her from the blazing sun. Shamus had gone to fetch Lindsay who had spent the last two nights sharing the cabin with Mark's brothers, James and William. Mark now shared the cabin with Shauna since their wedding at the Sunday services.

A wistful expression sat sweetly upon Mary's face as she recalled the beautiful picture the bride had made dressed in pale blue. The colour of the dress brought out the sea green of her daughter's eyes and blended nicely with Mary's grey outfit. To ensure the couple has a long and happy marriage, Shauna's attire included similar good luck charms Mary wore on her wedding day. The bride wore 'something old' (a brooch that had belonged to her Grandmother), 'something new' (a camisole Mary had planned on giving Shauna as a Christmas gift), 'something borrowed' (a cameo necklace of Mary's) and 'something blue' (the dress she wore). Never would Mary admit she may be superstitious, just cautious. They paid special attention to the pinning of Shauna's auburn tresses high upon her head in a manner to enhance the small feathered Sunday-best hat she wore.

Mark and his brothers had looked very smart in their Sunday-suits, too. James and William impressed Mary. They were nice lads. Well-mannered and good looking. It was apparent, the three boys had a good upbringing. The quiet but special ceremony led by the Methodist Minister, Mr. Cameron, went smoothly. Mary's pale fingers touched her face where the tears had fallen when the couple had been pronounced husband and wife. Mark's mother had given him and his brothers, each, a small circle of her plaited hair. Several small plaits of hair had, themselves, been plaited into a bigger circle. The end result fitted snugly over Shauna's little finger. It was an amazing example of fine work and patience. Of course, she did not wear it after the ceremony. It was very fragile but it had made a wonderful sentimental substitute for the real thing. The couple planned to buy a traditional ring whilst in Townsville.

For a brief moment, Mary had shuddered when she noticed the look upon the face of James, the middle McIvor brother. She knew beyond doubt, the man was in love with her daughter, with his now, sister-in-law. Like the passing of a black raven, a foreboding had washed over her. Now as she stood on the ship's deck, she again felt that wave of fear. Mary shook herself. This was all nonsense. Probably something she had imagined in her state of nervous tension on the day. The man had behaved impeccably.

Mary admitted to herself a concern considering the couple had known each other for such a short time. But looking at them together and seeing how much they adored each other, she felt some reassurance. It had been a stroke of luck to find a photographer on board. Mr. Smithson was on his way to take up a post with the Townsville Bulletin Newspaper. Mr. Smithson instructed them to call into the newspaper office two or three days after they docked, to collect the photos.

With a lace handkerchief, she patted her face.

Whew! she thought, *I knew it was going to be hot but this is boiling hot. Shauna and I'll have to buy some light material here in*

Townsville before we take the train to Home Hill. She peered left and right. *I do wonder what's keeping Shamus.*

Mary found it all very exciting to watch the gangway being set into place. There were many people with horses, carts, drays and other means of transport including one of those new fandangle motorcars; waiting to meet friends and family, Mary guessed. A raucous mixture of loud voices calling in various languages accompanied the sounds of cargo being loaded onto the drays. Horses stomped their feet and snorted impatiently. There were several large buildings on the wharf which looked as if they may have held stores of some kind. A smaller building, looking very much like a government office, stood to the side and was most probably the customs office. It seemed a very chaotic scene but Mary assumed the people knew what they were doing. The commotion drifted up on the hot air.

She looked up from her musings at the sound of laughter. Mark and Shauna had joined her.

They do make such a handsome couple, Mary thought.

"Good morning, Mam," greeted Shauna. "Isn't this so exciting? I feel a little nervous though. How about you?"

"Hello, dear, Hello, Mark. Yes, there's certainly a crowd. Look, the people are starting to leave the ship and see, they're unloading the cargo further down. Oh, I do hope my treadle sewing machine has weathered the journey safely. You did pack the new china set securely with the linen as I showed you, Shauna."

Mark let his mind drift as Mary prattled her worries to his sweet Shauna. As usual, it led him back to the wedding night with his beautiful wife. His heart again pounded at the memory of her shy glances as piece by piece her attire fell to the floor. A curtain of flaming hair had allowed tantalizing glimpses of a snow-white skin glowing in the moonlight streaming through their port-hole window. He twitched at the discomfort when he felt a rising in his loins at the recollection of his fingers as they traced the outline of her perfectly shaped young body. Again, he held his breath as he had when her trembling fingers made short work of the buttons of his shirt and trousers. A soft groan escaped his smiling lips.

Mary turned to her son-in-law. "Are you alright?"

Mark's face reddened. He pressed himself into the ship's rail to conceal the evidence of where his thoughts might have travelled.

"Yes, thanks, Mrs. Doolan. Er … I was just watching those kids down on the wharf. One of them will surely end up under a horse's hoof or a dray wheel."

Shauna looked closely at her new husband and grinned. She rescued her lover.

"Mam, I wonder how long we'll have to wait before we can disembark?"

"Oh dear, where are your father and Lindsay?" Mary started to fluster.

"I'll go and hurry them for you," said Mark. "Will you two ladies be safe here?"

The ladies smiled at his concern.

Below deck, Mark found Shamus, Lindsay, and his two brothers just coming out of the cabin.

"Mrs. Doolan's becoming anxious," commented Mark with a smile. "The stewards will deliver our travelling luggage to the Customs on the wharf. I'm not sure she trusts you with the packing, Shamus."

"Don't be smart now, young pup," returned Shamus with a grin. "Lindsay and I've just finished up and we're on our way. I think you may get the edge of my wife's tongue if you don't stop calling her, Mrs. Doolan. She wants you to call her, Mary." Shamus turned to

James and William. "I know you're staying at Buchanan's Hotel but you'll come and have dinner with us at the Queen's Hotel tomorrow night, won't you? Who knows how long it may be before we meet again, once you begin on your travels?"

"To be sure, Mr. Doolan, to be sure," Mark's brothers replied in unison.

When they found their way to the Custom's building, Mark commandeered chairs for the ladies. Now on the docks, the noise assaulted their ears. It appeared they were in for a long wait when a well-dressed middle-aged man approached them.

"Excuse me. Would you be the Doolan family?"

"Yes," replied Shamus, "may I help you?"

"I think I may be able to help you. My name's Jonathon Chiswell. I'm Michael Doolan's solicitor here in Townsville. It was I who forwarded Michael's letter to you regarding his property, Emerald Flats."

"Oh, yes, thank you," said Shamus. "May I introduce the family to you? My wife, Mary, my son Lindsay, this is my daughter, now Mrs. Shauna McIvor, and her husband, Mark. These two lads with us are Mark's brothers, James and William. They'll not be staying at the same hotel as us but have other plans."

Everyone greeted the solicitor and made small talk about their journeys for a short time until Mr. Chiswell held up his hand.

"I should be able to help you through this process a lot quicker. If you wait here a moment, I'll see the head clerk who just happens to be a personal friend. Please give me your cargo luggage identification and my assistant will arrange transportation."

James, William, and Mark only had the duffle-bag and Gladstone bag they each carried with them.

At the hotel, Shamus and his family shared a light lunch with Mr. Chiswell, to whom they were very grateful. Without his help, the wait at the Customs' shed would have been long and arduous. They would have had to organize transport for themselves and their luggage. They learnt Mr. Chiswell and Uncle Michael were old friends as well as business associates. Mr. Chiswell said he did not understand why Michael was not here to meet them, as planned. No doubt a telegram would be waiting for him at the office today or tomorrow. He explained it would depend on someone from the property travelling a considerable distance to the Home Hill Post Office to send it. This did make communication less than reliable. Once arrangements were made to meet with Shamus tomorrow morning at ten o'clock to finalize the official business, Mr. Chiswell returned to his work.

"Shamus, this hotel has a lovely setting looking out over the water." Mary took the last sip of her lemon drink. "I don't know about anyone else but I plan on lying down for a little, once the room has been put to order. How about everyone else?"

"If you don't need a hand, I think Lindsay and I'll explore the town," replied Shamus. "What do you say, Lindsay, not too old for a long walk?" he chuckled to his young lad.

Mark smiled at Shauna. "Would you mind if I left you alone for a while? I'd like to seek out the banks in the town and assure myself my finances are available to me here? I'll need to ask if they have a branch where we're going. I'm sure you'd find a visit to the bank ever so tiresome. Tomorrow, while your parents are doing business with Mr. Chiswell, we can select a proper wedding ring for you, if you wish."

"Yes, of course, my dear. I like Mam's plan best and will close my eyes for a bit."

The group broke up and all went their separate ways; Shamus and his son to walk the waterfront and Mark on his errands.

"Will you look at this?" James McIvor spoke to his brother who peered in through the door of the saddler's shop. William stepped back under the shady tree. On the opposite side of the street, a black horse and sulky stood parked outside a business house. A prim looking young lady of about ten or eleven years sat on the seat of the sulky. Two mischievous boys were on either side poking their heads around the wheels giving cheek to the little miss.

If James and William had been closer, they would have heard the boys saying,

> "Who do you think you are?
> A little miss with hair so fair
> Holding your nose up in the air,
> Just a galah, that's who you are."

They chanted before diving back behind the sulky where they burst into giggles at their perceived brilliance at poetry.

James turned to William. "Threepence says the little lady throws a tantrum."

"I'll take your bet. She looks every bit the lady. Look at the way she's dressed in all the frills and shoes with socks on her feet, no less. She'll just ignore them." replied his brother.

Hardly had the bet been taken when they saw the little miss stand up, stamp her feet, and say, "You little dingo pups! You get away from me or I'll wrap this driving whip around you both." In one motion she grabbed the whip out of its stand in a hand comfortable with its weight. "And I'll lay you out for the horse to stomp on ten times. Drongos!"

James and William laughed quietly for a moment. "I'll take your three pennies brother. Oh, no! What are the blighters up to now?

That's firecrackers they're lighting. This could be dangerous. William, run!" James and William began to run towards the horse. The crackers went off. The horse kicked out savagely with its back legs, reared up screaming a loud whinny and started to bolt. James and William grabbed a hold on either side of the bridle but the terrified horse dragged them for seventy yards before they could bring it to a stop. Their hands gripped around the harnessing held them upright. Waves of tremors rippled through the animal. Salty sweat foamed its sides. Only the whites of its eyes could be seen. James and William looked back at the young girl who sat pale, still, and silent on the seat. White knuckles gripped the edge of the sulky. The brothers assumed she was in shock. But the little miss stood up, climbed out of the sulky and walked to the head of the horse.

"Steady, Blackie," she said quietly. "If I ever see those idiots again, I'll tear their ears from either side of their heads. Steady, Blackie."

A look of disbelief passed between the brothers.

A well-tanned man wearing countryman's trousers, boots, white shirt, and jacket ran towards them. A large hat, held in his hand, flapped against long legs.

"Maryann! Maryann! Are you all right?   What on earth happened?"

"Don't blame Blackie, Father. Two stupid, brainless, fat-head, idiot boys lit firecrackers under his back feet. I'm going to rip their guts out." The little miss replied.

"Steady on, girl. If your mother heard you talking like that you'd be locked up in your room for a month," her father said with a grin. "Obviously, you're not seriously damaged."   He turned towards James and William who were still holding the slowly recovering horse. "I must thank you boys from the bottom of my heart. You've saved my daughter's life and a very precious one it is too. How can I thank you?"

"No thanks needed," they replied in unison.

The men stood and spoke for several minutes. James and William learnt the girl's father hailed from a cattle station outside a town called Charters Towers. His name was Matthew Littlewood. He introduced his daughter, Maryann. Mr. Littlewood was in town on business after having delivered cattle from his property to the Ross River Meatworks. He hoped to hire more stock-hands before his return. James explained they may be interested in a job. The group made arrangements to meet that evening to discuss the idea.

"I wish I'd been there!" exclaimed Lindsay as he heard William and James relating their experiences of the previous day. "Tell us again how you raced out and dragged the horse to a stop? Oh boy, that would've been so exciting. What did the father say? What did he do? I bet he was pleased. The girl sounds pretty good – for a girl, that is."

"Lindsay! We are at the meal table remember; little boys should be seen and not heard," stated his mother. She turned to James who, with William, had joined them for the evening meal on Thursday. "What did the father say?"

At first, James did not hear what Mary had asked. His bowed head hid the confusion swarming through his body like a host of bees. His and Shauna's eyes had met, accidentally, across the table. The pumping of his heart deafened him. It was his brother, William, who spoke up with a grin.

"He was very grateful. The upshot of it is, James and I will be joining him on his return journey to Charters Towers tomorrow. Our travels are just beginning. Apparently, we're now called Australian

Stockmen and droving cattle will be our current form of employment."

Shauna had glanced across the table to hear James's answer to her mother's question. The lurch of her stomach when her green eyes locked into the serious blue of James's eyes caught her unawares. They had both dropped their heads immediately. She felt the heat creep up her neck to suffuse her face. Her breath caught in her throat. Her thoughts swirled. What just happened? Trembling fingers smoothed the tablecloth as if the linen might represent her turbulent feelings. Her fork clattered on the china plate as she played with her food. Her mind was so taken with her thoughts she didn't notice, at first, when Mark leant towards her ear.

"Are you alright, Shauna?"

She turned with a whispered reply, "Yes, yes, Mark. I'm fine."

"You are quite flushed. I think you need to rest."

She smiled at her husband, grateful for his discernment.

Later, when James and William were preparing for an early start in the morning, Mark said, "James, you take care of little brother now."

"Don't you think he's big and ugly enough to look out for himself?" A chuckle accompanied the answer.

While Mark was downstairs saying goodbye to his brothers, Shauna sat in their room writing a letter to the family back in Ireland. Frequently her gaze fell upon the wide band of gold snug upon her left, third finger. Tomorrow, Shauna and her mother had plans to shop for whatever they might need at their new home. McKinnon's shop looked to be a likely place to buy materials. They were to make a call to the newspaper office and collect the wedding photos also.

Shamus, Mark and Lindsay intended to explore inside the Burns Phillips warehouse down near Ross River.

Busy with her plans and struggling not to recall her reaction to her eye contact with James earlier in the evening, Shauna did not hear Mark's quiet return.

He bent to kiss her head. "Come to bed, woman. Everyone else has had your attention for the last few hours. Now it's my turn, wife."

Shauna looked up in surprise. Not at the words so much as the note of flint within them which was reflected in the narrowed darkened blue eyes surrounded by a tight smile.

She gasped. "Mark, are you angry at me for something?"

"No, of course not. Sorry, I didn't mean to sound so abrupt. It's just," he paused for a brief second, "you seem to have been surrounded by people all day, including my two brothers; now I want some attention myself."

He bent and kissed her gently. Shauna kissed him back but hurt still gnawed at her mind while guilt at her reaction to James's earlier glance buried deeper into her memory.

In their room, Mary and Shamus were discussing the day just past.

"Shamus, I do hope nothing is seriously wrong with your Uncle Michael. The telegram Mr. Chiswell passed on to us didn't say a lot. What sort of fever do you think he could have?" Mary looked over at her husband resting on their bed. On a bunk against the wall, Lindsay's eyes drooped as he lay reading.

"Mary, I'm sure it's nothing. This is the tropics and there are many types of fevers to be had, I should think. It's only a few days until we meet him so we'll find out then. This place of his, Emerald Flats, sounds more impressive than I'd first thought. It's quite a way from the village though. We'll be rather isolated and there'll be little company, I should think."

Shamus was surprised to find when they visited Mr. Chiswell this morning, his Uncle Michael had already signed the property partnership papers some months earlier when in Townsville arranging delivery of a farm irrigation pump. Uncle Michael had left a message with Mr. Chiswell asking Shamus to look at a horse-drawn plough on display at the Burns Phillip warehouse. He wanted his nephew's opinion on the implement. That errand was on Shamus's list for the following day.

On the train heading west towards Charters Towers, James McIvor rested his elbows on the open window of the carriage. His mood was pensive. His unseeing eyes missed the disappearing suburbia as they passed through the outskirts of Townsville. He was oblivious to the closing in of the bush from the changing green colours of the coast to the browner inland shades. James felt as though he had left something behind and he knew what it was – his heart. No amount of his mother's cod liver oil would heal this hollow lead weight in his belly. He loved his brother, Mark, and James knew it was best he be on his way. If it had been anyone else but his brother, he would have fought hard to win the love of the beautiful Shauna.

William shouted from the window frame beside him, "This is it, James. We're truly on our way."

Four days later, Lindsay was beside himself with excitement. For most of the train trip south, his head had been stuck out of the window. He ignored the smoke and dust as they stung his eyes but gazed, enraptured, at the passing countryside. The trees were so tall. They were gum trees; the man in the next seat had told him so. He had also been told, the birds making the big noise outside the hotel window each morning, were called kookaburras and they laughed every morning and again at night. That appealed to his sense of humour. The rattle of the train wheels on the steel tracks hypnotized. A thrill ran through his body at the loud hollow sound of the wheels on the tracks each time they went over gullies or creeks. The first sugar-cane came into sight near Donoghue's Siding. The guard on the train said this area was called the Haughton River and was the halfway point between Townsville and Home Hill, to where they were going. The sugar-cane swayed like a sea of green waves as the wind blew the plant tops.

When the train rocked and rattled slowly over the new Burdekin River rail bridge, Mark's thoughts were interrupted by his wife's call.

"Mark! Quickly! Hold on to Lindsay's feet; he'll surely fall out of the window if he hangs over any further."

Mark was torn between admiring the land they were passing and admiring the view of his new and beautiful wife. Pride filled his chest. He looked forward to when he could have her to himself. At her call, he grabbed Lindsay's feet, just in time to stop him from taking a swim in the Burdekin River.

Shamus had spent the journey watching the countryside with avid interest. He also felt a little humbled and hoped that, at the age of forty-eight years, he would be able to meet the challenge ahead of them in this developing land.

Mary enjoyed looking at the country through which they passed but her mind kept thinking of what may be ahead. What type of living conditions would they encounter? How would they access supplies? According to Mr. Chiswell, a Doctor Chambers and a Matron Grey ran a small private hospital at Ayr, on the north side of the river, called Wyndara. It might be a hell-raising trip to travel there if you were in difficulties. At least, the rail link from Home Hill to Ayr had been completed recently. The access to medical help particularly worried her now Shauna was married. God willing, her daughter would soon have a child of her own. A frown drifted across her brow as she remembered her own experiences in labour and those times when she had assisted other birthing women. Her mother always said delivering a baby was mostly a case of being a good catch, but if things went wrong, it could mean dire consequences. She shook herself, knowing it was unproductive to worry.

Mary forced her mind to think of other things. A smile sparkled in her eyes at the memory of the picnic on The Strand at Townsville when they listened to the local band practising. Lindsay and Mark had appeared to get on so well. They must have run for miles, up and down the beach, in the afternoon. A soft chuckle passed unheard as she thought how relieved Shamus looked when he was able to give in early and let Mark do the running. It was constant amazement for her just how little the suffocating heat seemed to affect the younger ones. Her gaze ran over her family. Everyone would be tired by the time they reached Uncle Michael's farm later, maybe even after dark. She had made sure to bring some bread and sandwich makings just in case there was not enough food. Shamus had laughed at her. He was sure Michael would be able to feed everyone.

Smoke poured out of the train's funnel as it strained to climb the south bank of the Burdekin River.

Shamus called to his son-in-law. "Look, Mark, that must be the Inkerman Sugar Cane Mill Mr. Chiswell told me about. They're hoping to have it ready for the crushing this coming year. There's the workers' camp next to it, I presume." Young cane, four feet high, grew nearby.

After a short stop at Carstairs, near the Inkerman Mill, the train built up a little pace. A few scattered buildings came into view from the left-hand side of the train. Shamus sat up with interest.

"The main street, I presume. I think I can see a grocery shop." He turned his head to Mark. "Does that say, 'Coutts'?" He pointed to a building further down the street. "You can see 'Teitzel Brothers Butchery' easily enough."

The train's whistle pierced the quiet town's streets as the wheels ground to a crawl.

"Yes, Shamus, and there's what looks like a boarding house and a café near those trees?" Mark pointed.

"I hope that's a newsagency. I like to keep up with the world news." Shamus pointed this time. "It's a bit difficult to see properly looking through the trees and past the railway sheds."

"I can see it! I can see it!" called Lindsay. "This is the Home Hill Railway Station. Look, there's the sign." The family all strained to peer out of the windows.

When the engine came to a halt, everyone scrambled for their light luggage and exited the carriage.

"Be careful, ladies, let me help you. It's quite a step to the platform!" called Mark who was beaten out only by Lindsay.

Porters were seen unloading the heavier cargo further along the train. A tall slim man, about Shamus's age, approached them. He twisted an old felt hat round and round in large hands. He wore clean but unironed grey trousers and a white shirt with the sleeves rolled up. By his side walked a tall and very straight-backed, dark-skinned, younger man who appeared to be encouraging the older man.

"Excuse me," the older man spoke to Shamus. "Would you be Mister Shamus Doolan and family?"

Shamus looked the man up and down. This could not be his Uncle Michael because his father had told him he was the spitting image of himself. This man did not look like him at all. Mind you, Mary was always saying he should lose a bit of weight.

"Yes, I'm Shamus Doolan."

"Sir, I'm Paddy McIntyre, Mister Michael's friend. Everyone calls me Paddymac. Mister Michael's still not strong enough to make the trip to town today to meet you but Haddi here," he pointed to the dark-skinned man standing by his side, "and I have come to take you home to Emerald Flats."

Shamus liked the sound of 'home to Emerald Flats'. His spirits lifted.

"Thank you, Paddymac. Pleased to meet you and Haddi. May I present my wife, Mary, my daughter Shauna, my son Lindsay, and my son-in-law, Mark."

Once introductions were completed, Paddymac took them to the front of the station where four horses stood harnessed into a large wagon already loaded with supplies. Next to the wagon, another horse stood patiently attached to a sulky.

"Mister Michael said the ladies may like to ride in the sulky. It wouldn't be a very comfortable journey on top of the loaded wagon," commented Paddymac.

"Sounds a good idea, Paddymac. I remember where I've heard that name. You're the young lad who used to write the letters for our Uncle Michael to his brother, my father, years ago. Uncle Michael said it was his way of teaching you how to write because there were no teachers or schools where you both lived. My father thought the letters were very good."

Paddymac blushed.

"Paddymac, how did this town get its name? I can't see a hill anywhere," asked Shauna.

Paddymac grinned. His blush deepened. "Mister Michael said it was named after a battle site on the field of Inkerman, during the Crimean War last century."

Paddymac drove the wagon around to the goods shed where the remainder of the Doolans' cargo was transferred quite easily by two strapping railwaymen, Paddymac, Haddi, and Mark.

The sun rested low on the horizon as they turned into the property. Shamus jumped down to hold the wooden slat gate open wide.

"This is Emerald Flats, Missus," informed Haddi turning towards the two women.

On the left of the sulky, a fence stretched ahead close to the track. A paddock with tall trees opened out to the right. A herd of cattle rested near some undergrowth. After travelling for almost a mile, they came to a second gate. Two medium-sized, black and white dogs circled the horse and buggy silently. Around and around they inspected and contained the visitors; like they were stray cattle at round-up time.

"This is house yard, Missus." This time Haddi jumped down to open the gate. He snapped a command at the dogs. They sat with tongues out and drooled from their mouths.

Shamus picked up the reins and with a light flick encouraged the horse through into the yard while Haddi shut the gate behind them. Through the dusk, they could see further back to their left a maze of cattle yards spread out with what looked like stables built beside them. Nearer the gate stood a raised rectangular timber building with a corrugated iron roof.

"The workers' barracks, Missus," Haddi explained at Mary's questioning glance. Rusty rooves of more farm sheds looked over a stand of fruit trees. A windmill and tank stood in the middle of the compound near where a high wooden building was in the process of being built. Haddi turned the horse and sulky right which brought them up to a small hut raised on posts five feet high. They rounded the corner of this building and stopped beside a large room built on the ground. Smoke drifted lazily out of the chimney. A large table could be seen through the open wooden awning windows.

"What's this building?" Shamus had said little all the way into the property. He absorbed everything he could see.

"This Mister Michael and Paddymac's house. They now in worker's hut leaving this empty for you until new house over there, done." A dark arm reached out in the direction of the new building under construction.

Mary gasped as a multi-coloured river of people flowed out from the kitchen. In the lead, an elderly, not so tall man, with snow-white unruly hair and a full snow-white beard approached the new arrivals. He was dressed in wrinkled dark trousers and a white shirt. On his feet, he wore a pair of elastic-sided boots with not a lot of elastic left. The two dogs came to a panting, tongue-lolling rest on either side of the man.

"I'm Michael Doolan." Michael extended his hand out to his nephew. Instead of shaking hands, Shamus drew the older man into a bear hug. Mary was sure she saw tears in both the men's eyes. After Mary and Shauna were introduced to Michael, he drew them forward to meet the group of people standing quietly at his back.

An elderly Chinese man of medium height and thinning grey hair shuffled forward.

"We happy to meet you, Mr. and Mrs. Doolan. We hope you have nice trip. You'll be hungry and tired. A meal is prepared. I'm Old Mr. Wong. My wife, Old Mrs. Wong." He indicated to the little Chinese lady with white hair and a bent back standing beside him. The long sleeves of his jacket fell back revealing skinny arms. These now spread out towards the others, similarly dressed, of all ages who stood around him. "My family."

Old Mr. Wong then pointed to a tall dark-skinned man and his plump dark wife. In the shadows, several pairs of eyes shone in the lamplight from the kitchen. "This is Harry and Mabel. They and their family work with Michael and Paddymac, here, on Emerald Flats. They live at Harry's Camp on the river. We leave now, you settle in. You very welcome. Tomorrow enough time to meet everyone proper."

By this time, Paddymac pulled the wagon to a halt nearby in a flurry of dust. Lindsay and Mark slithered down from the top of a high load. Lindsay stood goggle-eyed as he watched all the people making their way into the approaching night. He could see black people and Chinese people and other kids to play with. He knew this was going to be a wonderful place to live. Shamus introduced Uncle Michael to his son and son-in-law.

"This is a surprise; I didn't know young Shauna was married."

"It was a surprise to all of us, I guess. They were married on the boat the weekend before we docked," Shamus answered.

Michael congratulated the couple then turned towards the hut.

"I'll show you to your accommodation. This little house is only temporary until the new house has been completed, in the New Year, we hope, or before the cane crushing next year, at least." Michael took a lamp from a line of lamps on the kitchen wall just inside the door and lit it. Within its glow, he led the way up the stairs. "We've the two bedrooms and there's a bunk for the lad out on the verandah. You can move it into the hallway if you prefer. Each bed has a mosquito net and we even have some sheets. Please make sure you tuck the mosquito nets in tight at night. They'll keep out any nocturnal animals wandering around." Michael instructed. A shiver ran down Mary's spine. She looked over at Shauna who rolled her eyes.

Mary touched Michael on the arm. "Uncle Michael, I feel bad you've moved out of your house for us; especially when you've been ill. I'm sure we could've made do in the workers' hut."

"Now don't you go worrying yourself, lass. This'll be much more suitable for you ladies than in the shed; particularly when the workers return in the New Year."

By the time the group returned to the kitchen they found Paddymac preparing a pot of tea and setting out tin plates on a roughly hewn table on which a carbide lamp spluttered out a bright light. Looking about her, Mary first noticed the table with its wooden forms on either side which took up most of the area. A dish of hen eggs sat on the table beside the lamp. Rough wooden shelving and innovative cupboards made from kerosene tins, similar to those she had seen in the bedrooms, were down one side of the long room. A wooden bench held two large tubs and a bucket. At the far end of the room, on a wood stove, a large kettle whistled up a fierce head of steam. Near this, aromatic steam bubbled from under the lids of two small cauldrons. When Mary lifted the lids, she found a soup simmering in one and a meaty stew in the other. Her eye caught sight of a hessian-covered wire frame hanging near the doorway on the side closest to Michael's small hut. Water leaked from a small container on the top of the frame leaving the hessian damp. Turning to Paddymac she asked what it was for. Paddymac walked over and opened a wire door at the front. Inside were three wire shelves on which stood a plate of butter, a jug of milk and a bowl of meat.

"The breeze on the wet hessian keeps this food quite cool and we have it over here to be away from the hot stove and shaded from the afternoon sun. It's called a Coolgardie safe."

"And what's this floor made of?" Mary tapped the floor under her shoe.

"That's packed ant bed," Paddymac continued. "You'll find it is almost as hard as cement."

With a rueful smile, Mary placed the picnic food she had carried from Townsville onto the table.

"If you men sit, Shauna and I will serve up this wonderful meal. Did Uncle Michael prepare this Paddymac?" she asked.

Paddymac laughed. "If it was left to Mister Michael, we'd be eating bully beef and damper. No, I would think Old Mrs. Wong or her daughters-in-law have made the chicken soup and Harry's wife, Mabel, or her daughters-in-law have made the meat stew. A beast was killed yesterday so it'll be fresh. See the vat over in the corner? Inside will be the excess of meat soaking in the brine. Mister Michael and I have salted some of the meat and have it drying in the smoke shed. Mabel renders the fat down for us to grease the leather gear. Old Mrs. Wong and family boil the bones from which we'll all get some beef stock for soups and stews."

Shauna carried a large bowl of sliced yellow fruit to the table. "What's this, Uncle Michael?"

Michael smiled. "That, young Shauna, is mango, the gift of the Gods. Try it and tell me what you think. Don't worry about the strings in your teeth; they taste great too."

Shauna bent closer to the bowl and sniffed. "It smells sweet." Her slim fingers lifted out a thick slice of the fruit dripping with juice and slipped it into her mouth. Her teeth chewed the flesh. She smiled and wiped at her mouth with her hand. "Hmmm, that's very good." She turned to her brother. "Here, Lindsay, try this."

His eyes lit up as the flavour teased his taste buds. "Does this fruit grow here, Uncle Michael?"

"It does, lad; on the tree outside this kitchen. You're welcome to eat all you want. One thing you must remember is to wash your face and hands when finished because the sweet juice can irritate the skin."

A half-moon brightened the grounds outside the hut. Both Mary and Shauna, in their separate bedrooms, snuggled in closer to their partners as they remembered the warning from Uncle Michael regarding the nocturnal animals. Several times, Mary had checked the net around Lindsay was well tucked in. The lad was not at all concerned and like most small boys put full trust in the capabilities of the old dog lying softly snoring on the floor beside him. He was rather thrilled to be camped out on the verandah.

"What do you think, Shamus? Will Lindsay be safe out there?" Mary asked.

"If Uncle Michael thinks he's safe then I'm sure he's safe,'" was the reply. "Besides, they don't have lions or tigers in Australia. Uncle Michael said his dog, Just Dog, is his name, will remain on guard beside the bed all night."

"Just Dog – that's a strange name. Did he tell you what the name of the other dog was?"

Shamus chuckled. "That one's named, Old Dog."

Mary smiled in the darkness. "How original."

Meanwhile, in the room across the hallway where the large windows were pushed wide open to catch every little bit of breeze, Shauna also found sleep elusive despite their exhausting day.

"How safe do you think we are? What sort of animals do you think we have to be concerned about, Mark?" There was no answer. Mark lay in the arms of deep slumber.

Chapter Four

Christmas at Emerald Flats

"Mam! Mam! Are you awake yet?" called Lindsay as he came bounding up the stairs. His face was red, his hair had not seen a brush this morning and there were no shoes on his feet.

"Well, I would be now, even if I were dead," replied Mary as she rushed out of the bedroom where she had been trying to secure the mosquito net. "Shauna may be trying to sleep. Will you please keep it down? And where are your shoes?"

"Yes, Mam. No, Mam, Shauna's in the kitchen cooking breakfast. I was up at piccaninny dawn with Uncle Michael, Paddymac, Pa and our Mark. Guess where I've been," he continued with no intention of giving his mother the chance to respond. "Pa and Mark milked the cows for Paddymac. I gathered all the dry cow pats into a huge pile. Tonight, they're going to light the pile. The smoke smell keeps the mosquitoes away from the horses and the cows; then they won't be upset and make less milk. Akama, Sabbo, Cabri, Maani and Gabrel showed me where the carpet snake lives. It's a mile long and as fat as a cow. It had a slippery shiny skin. It won't hurt you if you leave it alone. The bite's not poisonous; might make you a bit sick though. It eats all the rats in the storage shed." Lindsay gabbled on without taking a breath or feeling any guilt at the exaggeration.

Confused at all these strange names but reassured no life-threatening event had befallen her son, despite all the noise, Mary instructed him, "Slow down, Lindsay. Now, repeat slowly what you've just said."

After Lindsay had calmed down a little and repeated his story, Mary wanted to know who were these people he was talking about.

"They are Harry and Mabel's grandchildren. They live at Harry's Camp, on the river. Akama, Sabbo and Cabri, she's a girl, fed the goats and let them out into the front paddock. Maani and Gabrel are the twins. I'm older than them. They fed the hens and ducks before putting them out to run in the yard. We collected loads of eggs. The boys know where their secret nests are. They took some eggs home to their families and I gave some to Shauna. After breakfast, we're going to take the rest over to Old Mrs. Wong. We have to make sure the hens don't wander over to Old Mrs. Wong's place. If the hens get into the vegetable gardens, they'll be chicken soup."

At this point, Mary had made her way to the top of the stairs, her head awash with all this news. She stopped abruptly.

"Lindsay, I do hope you kept well away from the snake. What did Uncle Michael say when you went near it? And what was it you said about piccaninnies?"

"Oh, that's what Uncle Michael calls the time, early in the morning, when the sky is just starting to lighten." Lindsay chose to ignore the interrogation regarding the snake. He was beginning to learn a lesson all boys need to know; sometimes when communicating with their mother, ignorance can be bliss. It was hard to get anything past his mother though.

Mary's thoughts had moved on. She was pleased to see between the bedroom hut and the kitchen, a rough wooden bench upon which sat two large tubs. A tap was attached to a house post.

"That's a good sign," Mary murmured, "running water."

A dead tree lay on the ground parallel to the kitchen and about ten yards away. Two kerosene tins with darkened bottoms stood upside down beside the end of the tree blackened with charcoal. Mary pondered for a moment. Eventually, she guessed she may be looking at the clothes' washing facilities. Light a fire at the end of the tree, boil water, soap and clothes in the kerosene tins then rinse in the large tubs on the bench. She noticed the wash-worn, three-foot length of stick used for lifting the hot clothes out of the boiler.

From the top of the steps, Mary surveyed the compound again, in daylight this time. She identified the ginger plants, banana and papaya trees as Paddymac had called them, growing thickly in the moist ground near the water tank and bathroom. Quite some distance behind this stood the toilet, or as Uncle Michael called it, 'the dunny', shaded by a huge mulberry tree. Uncle Michael had told them silk worms lived in the mulberry tree. Mary smiled as she pondered if it was true or was it a story for Lindsay. Shauna and Mary had the dubious pleasure of investigating this outhouse, seeking snakes and spiders, in the lamplight last night. A wood-framed box having a seat with a lid on top and a door at the front to give access for the black-tar covered pan inside, made up the "queen's throne". Mary figured this option was a lot better than the hole in the ground with a log across it to sit on, which is what she had been told to expect. A box of sawdust and piles of old newspapers were supplied inside. The walls were constructed of old canvas tied around four poles and the roof was several bark strips lying over wire netting then held down with a few branches and rocks. Mary headed there now. Later she planned a walk over to investigate the other farm buildings.

"Good morning, Shauna," Mary greeted her daughter later when she entered the kitchen. "How did you sleep, dear?"

"I was sure I wouldn't sleep a wink, thinking about those nocturnal animals Uncle Michael referred to, but it wasn't too long before I dropped off and slept soundly. The bed's quite comfortable. How about yourself, how did you sleep?"

"Good, thanks. Do you need a hand? I'll set the table for you. What time do you expect the men in for breakfast?"

Christmas morning, on Emerald Flats, promised a clear hot day.

"Whoa! Whoa!" Lindsay yelled at the two horses in the wagon he was driving. He used his deepest and loudest voice. Accompanied by raucous protests, brightly feathered birds exploded from the branches of the tall gums on the river bank.

Paddymac, sitting on the front seat beside the boy, smiled. This kid had a lot of grit. Lindsay's feet scratched for traction on the front board while his small body stretched back almost horizontal as he pulled on the four reins. Paddymac liked the boy because he seemed to have a similar affinity with the animals as himself. For some months, Paddymac and Mister Michael had worked at training a young filly. It was to be a Christmas present for Lindsay. At the moment, the horse was installed in the stables. All of the other youngsters on Emerald Flats had been instructed to keep Lindsay away from the stables until the surprise had been sprung.

Paddymac's thoughts returned to the struggle with the draft horses. Slowly the large animals began to concede to Lindsay's valiant effort and were coming to a stop. It was time to start unloading the trestle tables and set them out under the shady trees in the sandy river bed near the waterhole where everyone at Emerald Flats picnicked each Christmas Day. Amidst calls of protest, the ducks rose into the air in search of more peaceful waters. The sun glistened on the iridescent blue-green panels of their beating wings. The egrets with their sharp white plumage lifted into the branches of the overhanging gum trees. Waterfowl scattered to the thick grasses around the banks at the far end of the pool.

Harry Bobangle and Mark were in charge of the Hāngi. Mark had never seen food cooked in this traditional Polynesian way. They dug a large pit, earlier in the day, in which a fire had been lit. As the fire settled to coals, they placed a layer of rocks on them to heat up. Banana leaves lined the pit and a sacrificed goat, filled with herb stuffing, was wrapped in more leaves then lowered onto the hot rocks. Banana leaf baskets holding different vegetables were placed beside the goat. More leaves covered the contents before the pit was filled in with the dirt.

"We leave a few hours to steam, then we dig up and eat. It very good," said Harry. Mark was a little dubious at having his meal cooked in a dirt pit but Harry did seem to know what he was talking about.

As well as the meat and vegetables in the pit, Harry and Mark had several dampers cooking in the coals nearby. The rest of Harry's family were busy with their allocated tasks. The older ones carried food and plates while the younger ones kept away the dogs and the flies.

Tantalizing aromas from the contents of many baskets on trolleys preceded Old Mr. Wong and his family when they wandered down the track.

After unloading the wagon, Paddymac and young Lindsay returned to the house yard to collect Mary, Shauna and Shamus with their contribution to the feast. Under the watchful eye of his wife, Shamus held a fruit cake covered with icing and Christmas decorations. One of the wash-tubs held ripe mangoes which Shauna and Lindsay loved. Shauna carried a large plum-duff. Paddymac promised to keep the container of cream cool in the waterhole until it was needed.

Mary could not believe her eyes when they were introduced to everyone who lived on Emerald Flats. Despite Michael explaining slowly as he presented each adult, Mary knew it might be quite some time before she would be able to put a name to a face.

She learnt Old Mr. Wong and his wife had the three sons, Déhuã, Chang and Déshi. They also had a girl, everyone called Babygirl. Déhuã had straight black hair. It looked like fine sticks jutting out from his head. Uncle Michael nicknamed him 'Curley'. He and his wife Ching Lan had two boys and two girls all under ten-year-old. Chang and his wife, Lee, had two boys aged five and two-year-old. Déshi and An had twin baby boys. The daughter, Babygirl, and her husband were visiting from Townsville with their three children.

Harry and Mabel Bobangle's family was a large one. The two boys, Gabby and Haddi, were the eldest. Gabby with his wife, Sophie, had two boys and two girls all less than ten years of age – one a babe in arms. The next son, Haddi with his wife, Rosie, had two boys (twins) and two girls also; these children were all under nine years of age. Then there were the two girls, E'Mia (Milly) and Fadia (Tilly), with at least seven children between them. They would not arrive from Ayr until later.

An old canvas had been spread on the sand and everyone settled down to enjoy a fine spread. Uncle Michael produced some cordial which made him very popular with the children. The women drank numerous cups of tea made from the large pot simmering continuously on the coals. The men sipped on the liquid from the demijohn brought by Old Mr. Wong. They talked and laughed in the shade near the fire. After they distributed the food to everyone, Mary, Mabel Bobangle, and Old Mrs. Wong, who nursed a grandchild, sat together. The younger ladies, Shauna, Sophie, Rosie, Ching Lan, Lee and An supervised the children's meals. The children squealed with delight when they were given the Chinese sweets the Wong ladies had prepared.

Even though her new friends were from widely different backgrounds, one a Chinese, another an Australian Aborigine and herself from Ireland, Mary discovered they had the same concerns in life. How were they to provide for their families? What was the future for their children? Mary also learnt there was not a school nearby.

Old Mrs. Wong expressed great interest when she heard Shauna was a teacher and planned on giving Lindsay his lessons. She worried because her children had never had any formal schooling.

Mabel Bobangle wanted so much to see her grandchildren learn to read and write.

Mary sat for some time pondering on this issue. She knew she must speak to Shauna of the ladies' difficulties. The three ladies sat in silence for some moments watching the children's enjoyment.

"I understand this river has flooded many times." Mary's arm stretched out to take in the waterhole by which they sat and the thin trickle of water further across the river bed. "It seems hard to believe looking at this waterhole today."

"Oh, yes," both Mabel and Old Mrs. Wong replied together. Sophie and Rosie now joined the senior ladies.

It was Rosie who commented further. "Harry talks of flood in early eighteen sixties. It washed away the place called Wickham. That's downriver on Ayr side. A large boat, Harry said name *Three Friends* ..." Rosie paused and looked askance at her sister-in-law. Sophie nodded her head before Rosie continued. "Washed way out of the river bed. Long-time pass before they dug a large channel and re-floated it back to the river."

"The family don't talk about eighteen ninety-six flood; that the year Mabel lost her son. Do you mind if I talk about that, Mabel?" asked Sophie.

Mabel sat still and silent for a short time before she related the story herself. "Flood scare me. We sad for long time. I never forget my little boy but it might have been everyone lost. The river come fast. We collect things from the humpy we lived in. Was only a moment then we turned to climb the higher bank. The baby not anywhere. Harry drag me away. I try to look but waters rising fast. My baby's body never found. Harry, Paddymac and Mister Michael built the new humpy on higher bank. Every time river rise, I scared."

"The cyclone rain caused the flood," Old Mrs. Wong went on. "Many cyclones cause wreckage along Queensland coast. We had two bad cyclones I can remember. Many buildings in Ayr and Brandon were lost. The place dry for six years before and then down came the rain and the winds."

Mary felt her heart thumping in her chest. What kind of place was this they had come to? Cyclones and floods that damage and kill. Her mind flashed back to the night when news had been delivered to their door after Shauna's first fiancé, Kevin, was drowned at sea in a storm. Mary's anxious gaze lifted, searching for Shauna, hoping she had not heard the story of Mabel's baby lost in the angry waters of what now seemed the idyllic picture of an innocuous river. She sighed at the sound of her daughter's laughter from where she stood talking with Uncle Michael. She asked her new friends if they did anything special to bring in the New Year.

"We have quiet night," said Mabel. "Paddymac go to dance in Ayr."

Old Mrs. Wong's eyes sparkled as she told of her family's plans.

"The Chinese have New Year late next month. My family always travel to Townsville and celebrate with our daughter and friends. Be easier now with the tramway line completed. The Chinese New Year is full of traditional rituals which ensure good luck for the year to come. The youngest son, Déshi and his wife, Ching Lan, will stay to take care of the gardens. We'll take the babies with us."

"Oh, would they like to have dinner with us while you're away? They may feel lonely with everyone at Townsville," invited Mary.

Old Mrs. Wong stifled a giggle with her hand over her mouth.

"The boys argue over whose turn to stay. Most of my grandchildren born nine months after the parents have been left alone to care for the gardens."

"Oh," was all Mary could manage to reply.

It appeared everyone's appetites had been satisfied. Not only food filled the children but impatience as they waited for the nod to go swimming.

"Swimming too soon after food can bring on stomach cramps," advised Mary.

Sophie called to her husband, "Gabby, you been checked no sign of crocodiles making their home here."

Sophie did not see the impish grin on Gabby's face as he replied. "No, woman. Never had the chance. I'm sure it okay. The crocs not want us on Christmas Day."

"You, crazy blackfella!" yelled Sophie. "What you think you doing? You going to let these kids go swimming with the crocs?" At that point she noticed Gabby laughing. She picked up a large spoon lying on the canvas near her and chased her husband into the water. "Now you the crocs' Christmas lunch." Everyone laughed. The children shrieked with delight.

Mary nodded to Shamus who had hardly uttered the release word when an avalanche of children joined Gabby in the water with an eruption of splashing and loud squeals.

Shauna, Mark and Sophie organized several games later in the afternoon when the sun lost its bite. Haddi and Rosie's eldest daughter, Cabri, ran as if she had wings on her feet. At nine years of age and as tall as her older cousin, she took a lot of beating.

No one noticed Paddymac slip away. When he returned, half an hour later, he sat near the water's edge waiting his chance to corner Lindsay. It was not long before the lad joined him.

"Paddymac, the water's great. Why don't you jump in for a swim?"

"I may do so in a little while," replied Paddymac. "First, I want you to investigate some strange noises coming from behind those paperbark trees near the campfire."

Lindsay went off willingly, though he was secretly a little unsure. In the short time, he had been in the Australian bush, he had learnt to give it due respect. What if a crocodile was hanging about or maybe a bold dingo? There was no way he was going to show any fear in front of Paddymac. As he rounded the thick group of trees, he discovered a bay-coloured horse standing with one rein of the bridle resting on the ground. This was a trick Paddymac taught all of his horses. The animal stayed there until the rider came along and picked up the reins. A string wrapped around the horse's neck secured a large piece of paper. A grin split Lindsay's face as he removed the paper and read the words written in a shaky hand.

My name is Sugar. I belong to Lindsay Doolan.

Merry Christmas 1913 from everyone at Emerald Flats.

Lindsay gasped. He stared into the animal's brown eyes. The brown eyes stared right back. After circling the horse, Lindsay stroked its well-groomed coat. The horse stood still as the boy lifted each of her feet. He gave her a big hug. With tears in his eyes, he picked up the reins. Lindsay led the horse to a fallen log which he used to climb onto her back. A great cheer rang out as he rode back to the party with his head held high. He hugged both Paddymac and Uncle Michael.

Lindsay asked Paddymac what presents he had been given when he was a kid.

"Every year Mister Michael whittled timber into animal shapes for me. I still have the collection in a box, under my bed." Paddymac smiled at the memories.

"What did you do at Christmas times, when you were a kid?" Lindsay asked full of curiosity at what happened years ago.

"Not a lot. Mister Michael always made sure we had something special to eat and of course the little animal he made each year. Every year we said a prayer. Oh, I remember the time we had Christmas twice in the one year."

Lindsay lifted his head. "How can you have Christmas twice in the one year?"

"This was when we lived in Charters Towers. It was on one of our earlier trips with the supply wagon. After being held up in Townsville waiting for a ship to arrive with provisions, we were on the road to Charters Towers later than planned. At the camp, on the second last night, I was tearing up little strips of paper. We thought the next day was Christmas day. Mister Michael kept asking me what I was doing but I didn't say anything except, "It's a surprise.""

"Mister Michael had fallen asleep and was snoring loudly, as he does," continued Paddymac.

"I don't snore," was the indignant comment from Michael who had been listening nearby.

"Says you. Anyway, while he slept, I crept out to a little bush near the damped-down campfire. I hooked all those paper strips on the tree. A Christmas tree to cheer us up seeing as we'd be late home."

"Were you surprised, Uncle Michael," Lindsay turned to ask.

"Yes, it was a nice thought," said Michael with a smile at Paddymac.

"So, how come you had Christmas twice?"

"When we did arrive in Charters Towers, the people were out in the street singing Christmas Carols. The church bells were ringing and folks were coming out from the service. It was Christmas Day, that day, not the day before."

"This Christmas Day has been the best I've ever had," said Lindsay as he patted his new horse and climbed on her back.

A pheasant burst from the bushes when Mark jumped out in front of Shauna on the steep track. Her soft squeal lifted in the air along with the rush of the bird's wings. The basket of plates and cutlery she was carrying to the dray, parked at the top of the river-bank, almost came to a clattering end.

"Come with me, Shauna. I'm sick of all these people. Walk with me back to the hut. I want some peace."

A flash of annoyance marred her brow. She drew a deep breath.

"Mark, it would be very bad-mannered to walk off without helping to clean up. In fact, I'm enjoying the company of these people. They have a lot to teach us."

"Well, I'm really past good manners, Shauna. I'm tired of them all, even that halfwit Paddymac. They don't even have the same skin colour; savages if you ask me. I want us to get out of here and be alone for a while."

Shock hit her in the stomach like the kick of a horse. She gasped. Shauna snatched her arm out of Mark's grasp. Determination held back the tears when they threatened to fall as this bucket of cold disillusionment washed over her. Her mouth froze open.

Mark pulled himself up to his full height and slammed his hands on his hips. "Shauna, I'll not tell you twice. I want us to go home."

Shauna could feel the stubbornness creeping through her body like a serpent. She pursed her lips and stood with her fists on her hips. Her voice tightened as she answered.

"Mark, you'll have to go home on your own. I don't like to be spoken to in such a manner nor to be given unreasonable commands. And I don't like the way you talk about our friends."

Mark swung on his heel and ground out through gritted teeth. "Don't expect to see me waiting for you there, then." Sand spat up from his feet as he moved up out of the river bed.

Tears burnt Shauna's eyelids. She almost went to follow him but clenched her jaw and stood her ground. She ran to the dray where she hid, nursing her tumultuous thoughts. *Deep down, was Mark a racist and a bully? How had she not noticed this earlier? As his wife, would she be judged to be of a similar kind?* It was some time before she regained control of her emotions.

Unseen, stood a witness to her embarrassment. Michael Doolan slipped quietly back into the thickness of the paperback trees.

So, that's what you think of us, Mr. Mark McIvor. I'm glad I've got your measure. It seems Shauna hasn't a lot to look forward to. I wonder if Shamus has any idea of what you're capable of.

Kookaburras cackled in the branches of the tall trees on the river-bank. Several crows made frequent dives into the picnic site snatching food scraps lying in the sand. The hint of dusk eased in upon the group as Old Mr. Wong collected his wife. The elderly couple said their goodbyes and turned to walk along the river-bank towards their home. The younger women handed out leftover food. The children were particularly hungry after their exertions of the afternoon. Lanterns were lit to cast their pale glow. Everyone helped to pack up and load the wagon. Some carried items back to Harry's Camp or to the Wong's gardens. The moon lifted over the horizon as Paddymac guided the horses on their way home. Without Lindsay's help this time. The boy sat proudly upon his horse, Sugar.

"Make sure you give her a treat and brush her down before you let her out into the night paddock," called Paddymac.

"I'll not be surprised if, in the morning, they find he's spent the night sleeping on the back of the horse," chuckled Uncle Michael quietly.

Amidst fluttering wings and loud squawks, the ducks returned to their favourite waters. Evening lights reflected in the settling surface of the waterhole. Three wallabies emerged from the grasses to drink the cool water.

On hesitant feet, Shauna entered their bedroom with the lamp-wick turned low. She did not know if Mark would be there to welcome her and if he was, what sort of welcome she might receive. The unmoving shadow of his body on the bed said not a word. She slipped in beside him and spent the night worrying if she should speak first or not.

Mark's soft touch on her shoulder greeted a very tired Shauna as the morning sun entered their room. A puddle in the saucer surrounded the base of the cup of tea he offered.

"I'm sorry for my outburst last night, Shauna. I was just feeling lonely for you. You'll forgive me, won't you?"

Relief flooded through Shauna's body drowning the warning signals flashing in her mind.

"Oh, Mark, I'm sorry too."

Their bodies wrapped in a warm embrace as Mark struggled to rescue the cup and saucer.

On New Year's Eve, the family took a picnic lunch and travelled in the dray to visit Paddymac's block of land where he was in the process of developing a cane farm. Shauna watched with interest from where she stood on the paddock headland as the men manhandled the iron fluming channels. They looked like long continuous water troughs with trestles to hold them in place. A spear-well had been sunk not too far from the river-bank. Paddymac had a wood-fire heating up a head of steam in the shiny, new pump engine. It took a few tries and lots of advice from the critical audience before Uncle Michael and Paddymac set the machine pumping water. The fluming carried a considerable volume of water to a large channel dug into the earth. This channel ran beside the cane growing area almost parallel to the river itself. From this large channel, the water was diverted into smaller hand-dug furrows running at right angles to the river. A row of cane ran the length of the paddock between each of the furrows of water. Sugar-cane had been growing on the north side of the Burdekin River for over twenty years and Uncle Michael had learnt a lot from the experiences of these farmers.

Shauna watched Mark as he walked along the headland toward her. Sun penetrated his narrow-brimmed Panama hat giving only a hint of shade. His step was firm and his lips pressed together. The excitement in her day dissipated. She was beginning to learn the signs. Mark was not happy.

His tight voice fell on her ear like a block of ice. "Shauna, what are you doing standing out here in the paddock drawing attention to yourself. Shouldn't you be sitting over in the shade preparing the lunch with your mother?"

Shauna's surprise at the statement silenced any thoughts of an answer. Mark took the opportunity to offer a poor excuse for his outburst.

"Shauna, you have beautiful skin. You should be looking after it. I like to see you at your best, always."

Her teeth caught her tongue just as she was going to make some ill-considered remark about his thin hat compared to her own wide-brimmed, felt hat which allowed no sun to reach her face. Her eyes stared at his uncovered arms already reddening in the sun. She looked down at her own long, cotton sleeves.

Before she could calm her thoughts, Mark rested his hand on her waist turning her gently around towards the shaded picnic site. "Now, be a dear and do what I ask."

Shauna's teeth ground together at every footstep.

Chapter Five

Paddymac's Secret

Between the midday sun and the tropical humidity, the workers were glad to throw themselves down on the ground in the shade of the Burdekin plum tree where the women had set up the picnic lunch. Small grey birds danced along the branches to the higher foliage at this fresh intrusion of human beings to their cool retreat.

"Paddymac, you look different somehow. You look even more happy than usual. The smile has not left your face all day. Would it have anything to do with the gossip I heard of you going to the dance in Ayr tonight for the New Year's celebrations?" Shauna asked as she passed him a plate of corned-meat sandwiches.

A red flush glowed through the dirt and sweat covering Paddymac's face. He fumbled the plate and dropped his eyes. Paddymac was excited but he was not going to divulge anything to the new people just yet. Only Mister Michael knew what was going on in his life and he'd sworn not to reveal anything.

Later in the afternoon, when the others had returned to Emerald Flats, Paddymac toiled alone. The lift and fall of his well-worn hoe never missed a beat as he cleared the weeds from the last of the drains in the first section they had planted. When he reached the end of the last row of cane, he brushed roughly at the skin of his left arm and around his neck. The cane stood nearly five feet high. The cane tops bristled with the fine, sharp prickles of the hairy-maries which irritated any uncovered skin.

He chuckled softly. Tonight was going to be a very special night for him. All the regular residents at Emerald Flats knew he attended the dance in Ayr once a month when the river was passable. They didn't know what was going to be so special about tonight. He knew they were bursting with curiosity. If all goes to plan, they'll find out soon enough. That's if Thelma accepts his proposal. His face sobered at the thought she might not. Maybe she was only being nice to him because he was a bit different from the other blokes.

He hadn't yet told anyone here about Thelma – except, of course, Mister Michael. Paddymac knew Mister Michael wouldn't tell a soul even under threat of a slow death. She was a lovely girl, Thelma. Well, maybe not a girl. Thelma was thirty-four years old, unmarried and a slave to her family who owned a grocery store in Ayr. Paddymac was forty-eight going on forty-nine. He worried he may have been too old for her but she did not seem to mind. Thelma was a quiet girl but a very good homemaker having looked after her parents and brothers most of her life. It was time the wives of her brothers took on a bit more responsibility instead of letting her do all the hard work. He was not sure if Thelma saw things the same way though. Tonight, he would learn what she really felt.

As he rode his horse into Ayr his hands trembled; they ran with sweat. A bright moon and a million stars guided his way. His rib cage shuddered with his thumping heart. Maybe he was going to make a great fool of himself. Why would someone with her intelligence want to be saddled with an idiot like himself? When he entered the hall, his eyes locked into those of his love immediately. Her wide smile scattered his doubts. He took little notice of the streamers decorating the walls. With a brief grin to the band members, he strode over to the woman he loved. As he swung Thelma around the dance floor, tendrils of her brown hair hung loose curled over the unblemished skin of her face and neck. The pale grey gown with the red buttons was his favourite and brought out the colour in her grey eyes.

When midnight approached and the noise inside the dance hall reached a crescendo, Paddymac and Thelma sat in a quiet corner of the verandah draped in the light of a large clear moon. With many stops and starts, stutters and pauses, Paddymac popped the question. He held his breath. His love stared out quietly into the night. Paddymac's eyes roamed her face seeking some indication of an answer. She looked so beautiful. Thelma turned slowly towards Paddymac; her face was serious. Paddymac's heart slumped. She was going to refuse. The thought burrowed deep in his head.

"Yes, Paddy. I'd be honoured to be your wife."

"Oh, Thelma," was all Paddymac could say as he held her tightly to his pounding chest.

New Year's Day, 1914. Paddymac walked on a cloud. Mister Michael had been awake when he arrived home in the early hours. He was almost as excited as Paddymac when he heard the news. Paddymac worked his way through the daily chores by rote. The yells and yahoos heard in the distance, penetrated his consciousness. Harry's grandchildren, Akama and Sabbo, with Lindsay were out on their horses bringing the bull and his herd into the cattle yards. Mister Michael wanted to show Shamus and Mark what the blood-sucking, fever-inducing cattle tick looked like. The herd they had now was made up of cattle bred from stock which had survived the tick fever and had passed their acquired resistance onto their progeny but it was still a continuous struggle to keep the numbers of this pest under some sort of control. If the infestation of ticks on the cattle today required it, the men would push the stock through the arsenic chemical dip this afternoon. He jumped when a voice spoke.

"Paddymac, I didn't get the opportunity to thank you for the wonderful horse you and Uncle Michael gave Lindsay for Christmas. You've put a lot of work into breaking her in," commented Shauna who had come up quietly beside him.

It took him a moment to focus on what Shauna was talking about. Eventually, he was able to reply, "Our pleasure."

Shauna looked askance at the man. "Are you alright, Paddymac? You seem preoccupied."

"All's very well, Shauna." His grin escaped its usual control. It split his face.

Shauna raised her eyebrows. All during the day, she pondered on the subtle differences in the Paddymac she had come to know.

The Emerald Flats returned to the normal peaceful flow after the festive season's distraction. Lindsay was agog. Paddymac was bringing a lady to lunch today. Uncle Michael told them so. The pair should be here shortly. Mam and Shauna were fussing about in the kitchen, what on earth for, he couldn't imagine. After all, it was only a girl coming to visit. At least she must be able to ride a horse, he guessed. The dogs set up a cacophony of barking.

"Here they come," yelled Lindsay to his mother.

Tucking tendrils of their hair back into place and removing their aprons, Mary and Shauna came out to greet their guest. Pride and pleasure shone on Paddymac's face. A tiny and very lovely woman rode side-saddle on the bay horse next to his; her dark brown hair neatly tucked up under a large hat. Eyes unseen were downcast and a high colour glowed in her cheeks. Paddymac helped her to dismount and introduced Mary and Shauna to Thelma, his fiancé. After a short pause of surprise, Mary rushed over to their guest and enclosed her in a warm hug.

"Thelma, it's so lovely to meet you. Congratulations to you both. Please, come in and rest. Would you like a cup of tea? Lindsay," she turned to her son, "Go and tell your father, Uncle Michael and Mark we have company and everyone is to wash their hands and have on a clean shirt."

Contentment filled Paddymac like rain fills the water tank in the monsoons. His eyes fixated on Thelma as she talked with Mary and Shauna. He felt grateful to Mary, and indeed all of them. They made Thelma feel welcome. Everything was going to be hunky-dory.

At the end of the meal when the men sat enjoying the last of their pannikins of tea, Thelma insisted on helping clear the dishes. Mary, Shauna and Thelma washed and dried at the tub on the bench.

Mary asked, "Thelma have you and Paddymac set a date yet?"

The pale flush which had appeared several times during the meal when attention was drawn to her, once more infused Thelma's face.

"Paddymac will build a hut for us on his farm. When it's ready, we'll become man and wife. Neither Paddymac nor I want a big affair. Paddymac was hoping for a small ceremony here at Emerald Flats. I admit it would be lovely; if Mister Michael and you people agree."

Shauna's face lit up. "Thelma, how wonderful." She turned to her mother. "Isn't it, Mam."

Mary smiled at Shauna's enthusiasm. "It's for Uncle Michael to agree."

Uncle Michael sat nodding his head; a smile lit the blue eyes. He sighed. "Looks like we'll have to kill a beast and do an extra trip to town for supplies. All this kerfuffle happening, people will need a feed."

Mark lifted his head. "I'd planned on going to town on business next week. If you write a list, I'm sure I could take the dray and collect what you might need."

Shauna's eyes widened; her lips formed a tight circle. This was the first she had heard of Mark going to town. It sounded very much like she was not invited on the excursion.

The cool atmosphere had continued between Mark and Shauna since Christmas and New Year. Mark struggled within himself to understand why Shauna only gave short polite answers to any comment he made. Surely, she wasn't upset at his words over at Paddymac's farm. After all, it was his duty as a husband to ensure his wife does as he wishes. Occasionally he gave brief thought to his temper tantrum on Christmas day. It was she who didn't come home with him when he asked her to.

The idea she was expected to never do anything without her husband's permission, niggled at Shauna. Her mind pondered the words of the ladies at the Christmas party. She wanted so much to be able to start school lessons for all the children at Emerald Flats. Without Mark's permission, it could never happen. Following on that thought was the memory of his disparaging and insulting comments about her friends. Disgust filled her heart to bursting every time those words ran through her head. How could anyone think badly of a wonderful kind-hearted man like Paddymac or anyone else on Emerald Flats come to that? Everybody had gone out of their way to welcome her family here. She shook her head. With such an attitude, Mark would never permit her to have her little school class.

Two days later, after Mark had left for town driving the wagon, tears caught her unawares. How could he go off to town on his own without even inviting her along? Her feet dragged as she began her morning chores.

Reluctantly, Shauna admitted she needed a wiser head than her own to solve her problem. Mary listened to an edited version of the issue later as they prepared a pie for the evening meal.

Mary had noticed the ice between the newlyweds in the past days but did not like to interfere. She paused in thought before offering Shauna the advice of her grandmother. 'Two things a woman must remember, young Mary,' her grandmother had said. 'One is to always let your husband think everything is his idea. The other is to remember the old saying about there being more than one way to kill a cat. You can choke it with cream.'

Shauna was a bright girl. Her mind tossed the problem and the advice around in her head for hours.

But Mark did not return home that night. Anger boiled inside Shauna leaving sleep an impossible ambition. Her mind struggled from one scenario to another. Was he safe? Had there been an accident? Was he looking for another's company? Did he not love her anymore? He had talked of buying his own farm; was that what he was doing?

In the morning, dark circles rimmed her eyes. Mark was her husband and they had to make a go of the marriage. She must try harder to please him. Her mother's advice reclaimed her thoughts.

When Mark drove the wagon into the yard at lunchtime, dishevelled, tired with blood-shot eyes, he ignored everyone and strode off to their bedroom. Shauna found him later, unchanged, spreadeagled across the bed, snoring. She left him alone. But her resolve remained firm. She had made her plan.

After supper, she took Mark's hand and led him up the stairs and into their room. By the time she introduced the subject of the school lessons as the hint of dawn lightened the room, Mark was more than happy to agree to any madcap scheme his wonderful wife might suggest.

Chapter Six

Blowing the Stumps

A little sunlight shone through the grass and entered the small opening leading into the tiny dark space. The long shiny body lay curled up in a small ball that belied the length of the snake as it flicked its forked tongue in and out sensing the vibrations of the earth. The activity outside had disturbed the reptile's sleep. The wheels of the dray rumbled along the rough track with Paddymac, Shamus, Mark, Harry and his sons Gabbi and Haddi on board. With increased irritability, the snake sensed the voices of the men and the rattle of the mattocks, shovels and hoes being unloaded.

The men were here to clear some of the brush around the stumps left in the paddock by the timber cutters. Uncle Michael planned to let Paddymac use the gelignite to blow the stumps on his own. This would be the second paddock at Paddymac's farm to be planted with sugar-cane. Considerable work was needed if they were to have this area ready for planting by April. The forest rang with the fall of the axes used on the smaller roots. Mattocks and shovels scraped at the soil to make a hole to lay the explosive. The snake slithered out of its once peaceful resting place and began its silent journey through the grass around the base of a large tree-stump.

Gabby's eye caught the glint of the shiny body just as his axe started to fall. He was able to interrupt his action to some degree but not enough to escape the strike of the brown snake. The serpent latched its fangs with great determination onto the little finger of his left hand.

Without thinking, Gabby laid the hand on the stump. With his right hand, he brought the axe down in a swift blow. He chopped the top off the finger which included the attached snake. Gabby then belted the snake on the head with the back of the axe. It was over in a matter of seconds.

It took some moments before the pain hit. "Yeow!"

Haddi rushed to his brother's side immediately.

Back at the home compound, things were starting to slip into a comfortable pattern. Each morning was always an early start for everyone. This did not bother the newcomers. Having come from a farm in Ireland they were used to early starts. After animals were attended, Shamus, Mark, Uncle Michael, and Paddymac, when he was at Emerald Flats, with young Lindsay as his shadow, came in to enjoy a breakfast prepared by Mary and Shauna.

After things were cleared away, Shauna gave the children their lessons until lunchtime while the men worked in the paddocks. When lunch was over, the men rested for an hour before they returned to the farm work until dusk. Often Uncle Michael did not go out in the afternoon until the day was a little cooler. Lindsay completed another hour and a half of schoolwork while Shauna prepared lessons for the following day. When released, the boy spent time with Uncle Michael where he sat on the verandah in his squatter's chair. Lindsay hounded him relentlessly begging Michael to tell the stories of his and Paddymac's life.

Shauna's class had grown from one to eight pupils.

Her school roll book looked something like this.

Harry and Mabel's grandchildren
Parents Gabby and Sophie
Boys
Akama   10yo.
Sabbo   9 yo.
Girls
'Alya   6 yo.

Parents Haddi and Rosie
Boys
Maani,   6 yo.
Gabrel   6 yo.
Girls
Cabri   9 yo.

Old Mr. and Mrs. Wong's grandchildren
Parents Dèhuā (Curley) and Ching Lan
Boys
Angua   10yo.
Cai   9 yo.

Shauna thought the smaller children should wait until they were six before taking classes. Lindsay was more advanced than the others and worked at separate studies.

Mary sat at the kitchen table with a cup of tea, listening to the pure notes of the butcher bird's song in the mulberry tree. The carpenters were back from holidays and the continual sound of the hammers assaulted their ears from dawn until dusk. Their home was beginning to take shape on the east side of the compound. Four carpenters joined them in the kitchen for each meal of the day.

Looking out through the window space she watched as Shauna supervised her class of children sitting on logs under the mango tree. Mary's mind drifted back to when they had first spoken to Uncle

Michael on the subject of lessons for all the children. Shauna revealed she was writing to the Education Department regarding Lindsay's curriculum. Uncle Michael nearly fell off his chair when Shauna said she might enquire about the curriculum for the other children's grades.

"Whatever you do, don't mention the other children or their lessons. It's not so long ago the government sent many of the Chinese and the Kanakas back to their home countries."

Uncle Michael had explained further how many white workers were afraid for their jobs. "In fact, the Wong's and Harry's families were lucky to be here at all."

Mary learnt it was Uncle Michael and his friend, the solicitor, Mr. Chiswell, who had been instrumental in claiming the exemption clause in the policy. Now the Wong family and the Bobangle family had their legal papers giving them the right to live in Australia.

Michael went on to explain further. "Mabel's aboriginal and all of her and Harry's children are married into the Aboriginal Bindal family. Harry and Mabel's daughters-in-law, Sophie and Rosie had Melanesian fathers who were returned to the islands. They all prefer to keep a low profile."

Lindsay shattered Mary's recollections when he rushed into the kitchen seeking biscuits and milk for the just-released children. Shauna entered more sedately with a smile of satisfaction upon her face.

"You know, Mam, it's such a pleasure to teach these children. They're so keen."

"Well, Shauna, you may feel even more pleased to know Old Mr. Wong has invited Lindsay over twice a week to learn what he can teach him of the Chinese language and culture."

"How good of him, Lindsay will be thrilled, I think."

"I asked Old Mrs. Wong to visit as often as she wishes to practise her English in conversation."

"Lovely."

At this point, Uncle Michael himself came into the kitchen looking for a drink.

"How's the school going, Shauna?" he asked.

"Next time we go to town, I'll buy a blackboard and some slates for the children, Uncle Michael."

"You know, I think I'll talk to Shamus about building a small classroom under the new house," Michael suggested. "It shouldn't be too much extra work."

"When it becomes too hot or when the rains come it'd be very much appreciated." Shauna smiled her gratitude.

As Mary placed his tea and the biscuit tin in front of Uncle Michael, she broached a subject that had been on her mind since Christmas.

"The ladies at Christmas were talking about the cyclones and floods you get here. What'll happen when they come again?" A worried frown marred Mary's face.

Michael sighed. "Yes, we've had a few nasty ones. We build high and we build strong in the hope of being prepared. What will be, will be." Seeing the look of horror clouding Mary's features, he added, "Mary, girl, there's not a lot you can do. This area is a highpoint on the property and includes the Wong's house. Harry has his house on the highest bank of the river. The cattle have a couple of small elevated areas in the paddocks, we hope they have the chance to reach these, in the event of the water rising."

Mary looked anxiously out of the window searching her surroundings. She turned back to Uncle Michael. "Have you had the water up near this hut?"

"No, lass, not enough to bother us. It's not just wind and water sent to give us headaches, you know. We've had some nasty droughts also. You'll find it's not a lot different than the farm in Ireland. Wherever you live on the land there's always some trouble threatening. You can't spend your time worrying about what might be. You just get on with what is now." Michael paused for a moment to give Mary a chance to absorb this advice before going on. "You know, the first white man in this area was from a ship wrecked not far from here. He lived with the blacks for many years before he re-joined the white man. You should ask Sophie about it. Her grandmother was with the tribe then."

Their discussion was interrupted. Michael jumped up and moved to the door. Two black crows cawed their protest as they scrambled into the air from where they had been scavenging under the mango tree. The rumble of the dray wheels and the sound of galloping horses heralded trouble. Mary knew the men had gone to the newly cleared land where more sugar-cane was to be planted in the autumn. They were to clear some more stumps ready for Uncle Michael to blow out with the gelignite. Dust billowed up around the dray as Paddymac pulled the team to a halt. Something serious was amiss. Paddymac would never drive the horses so hard otherwise.

Looking out of the window, she observed Shamus and Haddi helping Gabby down from the seat. Gabby was holding one hand covered with a dirty rag in the palm of his other hand. Paddymac started the horses again and headed towards the Wong's gardens.

Mary took a big breath. She knew it was bad and she knew she had to be steady. The men led Gabby into the kitchen and sat him at the table. Mary immediately bought a basin of water and soap to clean up whatever was hidden under the bloody cloth. She instructed Shamus to collect her medical kit and her sewing box. When she saw the amount of blood that had soaked the rag and was now running down the arm to Gabby's elbow, she knew there was every chance this may require both. Mary gasped when she removed the rag. She took a hold of the table edge.

Steady girl, steady, she told herself as she caught sight of what was left of the finger. *This fellow needs your help not a fit of the vapours.* Willing her hands to remain steady, Mary gently cleaned up the finger and instructed Gabby to put pressure on a point nearer the web-space to reduce some of the blood spurting out of the wound.

"Paddymac has gone to fetch Old Mr. Wong," commented Haddi. At this point, Gabby's head dropped to the table. Consciousness deserted him.

Mary felt relieved to know Gabby would not be aware of what she was about to do.

"Haddi, I want you to hold the pressure on the finger while I remove that little bit of bone above the middle joint." With a short, sharp and pointed butcher knife she carefully trimmed the joint attachments and shaped the skin as best she could to fit over the new end of the finger. Mary then took her sewing needle and strong thread and sewed the two skin edges together. At this point, Old Mr. Wong, his son, Curley, and Paddymac returned. Old Mr. Wong gave her a poultice to place on the suture line. Gabby groaned. His eyes fluttered. Haddi held his brother as he struggled to rise. Mary laid a clean piece of linen over the wound and padded it well. With further strips of the linen, she was able to bind it firmly.

"How on earth he didn't chop off all of his fingers when he brought the axe down, I don't know," remarked Paddymac after Mary had been told of the accident.

"Intuitive reflex made him draw the others back out of the way, I guess," replied Mary as she poured a not-so-small amount of brandy into a pannikin and offered it to the slowly recovering Gabby.

Mary gave Haddi instructions to keep Gabby in bed tonight and he was not to leave his hut until she came over to see him in the morning. If anything goes wrong before then they were to send for her immediately. Old Mr. Wong sent a small bottle of herbal medicine accompanied by oral instructions for Sophie to heat the mixture and give it to her husband. "It will relieve some of the pain and help him to sleep," he advised.

While Mary and Old Mr. Wong had been treating Gabby's finger, Shamus and Michael made their way outside. They moved away from the goings-on to squat under the mulberry tree. In silence, they drank from their pannikins and ate the biscuits filched from Mary's baking tin.

It was Shamus who broke the companionable silence. After a false start, he spoke. "Uncle Michael, I've been meaning to ask you something for a while now. It's about Shauna's Mark." Shamus brushed imaginary biscuit crumbs from his trouser legs. "How do you find him?"

Michael felt the tension emanating from Shamus. He wondered if his nephew had heard about Mark's outburst on Christmas day. He considered his answer with care.

"Shamus, it sounds like something's bothering you about the lad. He's a good worker and handles the cattle brilliantly."

'I ... er... there's something. I don't know; maybe I'm just being a fussy father. I mean, I can't fault the lad with his ability to work. He certainly carries his weight around here. No one could say he's short on courage either." Shamus fidgeted with his boot laces.

Michael's back straightened. "Do I detect a 'BUT' coming?"

"It's just our Shauna; she doesn't appear too happy lately. Maybe we made a mistake letting her marry a bloke we didn't know all that well."

"Many marriages start with less. Even with everything going for a couple, it takes a while for them to adjust to each other." Michael nearly smiled at the irony of him, a confirmed bachelor, offering such advice.

If Shamus noticed the irony, he ignored it. "Mark seems to want to dominate the girl and I know for a fact she'll not tolerate too much of that." Shamus swatted at several flies around his face. "Och, maybe I'm just worrying about nothing. No doubt, she'll work it out with him. But I do hate to see her unhappy." Shamus stood up, then sunk immediately back down onto the stump. He spoke in a hushed tone. "I don't like his attitude to your friends, the Bobangles and the Wongs. They're good people. Mark seems to hold himself aloof. He can be quite arrogant at times. We've seen enough pain and hurt between people of different backgrounds in Ireland. We don't want to bring it here with us."

Michael reached out and rested his hand on Shamus's forearm. "If there is racial intolerance in the boy, it hasn't been too obvious. Like you, I'll not tolerate it on Emerald Flats. As for young Shauna, she's a strong girl and no one's fool. I don't think you need to worry too much. Give them both some time."

As Lindsay helped Mary restore some order to the kitchen he commented, "Mam, yesterday Haddi was showing Sabbo how to catch a snake by the tail."

"Good grief, Lindsay! I hope you didn't try that? Don't you go touching those horrible things. The bite of some snakes will kill you, remember."

"No, Mam, I won't," replied Lindsay with his fingers crossed behind his back, which cancelled out the lie. "It was only a green tree snake. The trick's to grab the tail then keep twisting it back and forth. The snake can't get his balance and is unable to strike."

"Yes, well, that's as maybe but I still don't want you playing with snakes; do you understand?"

"Yes, Mam," Lindsay dutifully answered with his fingers firmly crossed this time. "Anyway, Just Dog keeps the snakes away."

"I'm pleased to hear it. Try to remember what I said?" Mary instructed as she followed her son out through the kitchen doorway.

The following day, Uncle Michael prepared the eight-inch wax-coated orange-brown stick of gelignite. He pushed the one-and-a-half-inch detonator with a length of fuse attached, into the end of the gelignite stick. All the men and boys gathered around.

"Whatever you do, you must use the brass crimpers to attach the fuse to the detonator. Never use metal pliers; unless you want to go to Kingdom Come." Michael straightened his back and stared vacantly into his past. A smile tweaked his lips. "Back on the goldfields, years ago, we didn't have such things and had to crimp the detonator onto the fuse cable using our teeth with the detonator held in our mouths." He grinned. "Now, where was I? Oh, yes, don't forget to leave plenty of fuse, or again, you'll go sky-high in little bits. And another bit of interesting information – never wipe the hand that has handled the gelignite over your forehead or you'll end up with a violent headache."

Everyone listened attentively as Michael knelt beside the cleared tree-root. "Place it snugly beside the big root and as far down as you can, preferably underneath another root coming out the side," he said as he laid the prepared explosive in place. "Now everyone, you must go back as far as you can and hide behind some of those other roots or trees." Michael stood and gazed around seeking his own retreat. Once he lit the fuse his short legs pumped like pistons as he ran to his own cover.

BOOM! The noise was deafening and bits of tree roots, clods of dirt, and smoke were hurled many feet into the air. The young lads squealed with delight at the sight. The work continued.

Using the cover available, Akama, Sabbo and Lindsay made their way carrying the flour bag with its secret contents towards the largest waterhole. It was imperative the adults did not see them and to their advantage, if the other smaller kids did not spot them either.

"You sure you brought the brass crimpers Uncle Michael spoke about?" Lindsay asked Akama.

"Course, I did, and the detonator and the geli?"

They sat in the thick scrub on the bank beside the water.

"Maybe crocs living in the waterhole?" asked Sabbo nervously.

"Sure won't be once we blow 'er," was Akama's reply.

With Lindsay and Sabbo supervising closely his every move, Akama set the fuses and detonators into the two separate sticks of gelignite they had removed from the shed. "The trick's not to chuck the thing into the water until it's ready to blow. I heard Uncle Haddi and my father talking about it the other night. They used this once to catch fish."

"Who wants to light it?" asked Akama. The two younger lads declined the generous offer. "Right, settle in behind that big gum tree and don't come out until they've both gone off."

Akama's heart pounded with excitement and nervousness. He lit the first fuse, waited until it was almost to the detonator, then let it fly over the water. As quick as a flash he was down behind the nearest tree trunk. With an almighty BOOM, the thing exploded. Water erupted well into the air. His hands were shaking as he lit the second fuse but he made himself wait until it had burnt down before he threw it out into the waterhole also. BOOM.

This time the water covered all the conspirators. They did not worry as they scrambled down the bank to see the result of their clever plan. Fish, large and small floated on the water surface stunned by the explosions. Eels were also in the number of shocked water dwellers.

"Greeeeat!" yelled Lindsay, "Look, there're two barramundi fish I can see and some large bream. This is a wonderful haul."

Amidst much splashing they gathered their catch, bringing them onto the bank where Mr. Déshi Wong was waiting to greet them.

"You lads going to be in big trouble," he said as he offered a large basket in which to carry the rewards.

With the arrogance of youth, they figured the gift of fish would override any misdemeanours they may have committed. Mr. Déshi Wong took home a large barramundi and some bream and eels for his family and let the boys carry the rest of the fish in his basket.

It was only a few days after the stumps had been blown in the new paddock when Michael and Paddymac sat enjoying doing nothing but drinking tea in the kitchen. Mark, Shauna and Shamus had taken the horses out to inspect the boundary fences. A windy storm had engulfed the area last night. Trees and branches fallen across the fences would need to be removed.

In the kitchen, Mary's biscuits were copping a fair hiding when Paddymac suddenly raised his head.

"My God! Mister Michael, did you hear that? Someone's using gelignite down at the river." They both listened intently for another bang.

Mary came into the room, "What's going on?"

"Listen," instructed Michael. "Are you sure it came from our part of the river?" he asked Paddymac.

"Just down from Mr. Wong's place, I think," was the reply.

They sat listening for a while then Harry's older grandchildren and Lindsay came up the track carrying a large basket between them.

"I'll skin them alive," stated Michael as he rose from his seat and stomped outside.

"What've you smart alecks been doing? Do you want to blow yourselves to smithereens? I thought I made it plain; playing with gelignite's a fool's game. Have you got any idea how much trouble I would've been in with your parents if anything had happened to any of you? Yes, well it doesn't bear thinking about. Now, take the fish into Mrs. Doolan and you can all go to Paddymac's farm and dig a full length of furrow for the irrigation water."

"But we were very careful like you said, and we've caught some lovely fish, a couple of barra even," wheedled Lindsay.

"Make that two furrows – for each of you – to be done by nightfall. Now skedaddle," was Michael's non-sympathetic reply.

As the boys collected the tools from the shed, they also grabbed a couple of empty sugar-bags. Experience had taught them, the number of blisters at the end of the day would be fewer if they wrapped a bag tightly around the handles of the hoes and shovels.

When Michael re-entered the kitchen, he spoke to Mary. "I'm sorry if I reprimanded Lindsay out of turn, but the boys must learn never to put themselves in unnecessary danger. There's enough to be had around here without looking for more."

"My thoughts exactly," Mary responded. She looked over to see Paddymac smiling broadly, "What's so funny, Paddymac?"

"Mister Michael. You big fat hypocrite. Who was it, when we first started learning to use the stuff, nearly blew his leg off, and mine, if I remember, when fishing with the gelignite sticks?" Paddymac was laughing as he turned to Mary. "Mind you, we caught some great fish though." The two men chuckled at the memory. "I'd better take these wee devils over to my place then and set them to work."

Old Mr. Wong had poked his head inside the kitchen window which was wide open in an attempt to catch a little air. "I've brought over more salve for the blisters. When my son say what the boys been up to, I knew they'd get punishment ending with blisters. They give Mrs. Wong a barra for tea. Reminds me the time you and Paddymac went fishing with the geli," he said with a laugh.

"I'll take some of the fish and the salve over to Harry's Camp. They'll need to know where the boys are," said Paddymac.

"No need," said Mary, "I can see Gabby coming along the track now.

Late in the evening, Lindsay left his bed with Just Dog at his heels. He avoided the kitchen where his parents sat reading and knitting. Using the moonlight as a guide, he made his way over to the Worker's Hut where Uncle Michael was still ensconced. As expected, he found Uncle Michael in the squatter's chair comfortable with his thoughts. Old Dog rested at his feet.

"It's a bit late for you to be wandering around, young man. You want to be careful you don't step on a snake in the dark."

"Uncle Michael, I wanted to say sorry for this afternoon."

"Och, well lad, there's not a one of us who hasn't made a foolish mistake at some time in our lives. The wisdom is in whether you can acknowledge the mistake and then ensure you never make the same mistake twice."

Lindsay considered Uncle Michael's statement for a bit. "Uncle Michael, what are some of the mistakes you've made?"

There was a drawn-out silence from Michael for some moments. "You know I've made so many I'm not sure where to start."

"Tell me about when you were my age, living in Ireland?"

"Well, I didn't go fishing with gelignite, that's for sure but I loved to fish in the brook near the farm. I caught the odd nice pike for my

Ma to cook. That was the same farm on which you were brought up. In those days, my parents, my siblings, brother George and I lived in the main house. Our grandparents lived in the little cottage with the rose vine over the gate. Is that still there?"

"Yes, Uncle Michael, Grandpa and Grandma Doolan live there now. Their eldest son, Mick and his family are in the bigger house now."

"We had to work hard, right from the time we could walk. Even though we had several farm hands living in the other cottages there were many smaller jobs for us to do. After helping bring in the cows for the morning milk we churned the butter for our mother then walked four miles to the village school. Most days we went to school; when there wasn't too much to do at home. Hardly ever during haymaking season. The hay had to be brought in before the rain, you see. I did love school. I still enjoy learning all sorts of things from books. Grandmother always said, 'Young Michael, every night when you go to bed you must think over everything you've learnt in the day. If you've not learned at least one new thing you have wasted the day God gave you.'" He looked over to where Lindsay sat on the top step almost invisible in the darkness. "I guess you've learnt something today about the danger of gelignite," Michael said with a chuckle as he reached down and fondled the dog's ears.

"Uncle Michael did you know Mam checked Gabby's finger today. It's completely healed. He sits with it just under his nostril and it looks as if he has his finger up his nose. We laughed like mad until Mabel came and chased us on our way."

Michael laughed at the vision in his head. "He'll get some mileage out of that I should imagine. Now lad, head off back to bed, it'll be another early start tomorrow."

Chapter Seven

The Flood

Shauna added the final touch to the icing on the wedding cake. One of Mary's fruit cakes sat on the table sculptured into the shape of a little church. The steeple of marzipan trembled when first placed on the top of the creation.

"Where are we going to keep this until Paddymac and Thelma's wedding?" asked Shauna as she slipped scraps of the marzipan into her mouth. "I'm not sure it would last the distance if the men or children caught sight or smell of it."

Mary laughed. "Leave it here for a little while, to set. We'll take a walk over to the big house. If the fresh paintwork has dried and the smell has settled, we can begin to move across." Mary bent over the cake to examined Shauna's work closely. "Looks great, dear. I'm hoping Shamus will take me in the buggy tomorrow to see how Paddymac and Thelma's place is coming along."

With eyes shining and hair flying, Shauna's feet barely touched the timber. She flew up the back steps of the new house, two at a time.

"Not the behaviour of a lady, my girl." Mary grinned at her daughter.

"Oh, Mam, aren't you excited?" Shauna laughed as she spoke. "This is your own home, your home in Australia."

"Our home, dear; this home is also for you and Mark. It's certainly big enough." Both women paused at the top landing. Shauna stood back and let Mary open the door.

The doorway led into what they called the vestibule. This wide extension jutted off the verandah which surrounded the main part of the house. It opened into what was to be a large kitchen but at the moment that area only had a roof and a floor. The main part of the house consisted of a wide hallway separating two rooms on either side before opening out onto the front and back verandahs.

Mary and Shamus were to have the use of two rooms on one side and Shauna and Mark were to utilize the two on the other side. A small bedroom for Lindsay had been built in the corner of the back verandah with a narrow access passage allowing a walkway around the house.

Mary leant out over the verandah railing. "Oh, Shauna isn't this wonderful? Can you imagine the sound of this house full of your children?"

A strained smile on her daughter's face did not fool Mary at all. She would be deaf and blind if she hadn't noticed periods of icy atmosphere between Shauna and Mark. It broke her heart to think of her daughter unhappy. She tried to brighten the smile.

"What'll my chances be of getting Uncle Michael into a new set of clothes for Paddymac's wedding, do you think?"

Shauna chuckled at the thought. She opened her mouth to speak but closed it again. Her mother looked so happy. How could she ruin her mother's moment with her own complaints of woe?

When Mary moved into the hallway, Shauna continued to gaze pensively over Emerald Flats. She had grown to love this place very much. Lately, Mark continually begged her to consider moving with him to a cane farm of their own. More than once she reminded him of the promise they had made to her parents, to spend at least twelve months helping them settle into their new life. Mark was not interested. Two farms had become available for sale when the men who had won them in the ballot could not meet the guidelines of ownership. One farm was only a few hours horse-ride away. But Shauna's instinct held her back. If she moved away, her little school would disintegrate. She owed it to these families to give something back. Besides, her mother was her best friend. They would both fret if away from the other for too long. Most of all, her thoughts took her to a place she did not want to visit. She was concerned at the way Mark constantly endeavoured to separate her from her family and new friends. One side of her conscience told her it was just the way of things when one married but the other side knew this need not be so. It was good to have friends when in a new and strange country. Perhaps Mark was impatient to make his own way on his own farm. The previous experiences of his controlling behaviour and those occasions of his disrespect regarding the Wongs and Bobangles burrowed away in her mind.

Mary's call drew Shauna away from her depressing thoughts.

"Shauna, can you imagine having the bathroom just underneath the building? No more braving the jungle in the dark of night."

The two women completed their tour. At the top of the front steps, Mary asked Shauna, "I wonder how long Mark and the boys'll be?"

They had gone out on the horses after lunch, to check the cattle. When Easter and the wedding were over, next month, there would be bullocks to be sold. Uncle Michael had explained his two options. He could deliver the cattle to the new stockyards at Carstairs where they would be loaded onto the cattle rail-trucks and sent to the Townsville meatworks. His other choice was to drove the cattle to Bobawabba, south of Home Hill, for delivery by rail to the meatworks at Bowen.

He was considering giving the young lads the experience of a droving trip for a few days. The boys had been working very hard physically and mentally. Their schoolwork was a credit to them all. It would be a great treat for them to drive the cattle to the railway yards at Bobawaba.

"Mam, perhaps we'd better make afternoon tea – oops, no, I forgot, Uncle Michael and Paddymac call it smoko, not afternoon tea. I can hear their voices coming from the shed." The two women looked out across the yard.

Mary squealed. "Oh, no! Look! The gate to the compound has been left open. The goats! The Cake!" she wailed, "I'll roast every last one of them if they find the cake."

Dust shot up with each footfall as Shauna's feet pounded across the yard to the kitchen. The piebald goat was just climbing in through the window as Shauna ran around the corner calling out and shaking her apron.

"Get out! Get out! You mangy four-legged eating machines. Out! Out! Out!"

The cake had made a narrow escape.

The trip to Paddymac's farm was deferred; the rain had been falling on and off for days.

In the classroom, Shauna's head swung up. The pencil dropped from her hand. Her half-prepared lessons for tomorrow were forgotten. Lindsay beat her to the gap in the walled sections protecting the under-house area.

Mud and water splattered up around them as Gabby's two boys, Akama and Sabbo ran towards the kitchen. They yelled for Mister Michael with every step. White teeth shone in their dark faces.

A bellow sounded from the shed. "Over here, boys!" Michael shuffled outside jamming his hat on his head as he did so. "What's all the fuss?"

When the lads skidded to a halt in front of him muddy water sprayed his dark trousers.

"Thanks, for nothing," grumbled Michael. "I'm wet enough with all this rain we've had. Are you trying to drown me?"

But the boys did not hear his sarcasm. Bent nearly double, they struggled to suck oxygen into their lungs. Michael waited patiently.

"Flood's coming."

"Dad said to tell you."

"The muddy water's swallowed up all the waterholes in the river."

"It's right across the river bed to the other side, already."

"It's rising fast."

"Grandma's crying."

Michael patted the boys on the shoulders. "Now, there's no need to worry. Your father and Uncle Haddi know what to do. You go back and help them lift everything into the house. Tell the family they can camp in my hut here until the waters have gone down again."

Shauna and Lindsay met Michael at the kitchen doorway. Lindsay's wide eyes glinted with excitement.

Shauna asked, "Uncle Michael, why don't you join us in the big house? It'll be a tight squeeze in your hut with the Bobangle families."

"Thanks, Shauna. I think I will. Now, is there any chance of a cuppa?"

Mary bustled into the kitchen shaking the rain-water from the old mackintosh she had draped over her head. The rain had commenced falling again. "What's all the commotion? I heard it all above the sound of the sewing machine and the rain on the roof."

Michael gave her a brief report on the latest happenings before drinking deeply from the pannikin placed on the table in front of him.

"What about the Wongs? Will they need to move to higher ground too? They can camp on the verandahs of the big house."

"They should be dry where they are. Old Mr. Wong built on a high knob. They've never had the water at their house before. If they do need to move further back here, they can use the worker's shed." Michael paused considering his plans. "Perhaps Lindsay should run over to the Wong's to make sure they've noticed the rising waters."

Lindsay needed no second telling. His body disappeared in the spray of water around his racing feet.

"And come straight back here after you've delivered the message," Michael called.

Shamus carried Uncle Michael's swag up the high steps of the big house and threw it on the stretcher near Lindsay's room. Mary and Shauna followed at the men's heels.

Michael scratched his chin for a moment while he gathered his thoughts.

"Right, that's sorted. Now, Mary and Shauna, will you make up a hamper to last a couple of days. If the river comes higher than usual, our kitchen may get a bit wet." He turned to his nephew. "Shamus, can you and Mark take the horses and push the stock out of the river paddocks. Mary, when Lindsay returns, ask him to come over to the shed and help me lift things onto the platform."

Within the hour, Harry Bobangle and the women of his family arrived carrying bundles of clothes and supplies hanging from their shoulders or in woven baskets held in their arms. Children seemed to be everywhere. They trooped up into the hut behind the kitchen. Michael disappeared into the depths of the shed.

When Mary asked Mabel where her sons were, she explained. "Gabbi and Haddi fix everything at our hut. They watch the waters. Come back here, if need."

Mary left them to their own devices while she went in search of Shauna. She found her helping Michael and the now mud-covered Lindsay as they lifted the hay, checked the sheds and the stock near the house.

Dust and hay erupted around him as Michael belted his hands against his trousers. "I think we've done all we can do here. Let's take a walk down to the river while there's a lull in the rain? You'll find it changed to your last visit there. Gabby will show you where his flood markers are."

Mud and water seeped into their work boots as Michael, Mary, and Shauna made their way along the track to the river-bank near the Bobangle hut. Lindsay, Akama and Sabbo who had joined them, sloshed in the mud.

The roar of the raging waters filled their ears long before they reached the river-bank.

"What's that noise?" Shauna asked Michael.

"That, lass, is the Burdekin River in full throat."

As the river came into view, Mary gasped. "Oooh, my goodness." She stood spellbound at the sight of the roiling brown waters carrying tumbling debris of logs, branches, twisted sheets of corrugated iron, and even an unfortunate beast caught up in the rising current. No more the placid waters of the irregular waterholes where they broke the monotony of the hot sands. "Uncle Michael are you sure we're safe here. Look, the waters are halfway up the sides of the river banks already."

Michael stood watching the turbulent currents for a moment before answering.

"Paddymac and I have seen several floods since we moved here in the nineties and never had any real problems. But we've learnt, one can never be complacent with such an unpredictable river." He turned to Gabby who had joined them.

"Gabby, you might want to check the weak point up near the cutting, regularly. If this contrary lady decides to break her banks, that'll be the most likely spot she'll do it."

"Yes, Mister Michael. Haddi up there now." He watched his sons and Lindsay playing at the water's edge. "Mister Michael, can the boys give a hand at your place?"

"Not just now thanks, Gabby. Everything's looking fine. Lindsay's a strong lad, he'll lend a hand, I'm sure." He nodded his head to Gabby before looking to Mary and Shauna. "I think we'll head back now and leave these fellows to it." He turned back to Gabby. "You make sure you leave here at the first sign of danger. There's room up at the compound for you."

"Yes, Mister Michael, you'll hear us coming if the water on our heels." Teeth gleamed in his dark face.

Mary and Shauna spent the little daylight left baking damper loaves and pots of salted-beef stew. Restless fowls clucked and shuffled in the branches of the mango tree outside. Mary looked up from kneading the dough when Shauna spoke from the corner where her arms were buried in the potato sack.

"I hope we've enough taties to last the distance. We should've asked Mr. Wong if he has any more in his shed."

"It's too late now," Mary advised her daughter. "If the track is passable, we'll look for some tomorrow morning."

"Do you think Paddymac will come to stay here with us? His humpy's so close to the river-bank and the new hut he's building is far from complete."

"If he does, we'll put him on the verandah of the big house with Uncle Michael."

Nobody slept soundly during the night. The lantern remained alight in the kitchen near Michael's hut and the kettle kept warm on the edge of a slumbering stove. The feet of Michael and Shamus rattled the back steps at regular intervals as they made forays outside inspecting the state of the compound. Due to the clouded sky, Shauna could not be sure of the time when she heard the shouting downstairs. Lanterns sent darting shadows around the foliage of the trees.

"Mister Michael! Mister Michael! The river's near to breaking its banks. The water's tearing through the river paddock. Haddi's on his way to let the Wongs know. You'll have water in the compound for sure." Gabby yelled.

Akama and Sabbo were swept up into the arms of their mother.

At that moment, Shauna's frantic call reached down from the vestibule of the big house to the group in the yard below.

"Look! Look!" Her shaking hand pointed. "Over there!"

Everyone's eyes turned to follow the direction indicated.

"Mother of God," Michael gasped.

Not a soul moved. All stood mesmerized. The sunrise revealed the wide wave of muddy water as it rolled relentlessly across the flat-lands filling the hollows and gutters before swallowing the paddocks. Islands of higher land dotted the brown lake. It seemed only moments before the water surrounded the compound. The liquid invader paused as if to draw breath. Horrified, everybody watched as it began its march higher and higher to engulf everything in sight. They retreated to the steps. Within less than an hour, the water flowed twelve inches deep across the compound.

The water swept up everything in its grasp including debris and small wild animals too slow to escape. Occasional flashes of the bodies of snakes as they whipped across the top of the water caught the eye of the wary spectators.

The water flowed under the gaps in the shed walls. It poured in below the floors of the worker's shed and Michael's hut. It gathered momentum. It developed a growl. Dirty water inundated the schoolroom where now the benches and stools hung from the rafters above.

Shamus and Michael moved swiftly to the top of the front steps of the big house. Just Dog and Old Dog sat alert at their feet.

"Shamus, I'm thinking perhaps we may have to bring the Bobangle families up here onto the verandah. This is something we've never seen here at Emerald Flats. Old Mabel will be terrified."

At that moment, a great commotion sounded above the roaring waters of the river. The two men ran to the back of the house. Lantern lights danced around the Wong families who carried their belongings in bags, on trolleys and wheel-barrows usually employed to carry the produce from their gardens. Crying babies added to the confusion.

"Up here! Up here!" Michael and Shamus went to direct the newcomers. Mary, Shauna, and Mark appeared at the window of the vestibule. Michael called to Mark. "Mark, bring the Bobangles up here, too? Who knows how high the water'll come?"

Mary strained to be heard above the noise. "Shamus, bring the food up from the kitchen." She turned to Shauna and a bleary-eyed Lindsay who joined them. "Do you think we can set up the new stove temporarily in this unfinished kitchen up here?"

"There'll be no vent system but as we're still waiting for the kitchen walls that shouldn't be an issue. We'll need to get the firewood upstairs too." Shauna thought aloud.

It was in the big house, an island in a sea of muddy waters, where the population of Emerald Flats sat out the flood of February 1914. The Wong family gathered with their things at one end of the front verandah and the Bobangle families filled the other end. Anxious eyes followed every change in the muddy rubbish-filled waters below. Furrowed foreheads told of the deep concerns for the fate of their home-sites.

Along with the cloying smell of the floodwaters beneath them, the sharp odour of many unwashed bodies filled the overcrowded household. Babies, sensing the tension in the air around them, cried fretfully. Soft voices soothed the young. Chattering voices never stilled.

Intermittently, the dogs sitting on the front and back stairs, set up an ear-splitting round of barking as wildlife sought refuge from the waters.

Seeking peace, Mark sat on the bench in the sluice room of the unfinished kitchen, but when the women congregated around the stove prattling without end, he retreated to his back corner of the verandah.

During that day and the next night, the water reached no more than three feet deep. It lapped at the top steps of the worker's shed and Michael's hut but did not enter those buildings. Its muddy flow wrapped around the stove in the old kitchen.

The heavy choking stench of flood-mud seeped into every corner as the waters receded. The relief was short-lived. It was time to discover the extent of nature's wrath. In the Wong's case, had any of their vegetable gardens and fruit trees survived this onslaught. The Bobangles had yet to learn if they had a home to go to.

Nervous ducks and hens, driven from their usual roosts, shuffled around on the steps when Michael and Shamus came outside.

"Shamus, if you can find the horses, I think you and Mark should take a ride around the boundary fences. You can check the cattle at the same time. We need to know what damage we're looking at out there and if we've any stock left at all."

"Lindsay and Mark are out now looking for the horses. I told them to keep a sharp eye out for any crocodiles which may have been washed in with the floodwaters."

"Oh, let's hope not. I'll ride over to Paddymac's farm. He should be safe if he noticed the river rising early enough. He'll have cane down though; I should think."

On the day before the flooding of the river, Paddymac had worked with the mattock and pick until late afternoon. When he noticed the rising waters, he secured everything at his camp. Exhausted, he threw himself on the hessian and timber-framed stretcher in the humpy on the river-bank. An hour later, he aroused from a deep slumber. He threw his feet off the stretcher to sit up and listen. The noise of the river waters had changed. His feet stumbled in the blackness as he rushed out through the doorway. In the faint light of a moon suffocated by rain clouds, he stopped, confused. The deafening roar of the river from the other side of the river-bank trees was an expected sound but a new and second rumble of rushing waters came from the opposite direction. Fear clenched his heart.

Instinct more than knowledge sent him scrambling to gather his swag. He swung it over his shoulder. It thumped against his back as his long legs ran in the direction of the only place higher than where he currently stood – his partially constructed new hut on the other side of the cane paddock. His feet sank into the deep mud of the tilled ground. The water's current dragged at his legs. His breathing laboured. Cane tops slashed at his face. Cane roots threatened his balance. Water splashed around his thighs by the time he threw his gear up onto the floorboards of his new hut, with himself not far behind.

"Where the devil did that water come from?" He tried to gather his wits as he sucked air into his lungs. "The river must've broken its banks somewhere." He strained his eyes to see his horse, but in vain; a black horse on a black night is impossible to see. With any luck, the animal had made its way to higher ground.

His retreat stood five feet above the ground and included only the floorboards and a roof. When the dawn delivered a stronger light through broken clouds, Paddymac sat staring at his crop of cane for this year; it lay flattened. Under this drubbing by the unmerciful muddy water, he knew little would remain of the topsoil they had prepared for the new planting. He dared not think of the irrigation pump and water channelling.

The disappointment, the despondency of wasted efforts, and the heartbreak built pressure in the pit of his belly like the pressure in a volcanic crater. It built up until it exploded in a gut-wrenching sob. He jumped to his feet and leant against a verandah post. Why did this setback affect him so much? It felt like a mule had kicked him in the guts. He and Mister Michael had been through hard times before. Mister Michael always said not to wallow in self-pity when things went wrong. On such occasions, Mister Michael reassessed the circumstances and started all over again. This is what he must do.

His heart broke for his wonderful Thelma and her disappointment. For her sake and their future, Paddymac drew himself tall took up a shovel and jumped down into the mud slush. He prepared to investigate exactly what damage the farm had sustained. He was alive. Things could have been worse.

The snicker of his horse, Blackie, behind him, lifted his spirits. Already things were looking up.

After waving farewell to their friends slopping through the mud on the track to their homes, Mary turned to Shauna.

"I don't envy them what they'll have to face today."

Shauna looked at their verandah splattered with the mud of many footprints. "Well, Mam, I think we may have a bit of a mess to clean up ourselves."

"I'm so glad we lifted everything we could from the old kitchen at Uncle Michael's hut. That room will take some cleaning up."

"Come, Mam, let's make a start there first. Talking about it won't get much done."

Chapter Eight

James and William McIvor

"Struth, William, do you think it could get any hotter?"

William laughed as he watched his brother James trying to cool off in a small puddle of water in the creek-bed. The weather had been hot and dry for some time. Only a few waterholes persisted. The pink and grey coats of the galahs flashed amongst the scant grasses growing near the mound of rocks under the tall gum trees opposite where William sat. Mr. Littlewood had assured the boys the rain was coming. His father had told him so. The man had never been wrong with his weather forecasts.

"Don't be a sissy. Come on and get some tea. It'll be dark very soon. There's a bit of this morning's stew left and some damper uneaten. A hot pannikin of tea will soon cool you down," William promised his brother.

The boys had been putting in a fence on the western boundary. It had been hard going. Later, as they sat in the dark watching the stars above, James pondered over the past two months since their arrival at 'Leaning Rock Station'.

When they had first entered the front gate, Mr. Littlewood called a stop for the cavalcade. The sulky carried Mrs. Littlewood and her two daughters. In close attendance on horseback, rode Mr. Littlewood and his son Thomas who was a twin of Maryann. James and William rode behind. The aptitude, with which the elder daughter Bella who looked about sixteen, handled the horse in the sulky, impressed the new Australians. Maryann had sat pouting all the way from Charters Towers because her mother had refused her request to take the reins.

"What inspired the name of Leaning Rock Station?" James asked as he admired the carving of the name in the large frame above the gate.

"See those hills way over to the east," Matthew Littlewood pointed to several grey hills in the far distance. "There's a short, deep gorge. At the entrance, the largest rock you can imagine leans out above the skyline. How it got there and how it stays there's a mystery. Not long after he arrived here, my father almost lost his life near that rock. He'd dismounted and was searching for a young calf when he lost his footing in the shale and slid over the edge of the cliff. He was able to grab hold of a small tree root and yell out to the blackfella, Toby, who worked for him at the time. Luckily the blackfella hadn't wandered too far away and was able to hear the call. Under Dad's instructions, Toby used the rope from the horse's saddle and dragged him back up again. If Toby hadn't been there it would have been lights out for Dad. Now the two of them are still alive and spend a lot of time reliving old stories."

James and William were kept occupied the first week riding the boundary line with Mr. Littlewood. They met a very unusual chap called Ding who was the official boundary rider on the property. The fellow never wasted words, read nothing but his bible, and according to their boss seemed to know everything going on in the district. Mr. Littlewood said he probably received all the news from the local aborigine tribe. Every day, Mr. Ding travelled from one line-hut to the next checking and repairing the fences as he went.

At the time, Mr. Littlewood pointed out to them where he planned to build a new fence on the western boundary. They learnt how to read the landmarks and recognize the horizon's characteristics. Mr. Littlewood was particular in showing them where and how to find water.

"In the heat we get here, you'll not last long if you don't have water," he explained. "After we get back to the homestead, I'll need you to help replace the buckets on the northern windmill rods."

Fixing the windmill had been a new experience for the boys but they were enthusiastic and quick to learn. William and a young black lad called Dusty climbed up to the top of the mill where they placed some wooden planks on which to sit, inside the mill frame. James and his boss had worked at the bottom of the mill clamping the emerging rod. With the use of ropes, chains, heavy steel clamps, and the power of two Clydesdale horses encouraged by Mr. Littlewood senior and young Thomas Littlewood, they pulled the rods up individually and stacked them against the inside of the windmill until the last rod with the bucket system attached revealed itself. A new bucket set replaced the old and the process was reversed until the mill was restored to working order.

"What are you chuckling about James? Something has tickled your fancy." William could not resist asking.

"I'm wondering how you're going to cope with 'Dynamite' back at the homestead." James rose upon an elbow on the bunk in the hut they shared. It was too dark to see his brother properly. "That Bella has her cap set at you, brother. I don't like your chances of an escape. Since our Christmas lunch with the family, the girl never takes her eyes off you."

In the next bunk, William felt the heat rise in his cheeks. He chose not to respond to his brother's teasing. He did rather like Bella. She stood tall and proud and had large brown eyes. He often felt those eyes upon him. When he caught her brushing her hair, counting one hundred strokes, he knew why her hair shone like black diamonds.

Anyway, she's only a young girl so stop even thinking of her, he told himself.

Silence reigned in the hut. William's mind filled with the young Bella.

James drifted off into his own dreams of a woman's face which often haunted his thoughts these days. *Beautiful Shauna; Mark's Shauna, remember! Stop thinking about her; forget her! Think of something else for Heaven's sake; find something to do*. He punched the rolled-up rug used instead of a pillow under his head.

Chapter Nine

The Wedding

When Shamus and Mary arrived at Paddymac's farm, they found Paddymac and Mark working in the paddock with the new horse-drawn plough. The draught-horses were not too keen on dragging the new implement. Paddymac encouraged them gently, taking them through their paces. Planting of the new paddock was to start soon.

Paddymac paused to rest the horse and himself. Sweat and dust mixed to mud on his face. He wiped at it with his sleeved arm. He stood tall. Pride shone in his eyes as he looked over the remainder of his crop which had survived the flood earlier in the year; even if it was a little bent and twisted. It was almost ready to cut.

He grinned and asked Shamus as he approached, "Did you know your Uncle Michael is already talking about having a tractor and a car one day?"

"Give me a horse any day," Shamus laughed. "I can't see Uncle Michael settling for a speed limit of 12mph as they have in the streets of Ayr. You've seen him riding like a young daredevil on the horses. It's hard to remember his age when you see him on horseback."

"You'll be coming with us next week to visit his friend, won't you, Mr. Doolan? The man has worked with a tractor on his farm on the Ayr side, for a few months now."

"Paddymac, you'll be going to the hospital, my lad, if you don't stop calling me, Mr. Doolan. Call me Shamus." He grinned then smiled ruefully knowing full well any altercation with Paddymac would no doubt put himself in hospital, not Paddymac. "You'll be looking forward to the cane cutting process, no doubt?"

"Oh, yes, Mister … sorry … Shamus, very much so."

In the basket, with the pannikins, Mary carried oat biscuits cooked that very morning. From her other hand hung a lidded billy of tea with the handle wrapped in newspaper to protect her bare hand from the heat. This was the afternoon smoko for Paddymac, Mark and any onlookers as they worked the plough horse.

She heard Paddymac laugh and say, "Mark, I think the idea's for you to balance the weight with your body so as the nose of the confounded machine runs just under the ground and not deep enough to bury you, the horse, and itself."

Mark picked himself off the ground. He belted the dust from his clothes and his hair. A frown hung for a moment on his face before it was replaced with what Mary thought was a forced smile.

"You're right, Paddymac. I'm sure this contraption bucks worse than any young horse I've ever ridden."

Her sudden relief surprised Mary when both men laughed.

Paddymac caught sight of Mary. "Oh good, here's Mrs. Doolan with our smoko – a sight for sore eyes."

They all moved over to the shade of a tree. When Mark and Shamus went off to examine the new plough, Mary spoke quietly to Paddymac.

"Why did Thelma insist on having the wedding here at Emerald Flats? I'm not complaining. As you know, we're looking forward to putting on a nice day for you both. I just thought it a bit strange she didn't want it to be at Ayr with her family and friends. As I understand, she's only invited her immediate family and of course, her church minister, to share her day. Thelma said they're to stay at the Crown Hotel in Home Hill. A horse and dray have been arranged for them to drive out here before ten on the morning of the wedding."

A flush appeared through the dirt upon Paddymac's face. "Mrs. Doolan, as far as I'm aware, Thelma's never really forgiven some of her family and supposed friends for making snide comments when she didn't marry earlier in life. There was a chappie she had her cap set on but he was killed at the Boer War. Anyway, Thelma thought it a good idea to have the celebration here. Thelma says we're all her family now."

"Now, Paddymac, I agree with Thelma. We're family and like my husband, I really would prefer it if you called me Mary, rather than Mrs. Doolan." Mary's eyes twinkled. "You wouldn't like me to forget and starch your flannels by accident one day, would you, now?" Her grin widened. "That might be decidedly uncomfortable."

"I'll try to remember, … er, Mary."

"Now, that wasn't so hard, was it?"

Paddymac grinned. "Starched flannels would be disastrous."

"It would, Paddymac. Getting back to where we were; you can rest assured Shauna and I are as pleased as punch to have been asked to prepare the wedding breakfast. I know Mabel and Old Mrs. Wong are very excited. They've already started giving their families instructions on what they must prepare. The cake has been finished and we've it hidden in a safe place; I hope."

"Thank you, Mrs. Doolan; you and everyone."

Mary smiled. "Paddymac, do I have to put you over my knee? You must call me, Mary, please."

"Yes, sorry, Mary."

Mary smiled before going on. "Will you and Uncle Michael bring out your best suits. We'll clean them up and do any repairs required." Mary's face held a rueful grin before she asked her next question. "Do you think there'll be any chance of getting those old work boots off Uncle Michael's feet? I know we shouldn't waste our breath asking him to shave."

Paddymac laughed as he visualized the kerfuffle such a request might generate.

Once again, Mary returned to the wedding plans. "Paddymac, you're bringing Thelma here the day before, aren't you? She'll be able to sleep in Lindsay's new room and we'll dress her there, in the big house." Mary made a mental note to ask Thelma if she wished to hold the ceremony and breakfast up on the verandah or underneath the big house.

Three days later, after their recent visit to the Inkerman Mill, where they had examined the plans of the tram lines built to transport cane trucks to and from the farms, Paddymac, Shamus, and Harry's boys worked in the shed at Emerald Flats building a high-sided wagon to carry the cut cane from the paddock to the railway siding. A winch had been built at the siding to assist the transfer of cane from the farmer's wagon to the rail trucks. Uncle Michael seemed to be everywhere at once offering advice.

Shauna's head lifted as raised voices fell upon her ears. She paused in her approach with the morning smoko.

"I'm telling you if Paddymac has to travel so far to deliver the cane to the railway siding it would be best if we had a larger wagon able to carry enough cut-cane each journey to fill two railway cane trucks. This would make fewer trips and save time," protested Shamus.

"Yes, but to do that we'll definitely need the four horses and maybe, even six, to carry such a load. Imagine the extra feed required for so many working animals," argued Uncle Michael. "A smaller wagon would cost a lot less to build and cost less in harness and chains for the horses. With two teams of horses, one team could rest, each on alternate days."

"With a bigger wagon, the horses wouldn't have to do so many trips. The cane cutting would continue while the wagon was away. Wouldn't it be cheaper to build a bigger wagon now rather than find you'll need to build another one later?" Shamus insisted.

"When we go to visit this farmer at Ayr, we'll ask his opinion. We'll see how they do things over there. Look, here comes Shauna with smoko; I'm parched," settled Uncle Michael.

Uncle Michael leant against the door jamb in the kitchen. "Only one week 'til the wedding, Shauna. Will everything be ready? I'm sorry, but the men won't be of much use to you. They'll be busy at Paddymac's planting the cane for most of the week."

Steam rose around Shauna's face as she lifted the porridge pot. She stirred vigorously. "There's no need to worry, Uncle Michael. Mam and I have it all under control. We're even planning a day over at Paddymac's ourselves." A grin replaced her smile. "Anyway, I'm sure the men would only get in the way."

Michael grinned in return. "More than likely, lass."

"What does the planting entail?"

"Hard work, blood, sweat, and tears – like all the farm work, I guess." Michael paused; his brow furrowed as he thought about his answer. "We plant the small pieces of cane along the furrows left by the plough. Each piece has one or more eyes from which the new cane-stool grows. Lindsay's sorted out some good bags in which the planters will carry the cut pieces of cane. For over twelve months Paddymac has been saving and redesigning the kerosene tins as drums for the cutters to deliver the chopped pieces to the planters."

Only the glow of the morning's sun peeped over the horizon the following day when Gabby halted the horses and wagon outside the kitchen. The men and the older children piled into the back alongside the hamper of food Mary and Shauna had prepared. The women and Uncle Michael sat on the front seat with Uncle Michael in charge of the reins. Extra shovels and hoes rattled against the sides of the dray fixed with odd bits of fencing wire. Planting was to begin on Paddymac's farm this morning.

When the willing workers arrived, kerosene tins dotted the paddock. Short sticks of cane poked over the lip of each drum. Propped up at the end of each row, short sugar-cane-sticks bulged the sides of sugar-bags like knobbly growths.

It did not take long for everyone to become organized in teams. The dropper, carrying the bags of short cane-sticks, walked along the drill laying the cut sticks in the furrow at every other footstep. Behind the dropper came the planter whose feet dragged in the side of the furrow to cover the plant-cane before giving it a firm stomp. The flooding rains of February and lighter showers since had ensured plenty of soil moisture to nourish the new plant.

Harry Bobangle's grey hair stuck out from under his hat like stray bits of the hat straw. Shamus attempted to relieve him of carrying the heavy sugar-bag of cane-sticks.

Harry turned with a growl, "I'm not done for yet, young pup, just you keep shovelling and I'll keep dropping these bits of cane." Both men laughed.

Mark and Paddymac worked at the dray loaded with the plant cane. Their sharpened cane knives flashed in the sunlight as they cut the long sticks. Mark's frown deepened every time he looked over to see his wife working as if she was a navvy.

At the end of her first row, Shauna lifted her head to stretch her aching back. She found aches in muscles she did not even know she owned. The promise she had made to her mother not to overdo things in the heat came to mind, but this mindless chore left her brain free to contemplate Mark's recent offer to take her away to Townsville for a week's holiday. Maybe that's what he needs – a break from all this. On the other hand, the children in her class were just settling down to their lessons. It would be a shame to disrupt them with her absence. Then again, a holiday might be the opportune time to tell him about her possible pregnancy. She might even visit a doctor there. She stopped and stretched again as another thought flowed into her head. Is *Mark insecure? Is that why he shows these signs of jealousy*? Her eyes panned the paddock to lock into those of her husband. Shauna's heart dropped at the sight of his deep frown and tight-lipped expression.

At the end of the second row, she turned to the planter following her footsteps.

"Lindsay, will you fill the bag from the drum and take over for me. I think I may have to sit for a bit".

Lindsay jumped at the chance to be a dropper. All his mates here today had the job of planters – following the men who dropped the cane. Haddi's wife, Rosie emerged from the shade of the trees and slipped in behind Lindsay.

Mid-morning found all the workers resting in the tree shade drinking from their water-bags. Sweat on their bodies mixed the dirt into mud layering their faces, hands and clothes. Shauna and Mary offered biscuits from one of the baskets to everyone.

With the sun high in the sky, the workers had been back in the paddock for two hours when Uncle Michael's calls drew them again to the shade where Mary and Shauna presented corned meat sandwiches for lunch. Many groans accompanied the toilers as they eased their bodies to the ground. Uncle Michael filled the pannikins with hot, black tea.

At the end of the day, the paddock had been planted. Raucous shouts and squeals rose from the river-bank where the men threw themselves into the water to cool off.

"I hope you've checked this waterhole for crocs," Gabby called to Paddymac.

"Nah, I thought you'd do that," came the laughing reply.

Further along the river-bank away from the swimmers, Mary turned to Shauna and Sophie, "Listen to the racket down there. This is one of those times I wish I was a man."

The dusk fell lightly over the front paddocks when Lindsay questioned Michael. "Uncle Michael, why does everyone make such a fuss for a wedding? Why do people get married anyway? I know for sure I'll never EVER be getting married," said Lindsay with utter conviction.

Michael smiled. *Out of the mouths of babes*, he thought to himself. "Yes well, lad, hmmm, it's just one of those things in life been sent to try us. There's no use chewing on the bit; just grin and bear it. You get to learn, at times like this, it's best to let the women get on with things and keep well out of the way."

Lindsay contemplated Uncle Michael's advice for a while before asking, "Did you ever get married Uncle Michael?"

The silence went on for so long Lindsay thought he had not been heard. He was just about to repeat the question when Michael replied. "Who'd want to marry a grumpy old codger like me, well set in his ways?"

This gave Lindsay food for thought as he sat under the mango tree with Uncle Michael watching an ant carrying a gargantuan load to its nest. After a while, he asked his companion to tell him a story of the old days. "Please tell me the one about Red Shirt and Blue Shirt when they tried to steal Paddymac's horse?"

Michael chuckled. "I must have told you that yarn at least a hundred times."

The call from Paddymac saved Michael another repetition of Lindsay's favourite story.

"What! What do you mean, the ladies want to trim my hair and beard? They'll have to catch me first," shouted Michael.

"I guess that wouldn't be too hard," said Paddymac with a straight face.

"Bah! Next thing they'll be wanting me to shave my splendid beard off altogether," complained Michael.

Paddymac remarked, pokerfaced, "Yes, I do think that's been mentioned."

"Over my dead body! Why do women want to make such a fuss just to get married?" Michael repeated the same question Lindsay had asked him earlier. "Why can't they just sit down at the table when the men come in for smoko, have a cup of tea, say 'I do', and give the preacher man a cup of tea and biscuit for his trouble, then everyone can get back to work."

Paddymac could not keep a straight face any longer. "Do you think Mary, Shauna, and Thelma would let us get away with that?" he asked with a laugh. "I'm not going to be the one to bring it up." They both began to chuckle. In the short time they'd known Mary and Shauna, they had grown to love and respect them very much. They were also quite aware both women had determined streaks. Women who were going to survive in this country needed such determination. It was a necessity to be admired.

"Aw, Mam! Do I have to have a shower again this morning? I had one last night. I'll end up washing myself away and I'll disappear down the drain hole."

"Well, don't block up the drain on your way through. Now! In the shower and I want to hear the water running," was the unsympathetic reply from his mother.

Not brave enough to even think the thought in front of his Mam, Lindsay waited until the door was closed and the water running before he whispered, "Damn women! Damn weddings! Damn! Damn! Damn!"

Saturday, the 11th of April, and everyone from Emerald Flats had gathered under the new house. Thelma's parents and two of her brothers with their wives were present as the minister gave a special Easter service after which he performed the wedding ceremony. To Mary, it all seemed to be over too soon but not before she had saturated her lace handkerchief and was sopping up the remaining tears with Shamus's much larger one.

Thelma looked so lovely. She had chosen to wear a simple grey frock knowing Paddymac loved it so much. Mary, with Shauna's help, pinned her brown plaited hair high upon her head. In her hand, Thelma held a white bible with a crocheted bookmark displaying exquisite little rosebuds in the pattern. A small hat with silk flowers completed the outfit. Beside Paddymac, Thelma stood like a small doll gazing up with adoring eyes.

"That's the long and short of it, I guess," whispered Shamus.

Laughter dotted conversations rolling around the trestle tables. Thelma was thrilled with the way the cake had turned out. She laughed when Mary and Shauna told her of its near escape from the goat's hungry attack. There was plenty to eat with a fresh beast killed the day before; ducks and a turkey had been sacrificed also. The boys had caught several lovely fish now baked with lemon and onions. Sweet perfumes, from the bunches of native tree flowers attached to every house post, drifted on the breeze.

Paddymac's new in-laws were polite to the Bobangle and the Wong families but Mary could sense the undercurrent of racial prejudice and knew she would never want to become close friends with them.

Thelma told the story of her mother's first attempt at cooking plum-duff not long after she had been married. Her father had looked at the sorry mess and threw it at the wall saying, "If it sticks, it'll be all right to eat, if not, it can go to the chooks."

Paddymac commented, "I'll be well fed. I've already tested Thelma's cooking."

One of the brothers piped up, "All Thelma's friends at our church have half a dozen wee bairns hanging off their skirts already. I guess our Thelma will have to hurry and catch up." This caused Thelma to blush furiously. Out of the corner of her eye, Mary noticed Shauna stood looking at her feet with a secret smile upon a pink face.

The other brother had taken many photos with the new Brownie camera he had recently acquired. The completed film would have to go to Townsville to be developed so it would be quite a wait to see the results.

Several eyebrows lifted when Lindsay, along with Curley's eldest son Anguó, conversed comfortably in the Chinese language.

At two o'clock, Uncle Michael drove his wagon with a two-horse team around to the front of the house disturbing the family of grey doves pecking the crumbs thrown by the children. Onboard were the bags and supplies Paddymac had instructed him to load. Thelma climbed up, assisted by her new husband. In a single leap, Paddymac landed on the footplate. Many kisses were thrown and goodbyes called as the wagon made its way towards the front gate. The younger ones ran beside the happy couple for at least half a mile, calling out to Paddymac to take them with him.

There'll be no hope of that happening, Paddymac thought with a smile.

"I suppose they're going to Townsville for their honeymoon?" Thelma's mother queried Mary.

"No, I believe they're spending a week or two travelling in the wagon out towards Charters Towers. Paddymac's going to show Thelma where he lived and enjoyed many years of his younger life."

"They'll stay in a hotel at Charters Towers, then?" the interrogation continued.

Mary shrugged, "I believe they plan to camp under the wagon in a swag; similar to how Michael and Paddymac travelled for many years."

Mary could not deny the wave of relief she felt when Thelma's family, along with the Minister, said their goodbyes and climbed into the dray.

The left-over food had been divided up and the families from Emerald Flats returned to their homes. Shauna and her mother were tidying up the last of the dishes in the kitchen when Mary could not contain her curiosity any longer.

"Shauna, my dear, have you got something to tell me?"

A soft blush perfused Shauna's face. "Whatever do you mean, Mam?"

"'I may be getting old, dear, but I'm not silly yet, nor am I blind. I couldn't help but notice your reaction when they mentioned the wee bairns Thelma's friends had."

Shauna held her hand over her mouth as she smiled widely. "Mam, I haven't told Mark yet but I think I'm pregnant. I didn't want to say anything until I'm sure. You'll not say a word now, will you?"

"No, my dear, I'll remain stum."

"Thelma, are you comfortable enough? Are you warm enough?" Paddymac fussed at their first campsite.

Thelma smiled and said, "Paddy dear, I'm not made of glass. I can think of nothing better than lying beside you watching the stars and the moon. You've been so kind in agreeing to take me on this trip for my honeymoon. This is so much better than being shut up in a hotel room, having to be dressed up all the time. It makes me cringe when I have to constantly be polite to people I don't know or whom I don't particularly wish to meet." Thelma sat on the ground watching the flickering flames of their dying fire. Her hands idly fondled the ears of the black pup the Bobangle family had gifted her and Paddymac as a wedding present. "Paddy, what are we going to name this little one?"

He walked over and dropped to the ground beside his bride. The pup wiggled with joy as the calloused hands lifted him high into the air. The two contemplated the squirming bundle as Paddymac turned it back and forth.

"Thelma, what do you think?"

She laughed. "He'll twist himself inside out if he keeps that up. Why not name him Twister?"

"Done." Paddymac grinned. His arms slipped around Thelma's shoulders. He breathed in the perfume of her hair. His lips wandered idly around her face, her neck, her shoulders – savouring the pleasure.

Thelma sat Twister on the ground beside their swag and turned to her lover. Their lips met. Discarded clothes lay about them as the melting heat fused their bodies as one.

Unshed tears of emotion almost choked Shauna as she began undressing. Mark lay silent on the bed.

Should she tell Mark she was pregnant, or not. This should have been a moment of pleasure when both parties shared the ecstasy of anticipation but all she felt was dread. How was he going to react? Her thoughts were rudely interrupted.

"Well, at least that idjut won't be drooling all over you anymore. He has his own wife to take care of now."

Shauna gasped. She took up her hairbrush and moved to the window from where she gazed out into the night. Her hands shook as she brushed her hair again and again. Her scalp tingled with the scrape of the bristles. Shauna could not speak. She didn't want to speak. She didn't want to be anywhere near this evil stranger. This man who made her feel dirty. This man her husband.

Chapter Ten

Droving

A few days later and Lindsay was beside himself with excitement. Sugar, with her bay coat shining in the early morning sunlight, smelt the boy's joy. She pranced a little and tossed her head at the other horses. Lindsay's hand strayed with regular frequency to the whip in its holder on the saddle before slipping around his back to touch the small swag secured behind him. Both legs hugged his saddle-bags loaded with supplies.

The bullocks were on the road to the cattle yards at the Bobawaba railway-siding. They would be loaded onto the cattle rail-trucks for delivery to the Bowen meatworks. Gabby and Akama were on the one wing. Mark with Sabbo rode on the other. Lindsay tailed up the small herd. Uncle Michael, with the tucker wagon, had gone on ahead to choose the first night's campsite.

When Lindsay asked Gabby how he knew which way to go, the answer had been, "Just follow your nose." Lindsay knew he was joking. Later he would ask Uncle Michael.

A small creek, south of Home Hill, had been selected as the first night's campsite. This trip was a treat for the boys. The men did not push the cattle too hard. Lindsay and Sabbo prepared the fire, boiled the billy and heated the tins of bully beef. They did not think at the time to remove the lids first. Amidst lots of laughter and ribbing, everyone had a hot job trying to open the tins later. The drovers were grateful for the several loaves of freshly baked bread Mary had packed for them. The younger members on the trip had been warned, it would be their chore to cook damper on the second night's camp. Gabby, Akama and Mark had the cattle watered and settled around a nice patch of grass before they come in to eat.

"Lindsay, you and Sabbo are to take first watch. I want you to walk your horses quietly around the herd as they eat. Soft singing will help to keep them settled. You know all the animals now so keep a watch. Don't let any go astray. There's plenty of moonlight. You'll see well enough," instructed Uncle Michael.

Akama could hardly speak for laughing. "If Sabbo starts singing we'll be chasing these beasts to Brisbane."

"Ha! Ha! Ha!" retorted his offended brother.

The eyelids of both the guardians drooped when Mark and Akama came out to take their turn at minding the herd. The boys fell into their swags, asleep before they landed. Nothing disturbed their slumbers, not even the call of the dingoes in the hills nearby. The cattle become restless towards midnight as the dingoes moved in closer. This herd consisted of full-grown beasts and the dingoes were unlikely to attack but the bullocks did not like the proximity of these predators. Their howls were enough to send a shiver down the spines of man and beast.

Gabby heard the shuffling, stamping, and snorting of the cattle and rode his horse out to keep watch with Mark while Akama was sent to his blankets. The eleven-year-old boy had done a man's job that day. At one stage, Mark and Gabby controlled a short-lived half-hearted disturbance with ease. The remainder of the night passed smoothly.

Mark felt sleepy but the swirl of thoughts in his head kept him wide awake. He struggled to understand why he felt the way he did. He loved Shauna; he really did. She was a beauty, there was no doubt but too beautiful and too friendly. His stomach churned as jealousy plagued his insides. He didn't mean the nasty words he threw at her sometimes but she was so damned stubborn and wilful. She didn't seem to understand the man of the house was in charge. Maybe it was because they didn't have a house of their own. She seemed to think more of the others and not enough of her husband. Even when he offered to take her on a trip to Townsville, she wasn't enthusiastic. She said she'd think on it. She can't leave those damn coloured brats in her school class, more like.

The boys had the fire alight and breakfast prepared when the men returned to camp. Mark and Gabby had snatched a couple of catnaps during the night.

"I could kill a hot cup of tea, fellas," said Gabby.

Lindsay noticed his butt was feeling rather raw and sore having spent more time in the saddle in one go than he had ever done before. He didn't say a word. He cringed as he thought of the teasing he'd receive if his mates discovered his discomfort. No thanks, hell would freeze over before he'd complain.

The second night was uneventful. On the third day, mid-afternoon found the team beside the triangular tramway turn-a-round near a rusting tin shed. In the far distance to the east, through the gaps in the trees, sunlight shimmered on a large salt-pan. It was a short lap to the rail yards where they settled the herd ready for collection by the night train. With the paperwork completed, Uncle Michael handed responsibility over to the rail workers.

"Come on, boys, we'll make camp at the same place as last night. With a bit of luck, the coals of our fire will still be warm. One of you can cook us a damper to go with the bully beef tonight," called Michael as he encouraged the dray horses into a trot.

Thelma's wide smile and sparkling brown eyes at the sight of her new cottage drew Paddymac's arm tighter around her shoulders. She had enjoyed her adventurous honeymoon but now she was ready to start her new life. "Paddy, look! We're home, dear."

Paddymac smiled at this woman who had come to mean so much to him. "Yes, my love, we're home."

His land held Paddymac's attention. He stopped at the edge of the track and jumped down to check the soil where the cane was planted. He felt the small bud of new cane. He spread the dirt lightly back over it. Waves of gratitude flowed through him like warm sunlight on a cold morning.

Thelma's voice caught his attention. "Oh, Paddy, look. How lovely. The hut's been painted. It looks grand. The family has worked so hard. We must go over and thank them straight away."

"Can we unpack the wagon first, my sweet one?"

As they drove up to the gate of Emerald Flats, Paddymac was surprised to notice the place appeared to be deserted. Not even a dog came out to bark at them. He pulled up the horses and wagon at the kitchen behind Uncle Michael's hut.

Under the big house, the children in Shauna's class were quick to notice the arrivals. From her work-table upstairs, Mary dropped her mending. In her progress across the compound, she was overtaken by the students released from their class.

The excited children swamped Paddymac and Thelma.

"Come, Thelma," Mary caught her hand. "I'll make a cup of tea. I want to hear all about where you've been. We expect the men back from their droving trip today, sometime."

Chapter Eleven

War is Declared

The cooler mornings did nothing to improve her blue fingers as Shauna lifted the large pieces of corned meat from the vat where they had been soaking in the cold brine solution. This was the fourth day in a row she had rubbed the mixture of saltpetre and brown sugar into the meat before returning it to the salt solution. Every day, for the next ten days, Shauna planned to turn the meat soaking in the vat. After that, some pieces of the meat would be removed and smoked for eight days. The remainder of the meat was destined to pickle in the brine to be eaten as corned meat.

Shauna wore the secret smile on her face which had not shifted since last night when she told Mark about her pregnancy. She had spent days worried he might not be pleased about this event but when he began jumping with joy and making plans for the little one to come, she relaxed. By her calculation, the baby should arrive close to Christmas time.

She paused in her work to watch fascinated as the varied expressions of emotion flickered across Uncle Michael's face like the changing lights in the sky on a stormy night. He sat at the kitchen table reading what could only be the Queensland Register, judging by the colour of the front page. The smaller children in her class loved to cut shelf liners and decorations out of the pink paper. On first coming into the kitchen, Uncle Michael had waited impatiently for his breakfast to cook, but since the young Wong lad handed him the paper, Michael's eyes did not lift. He appeared to have forgotten his empty stomach.

"I don't like this, young Shauna," Michael stated. He sat for a moment rubbing his hand across his chin. "If these European governments aren't careful, we'll all be drawn into a conflict we don't need or want. By the recent foreign policies of the German government, one has to ask, 'Do they want to start a war?' The Russian and the Austrian governments aren't far behind."

"Uncle Michael, they're so far away. I'm sure we don't have to become overly worried," soothed Shauna. *I certainly hope not*, she thought to herself whilst crossing her fingers for luck. At that very moment, she managed to drop the handful of knives she had been carrying to the table. Looking down she noticed two pairs of knives had crossed each other. A cold grip of fear clenched her heart at this sure sign of bad luck to come. Her face turned stark white. *Please God, let nothing happen to my baby,* her first thought flashed through her head before, *Please God, don't let there be a war.* Automatically, her arm reached for the salt jar on the bench. She threw a pinch of salt over her shoulder before she bent to scoop up the knives. *I'm getting as superstitious as Granny,* she admonished herself.

"Maybe you're right, Shauna, it's nothing for us to be concerned about," said Michael thoughtfully. "I do wonder though if our government knows something, they're not telling us. Remember last year, they opened the new Naval College in Victoria and it was only several months later Australia's fleet made a big show arriving at Sydney's harbour." The paper flapped and crackled as Michael held it up to fold over a new page. "Och, I guess it will all sort itself out." His eyes ran down the page before he looked up to speak again. "Look at this now. A Frenchman has flown one of those amazing flying machines carrying the mail from Melbourne to Sydney. It took him two and a half days. How incredible is that? You know, Shauna, one-day people will travel everywhere in these machines – probably not in my time, but soon."

Shauna laughed. "Well, I can assure you they won't get me into something like that. If God wanted us to fly, he'd have given us wings."

Mary led the family's return from the sheds. As they ate their porridge, more pressing day to day issues took priority in their minds.

"Uncle Michael, Mark and I are going to take a ride over to Paddymac's to look at the young cane. Will you be coming along, too?" invited Shamus.

"I might see you over there later. Paddymac's finished repairing the flood damage to the pump. He and Haddi plan to test it out, today," responded Michael. "I may have an appointment this morning." Michael turned his head towards Lindsay and whispered, "Have you asked yet?"

The boy's face split into a grin. He reached over and touched his mother's hand. "Mam, Uncle Michael's going out to shoot a wallaby for dog-meat today. Can I go with him, please?" begged Lindsay. He didn't tell his mother how Gabby was going to teach him to skin the animal and preserve the hide so it could be sold later. This was one of those things best kept to himself.

Mary cast a dubious look at her son and then glanced at her husband to get an inkling of what he might be thinking. Lindsay didn't miss the slight nod of his father's head. His heart lifted.

"You mind everything Uncle Michael tells you. You can't be too careful around guns." A worry-frown rested on Mary's brow.

The men and Lindsay headed out through the doorway. Shauna called to her husband, "When you yard the horses will you leave old Betsy in the yards for me, please? I think I may saddle her up and ride over to see Thelma later this morning. Maybe I'll ride back with you and Pa."

A look of horror distorted Mark's face. He turned back and took Shauna's upper arm pulling her back with him into the kitchen, almost knocking Mary over in his rush.

Surprise filled Mary's face. She went to speak then thought better of it. She strode out of the kitchen wiping her hands on the towel as she went.

"Shauna, what do you think you're playing at?"

Shauna's face held no less surprise than her mother's. "What do you mean, Mark? I'm playing at nothing. Let go of my arm, you're hurting me." Shauna rubbed her arm where red streaks had appeared.

"Sorry," Mark mumbled. He lifted his head. "Are you trying to embarrass me in front of everybody?" He held up his hand extending a finger to underline each point he wished to make. "Number One: You know I'll not allow you to go riding in your condition. Number Two: You can't wait to grab any opportunity to visit that …" He paused before spitting out the word, "Paddymac. Number Three: You're trying to make out I'm the mean one here who won't let you go anywhere." Indignation nourished his words.

Shauna felt her hackles rising. She gritted her teeth before drawing a deep breath. "Mark McIvor," Shauna also used her fingers to emphasize her points. "Number One: I'm not ill with some terrible disease; I'm pregnant. Of course, I can ride a horse for some months yet. Number Two: Paddymac is a kind and well-mannered person. I always enjoy saying hello to him. It's a pity you tend to forget your manners at times. Paddymac's not the reason I'll be going over there. I wish to see Thelma. She's going to let me copy some of her recipes. Number Three: The last thing on my mind would be to embarrass you in front of the family. Maybe you could offer me the same courtesy."

Mark gasped. "Shauna, I expect an obedient wife. Usually, I wouldn't hold with a man hitting a woman but sometimes it may be necessary to remind one's wife who's boss. Don't let me have to hit you, Shauna. That'd hurt me as much as it'd hurt you. Now, I'm telling you, you're not to go riding in your condition." He stormed out of the kitchen making his way towards the stockyards.

Without a sideways glance, he passed Mary and Michael on their way back to the big house. Mary's arms stretched around a pile of work clothes. Uncle Michael followed in her wake arguing strenuously about whether his clothes required a needle and thread just yet. Neither turned their head in Mark's direction. If Mark had been interested, he may have smiled at Mary's words.

"Uncle Michael, it's as hard as pulling teeth separating you and your old clothes. It'll be no trouble at all with my new treadle sewing machine. I'll have this lot mended in no time. Now, aren't you going to hunt dog-meat today?"

Fifteen minutes later, galloping hooves announced the departure of Shamus and Mark when they headed off towards Paddymac's farm. Silence hung on the air between the two grim-faced men.

Michael and Lindsay watched the pair leave as they prepared their animals.

"Uncle Michael, why does Mark always try to boss Shauna around? She won't stand for it you know. Granny always said she could be as stubborn as old Grandpa."

Michael stood quiet as memories shuffled the contours of his face. "Yeah, my father always tended to be a bit pig-headed but he was mostly right, you know." Michael reached down to squeeze Lindsay's shoulder. "Anyway, it'll be for Shauna and Mark to work out their difficulties. It's nobody else's business but theirs. All marriages take time to settle as couples blend into the ways of their spouse." A wry grin lifted his lips as he pondered the irony of himself offering advice on married couples.

"Yeah, I suppose so. Come on then, Uncle Michael, we've got work to do." Lindsay stood with the bridled draught-horse, Old Master. This nondescript brown horse with a cloudy near-side eye was the horse Uncle Michael guaranteed would not become upset at the smell of blood. He said it was the best horse to use for carrying the dead kangaroo back home.

"Did you get the small sack?" asked Michael. Lindsay showed him the flour bag he had tucked into the waist of his trousers.

Once everyone had left the kitchen, Shauna took her frustrations out on the pots and pans. Soon reflected sunlight from the shiny utensils streamed across the room. Next, her attention turned to the benches and shelves. By the time she reached the table her scrubbing arms slowed; a small smile lifted the edge of her lips. Her swirling thoughts began to rationalize. *Mark only said I wasn't to ride. He didn't forbid me to visit with Thelma. If I take the sulky, I'll not be riding; I'll be driving.*

In record time, having draped the cleaning cloths over the hook near the wash-tubs, Shauna strode outside on her way to the stockyards. The brown mare, Betsy, followed willingly as she led her up to the sheds using a halter rein.

At that moment, Mary arrived. "What are you doing, Shauna?"

"I'm going to take the sulky and go to visit Thelma."

"But didn't Mark say you were to stay home?"

"He said, I was not to go riding. He said nothing about travelling in the sulky."

"Shauna, do you think you might be deliberately trying to anger Mark further? Perhaps you should wait until he calms down a little then come at things from another angle."

"I'm sure that's the wisest thing to do, Mam, but what does he know about pregnancy and how I feel and what I can do? Mark can wait until I calm down."

"Dear, I think you're just waving a red rag at a bull."

"So be it. I'm not disobeying him and I wish to see Thelma today."

"Nothing good will come from irritating the man."

Shauna grunted as she drew up the final leather on the sulky shafts. "Now, I'm just going to collect my basket and notebook. Should I take some of those oatmeal biscuits we made yesterday?"

"Thelma will like that. And wait for me, I'm coming with you." Mary kept her next thoughts to herself. Those about hoping her presence might prevent Mark from really exploding when he discovered Shauna had defied him.

Lindsay rode his bay mare Sugar while Michael rode his favourite Midnight, a black horse with a white star on its forehead. Old Master followed on a lead rein held lightly in Michael's hand. The fresh mounts danced on tight reins as they travelled west towards the large lagoon.

Michael explained, "In the afternoon, wallabies and kangaroos rest on the other side of the water where it's cool and the grass is short and green. We'll make our way to the big fallen tree on this side. With the wind coming from the south-west they'll not smell our scent and we'll have a good view." During their journey, Michael went on to explain to Lindsay basic safety issues when handling a gun. In particular, the importance of making sure it wasn't loaded before starting out and how to hold the gun barrel towards the ground ensuring any misfiring would not blow his or his companion's head off.

Lindsay's excited prattling along with the soughing of the tree branches in the wind and Michael's silent thoughts carried him the remainder of the journey. His words to Lindsay took him back to the first day he had held a gun – his father's gun. A litany of instructions had passed over his head, chased away by the thrill of the moment. When the lesson was over, he accidentally shot the ear of his dog because he hadn't cleared his gun properly. Today, unconsciously, his hand slipped down to the gun-sheath as if to check his weapon again.

Having secured the horses, man and boy stalked over the small ridge using tree trunks and bushes as a shield. From here, the kangaroos came into sight just as Michael said they would. Stealth governed their progress. Michael and Lindsay made their way to the shelter of the fallen tree where Michael knelt with the gun barrel resting on the trunk. He explained to Lindsay how he planned to line the gun up with the chest of the large male standing by itself.

"Tuck the butt firmly into your shoulder. This'll lessen the kickback. Ease the trigger gently; don't pull it or squeeze it," instructed the older man just before he took the shot. The deafening sharp report echoed across the paddocks. The biggest kangaroo dropped. With tails thumping the remainder of the group scattered. Swishing wings and scrambling feet accompanied the waterfowl as they lifted into the air seeking the safety of a quieter retreat.

Michael and Lindsay walked around the edge of the water to ensure the animal was indeed dead. Once Michael was satisfied with the outcome, he led Lindsay back to the tree.

"Make a pad with the flour bag and tuck it into your shoulder, tightly, with the gun butt. This gun has a kick better than most mules and I don't want to take you back with a huge bruise or worse, a broken shoulder."

Lindsay chose a few identifiable branches to aim for. He took a few practice shots before clearing the gun as Uncle Michael instructed. Lindsay's feet danced over the broken ground covered in fallen leaf matter, sticks, and branches on his way to bring up Old Master. He helped Michael load the corpse – dog dinners for a few days to come.

During the journey home, Michael asked, "Have you checked the gun is unloaded?"

Lindsay smiled. "That's the third time you've asked, Uncle Michael."

"Can't be too careful, son. Tonight, after we've eaten, you can help me clean the gun and oil the barrel. You've done very well today. You know, Paddymac can shoot the eyelash off a lizard at one hundred paces. I'm not sure you're as good as him yet but with a bit of practice you'll be pretty close."

"Does a lizard have eyelashes, Uncle Michael?" Lindsay looked askance at his mentor.

"You'll have to catch one and find out, I guess."

The heat of the early afternoon beat down upon the passengers of the sulky with its two outriders as they returned in silence to Emerald Flats. Shauna's rigid back lifted her head high. Her previous concerns about discovering a Mark she didn't know rode high upon the stormy waves in her mind. Her heart broke at finding she was losing respect for the man she'd loved so deeply such a short few months before. Mary, sitting at her side, may have noticed the trembling of Shauna's capable hands inside her brown work gloves.

From his position in his saddle, Mark's face resembled a block of stone. His blue eyes glared, cold as chipped ice. Thoughts bounced back and forth inside his head. *How can this woman, who's so wonderful and intelligent in so many ways, not see how her behaviour reflects on him? His only concern is for her and the child's well-being; surely, she can see this.*

Shamus did not know what to say to ease the tension. He hummed tunelessly. He hated strained atmospheres. His thoughts were erratic as his melody. Shauna shouldn't have defied her husband but then Mark should never have spoken to her as he had earlier. That girl's so like her grandfather. If Mark did take a hand to her, he knew he wouldn't stand for it. Yet she really must learn to conform a little bit more. It's probably all that teacher's training. She's used to giving orders and not taking them. *Hopefully, Mary will come up with a solution.*

A few weeks later and even though the days had warmed up again, the evenings remained pleasantly cool. The carbide lamp spluttered out its bright light onto those at the table.

"Old Mr. Wong said yesterday there's talk in town the new school building in Home Hill has been completed. They plan to move the old tent school out to the Osborne area later in the year. It'll not be all that far from here," said Shauna.

Mark lifted his head; his eyes alert.

"As far as I'm concerned, I'm happy to have you teach young Lindsay for a few years yet," Shamus told his daughter. "What do you think, Mary?"

"I couldn't agree more."

"He's way ahead of his age-group. This may present problems if he were to be placed in a class with children his own age," Shauna explained.

Mark's eyes returned to his plate. His jaw clenched.

The evening meal was almost over. Shauna rose to begin collecting the dishes for washing.

"Guess what! Guess what!" They heard Curley Wong yelling. One hand waved the newspaper back and forth as he ran full pelt across the compound. From the other hand swung a kerosene lantern which threatened to snuff out its light from the abuse.

The family in the kitchen froze. Something bad must have happened. They did not realize just how bad things would be.

"It's war! Britain's declared war. Australia too! People all talking in town." His words were broken up by his gasps for air.

The silence hung like a black cloud over the group. Everyone sat stunned. Gradually they took in the import of this dramatic news. "Déshi gone tell Harry's family," continued Curley after a while.

Oh, those poor people in Britain. Our families in Ireland will be in danger also, were Mary's first thoughts.

"How will this affect us do you think, Uncle Michael?" asked Shauna.

Michael kept reading the article in the paper for a few moments before answering. "It says here, Britain declared war on Germany on the 4th August 1914 and Australia will join England in defending itself." There was quiet in the room as Uncle Michael read to himself before going on. "This declaration follows the invasion of Belgium by the Germans who declared war on Russia on the first of this month and France on the third. It goes on to repeat what I was reading a few weeks ago. This trouble has bubbled away since Austria annexed Herzegovina and Bosnia in 1908. Russia defended these provinces. This conflict between Russia and Austria has come to a head recently when a young Serbian assassin murdered the Austrian Archduke Franz Ferdinand." Quiet again returned to the kitchen, the dishes forgotten in the wash-tub. "Och, for goodness sake, look here. They say shots have been fired on a German merchant ship already. It's been prevented passage through Port Phillip Heads. Hopefully, this is all just a storm in a tea-cup. I guess we'll have to wait and see."

Later, when the men were by themselves and talking quietly under the mango tree, they brought forward their worries about how it would affect them and their families back in Ireland.

"We'll need to keep it as light as possible. It wouldn't do, to worry the women unduly," advised Shamus.

"I wonder how this'll affect the federal election campaign after the double dissolution in June?" pondered Mark.

"There's a bit about that in the paper too," replied Uncle Michael. "Both the main parties are supporting the war to the hilt. Our first round of officers hasn't graduated from Duntroon yet. Anyway, King George has sent a cable of appreciation for Australian support."

Chapter Twelve

Subtle Changes

The declaration of war, nine days ago, slipped to the back of everyone's mind where it prowled like a stalking shadow. The first crush at the Inkerman Mill had started. Work on Paddymac's farm took on a new urgency.

Light from the hurricane lantern spilled out into the compound each morning, while Mark and Gabby harnessed two draught-horses to the cane-carrier. When Shamus arrived, he jumped onto the front seat and took up the reins. He dropped their cribs of corn meat sandwiches, biscuits, and plain cake behind the seat. Bleary-eyed and grumbling, Haddi threw himself onto the departing work wagon – usually just in the nick of time. Each picaninny dawn found Paddymac at work with his cane knife when Shamus halted the horses near the ready-to-harvest cane.

The cool mornings evolved into hot sweaty days as the men cut the cane stalks low then lopped off the green tops. The hook end of the knife swept down the stalk to remove the dead leaves or trash. With a quick toss, the stalks landed in a tidy line across the crests of the furrows beside the other cut-cane ready to be loaded onto the cane-carrier. Following the flood earlier in the year, much of this year's cane crop remained bent over in an arch with the top leaves buried in dry silt. It was no easy task to cut each stalk individually and haul it out of the tangle of dirt and leaves. If the cutter did not keep himself aware of the wind direction at all times, the leaves dragged up a dusty cloud of dry silt around his face choking off his breath. Several times a day a shout went up from one of the cutters surprised as a large rat or snake streaked out from a clump of cane.

Back at Emerald Flats, it was up to Akama, Sabbo, and Lindsay to milk the cows and care for the other animals before their breakfast and school lessons. Uncle Michael supervised the youngsters, happy to toss in his two bob's worth of advice.

Each afternoon, after lessons and lunch, the same three boys harnessed a horse into the small dray. They made their way to Paddymac's farm to fetch the cane-tops. These were cut by hand into smaller pieces and used for stock feed. Every chance they got and using every wile in their armoury, the boys begged Uncle Michael and Shamus to purchase a mechanical chaff cutter. A chop-chop machine, as the boys called it, would make their job a lot easier.

"We'd lose much less school-lesson time if we had a chop-chop machine," Lindsay produced his argument stealthily.

One morning, as Paddymac and Shamus headed back to the trees where they took a break each day, Paddymac stopped, almost knocking Shamus off his feet. He bent and scraped about in the new-cane drill. Thelma approached holding two hot billycans of tea using a thick strip of cloth to protect her hands.

"You all right, Paddy?" Her voice brought a smile to her husband's lips.

"Yes, dear," he called before turning again to Shamus. "For goodness sake, Shamus, will you look at that!" He pointed a dirty finger. "All the soil's been disturbed around this new cane. Those dammed bandicoots have been eating the new shoots. We'll have to plant more pieces of cane in the spaces they've left," Paddymac grumbled. "Will you talk to the young lads and see if they'll start trapping the bandicoots? I'll ask at the next Farmer's Meeting if the Government's still paying for scalps."

"They'll do that – pay for scalps?"

"Oh, yeah, if we're lucky."

It was Uncle Michael who brought the subject up with Lindsay the next day.

Lindsay's eyes lit up. "How do we trap bandicoots?"

"It's not too difficult," replied Uncle Michael. "Harry's boys have been doing it for years. They sell the bandicoot skins with the kangaroo skins to their relatives down-river who then sell them on to the traders. Sometimes the Government pays money for scalps if the animal's a pest in the district. The boys use a stick, tied to the end of a long piece of string, to hold up one end of a wooden box or even a reshaped kerosene tin. With a tasty bait under the box, it's just a matter of waiting patiently. The lads'll show you."

With the household up before daylight, working all day and retiring long after dark, the arguments between Shauna and Mark were few and far between. It took all their stamina just to get through the day. Neither had the inclination or energy to argue but sadly neither had the energy to mend fences in their relationship either.

Every night, Mark lay with his hand on Shauna's swelling abdomen. He whispered, "I love you, Shauna."

In barely a whisper, Shauna replied, "I love you too, Mark." And each time she said this, guilt surged through her veins as her thoughts continued a silent addition, *I think.*

A warm Sunday morning sun and the serenade of the magpies brightened the mood of the family where they gathered around the kitchen table for their weekly session of bible reading.

"Have you any new thoughts on that 20hp tractor we looked at yesterday?" Uncle Michael asked Shamus when Mary closed the large family bible with a thump.

Shamus thought for a while before commenting, "I think the man may have been right; it's better for pumping than ploughing. We need to look at some of the others about the area before thinking of buying one for Emerald Flats." He reached over to take a biscuit from the tray Shauna had placed on the table before going on. "The telephone line now runs from Townsville to Ayr, why don't you contact Mr. Chiswell and ask his advice? With this war going on, we may have to hold back on buying a tractor."

Disappointment clouded the older man's face. "Maybe you're right, Shamus." Michael fiddled with the spoon in the pannikin.

"This war may go on for longer than we'd anticipated, Uncle Michael; I'm sorry to say. The papers are reporting the Australians have begun military air training at Point Cook in Victoria."

"Yes, Shamus, I read that too. It looks as if war will be with us for a good while yet. It's a terrible time for the families, with their young lads joining up and being sent away to who knows where. I guess my tractor's small potatoes when you consider them." Uncle Michael slapped his hands on the wooden tabletop. "Enough of the darn war. We need to take a day to go visit the farmer Down River with the electric power plant of his own? Wouldn't that be a good thing to have? We need to look at it sometime."

Shamus smiled as he listened to Uncle Michael going on about all the modern machinery he would like to have on the place.

He might be getting old but he's still young in his mind, thought Shamus.

The war seemed a long way away. Shauna enjoyed listening to the laughter and squeals of the students as she taught them how to make soap using caustic soda and fat heated in an old kerosene tin over the felled-tree fire where the washing was usually done. Both the girls were Harry and Mabel's grandchildren. Sweet 'Alya aged seven years, was Gabby and Sophie's third child. Brindle coloured hair stuck out from her head in crinkled knotted strands that curtained liquid black serious eyes. The promising athlete, Cabri, now aged ten, was Haddi and Rosie's first child. Cabri always loved the brightest colours and today was no different with her red and white patterned dress contrasting with the darkness of her skin. A red flower nestled in the knots of hair above her ear. The mothers, Sophie and Rosie, had come over to join the class. Broad smiles lifted their plump cheeks and sparkled in their eyes.

"I'm glad you teach us to make soap, Shauna. We use the bark of a red ash tree. It bubbles up when we rub it on our skin. Smells okay but not wash clothes like this soap you make," commented Sophie.

"Mrs. Doolan said she teach Cabri to sew patches on clothes. Will she mind we come too?" Rosie asked.

"Mam would be thrilled," was Shauna's reply before turning to Sophie. "Mark said your son, Akama, is going walkabout with your brother's family in a few days. What's a walkabout, Sophie?"

"He is, Miss Shauna. My Gabby, not mix a lot with the local aborigines. He more Polynesian like his own father, Harry. We not go on walk-a-bout. Akama's very close to my brother's children and wants to join them," explained Sophie. "They walk along the river to the place you call Charters Towers. Many will be there. The young boys are made part of the tribe. Everyone meets again with friends and family."

"Sophie, I remember Uncle Michael telling me of a white man who'd been shipwrecked off the coast not too far from here. He ended up living with your family for many years?" inquired Shauna.

"Oh, yes. The old people still tell story around the fire at night. My grandmother tells the stories her grandmother told of a whitefella belonga the family many years." Sophie's speech slipped into that of her grandmother. "Long, long time ago. Big, big canoe crash onto the rocks, and go down, deep in the water, way out where the sun gets up each morning. Only a few of his people floated to the land. The others died soon after but this white man lived long time until he go back to whitefella people. Only one of the elders of the time had seen a whitefella before. This whitefella he listen to the blackfella and learn how to live like him. Most of the whitefella not listen then and not listen now. Nobody learns anything now."

"Mister Michael said man's name James Morrill," offered Rosie determined to be part of the tale.

Cabri had drunk in the story with her mother's milk. She had heard it all before. She interrupted. "Why did Mrs. Doolan go to town with the Wong boys today?"

Shauna drew her attention back to her student. "The women in the town are making plans to help the war effort. They are to do things like fundraising events and knitting socks for the soldiers. Mam has gone to find out more and what we may be able to do here, to help also."

It was dark when Mary returned from her trip to Home Hill with Curley Wong. She edged her tired body onto the form at the meal table. Everyone peppered her with questions on the happenings in the town. Mary took a deep breath and attempted to throw off her mantle of weariness.

"A branch of the British Red Cross has been founded in Melbourne. The Home Hill people have commenced a Patriotic Fund to contribute to the war effort. Ladies have been asked to knit and sew for the Australian troops. Materials will be provided from the funds raised by picnics, concerts and dances in the district." Mary rubbed her face and stretched her back before going on. "The local carrier has kindly volunteered his time and labour in delivering these supplies to and from the contributors and the organizers in town. The headmaster, at the Home Hill School, has promised to encourage his older female pupils to join in. He has introduced a School Cadet Corps for the older boys."

While her mother had been talking, Shauna watched Mark reading his mail. His eyes squinted in the poor light of the lamp. A furrow marred his brow. When he stood without a word and walked outside, Shauna wiped her hands on the cloth she had been drying dishes with and followed him to the seat under the mango tree.

"What's wrong, my dear?" she asked.

For quite a long time, Mark remained silent. Shauna looked askance at him wondering if she had done something to upset him.

"This letter's from James and William." Mark waved the paper and envelope delivered earlier. "The silly blighters have gone and joined up to go to war. They've joined the 9th Battalion." Mark sat quietly for a long time. Shauna felt at a loss. She did not know what best to say. A tremor of relief ran through her body when he spoke again. "Is it really our war? We're Irish. What do we want with an English war? What were they thinking, is what I'd like to know? What'll our mother say when she receives the letter they posted?" Mark stared at the space between his boots. "Blame me, I guess."

Shauna thought about this news for a while feeling an ice-cold weight building around her heart. "Mark, will they want married men to join the army do you think?"

"Whatever does happen, Shauna, I'll not leave here until you have given safe birth to our baby," promised Mark. "James and William, they're only boys. I feel as though I should've gone with them, you know, to keep an eye out for them."

Both Shauna and Mark tossed and turned during the night. Suddenly, the dark tentacles of war seemed to be closing in on them.

Two days later, Michael noticed Mark sitting with his back to the shed post, chewing on a stick of grass and staring out at the paddock.

"Penny for your thoughts."

Mark looked up with a rueful grin. "They're worth ten bob or maybe even a Pound, at least, Uncle Michael." He threw the piece of grass away. "I'm wondering what I should do about this war going on out there. Should I volunteer to join up or not? Being an Irishman, I'm not overly fond of the British, but then again, I'm living in a British colony so I guess I do owe them a duty. As you now know, my two brothers, who came out to Australia with me, have already joined the 9th Battalion. I feel I should go with them but I have to consider my responsibilities to Shauna and our new baby. On the other hand, I did promise my mother to look out for my brothers."

Michael squatted on his haunches. He took up a short stick and began doodling in the dirt. "If you had asked me that question forty years ago, I would've said, 'Blast the British', but as you say, we're living in a British colony so that changes things. Maybe you need to discuss this with Shauna. She's very wise like her mother, I think," was Michael's advice.

Shauna, Mary, and Thelma looked ill at ease as they stood on the banks of the lagoon where the sun glistened on the calm water. Mark drew the gun from the back of the dray and removed it from its canvas wrapping. The box of bullets rattled as he dropped them into his pants pocket.

"When I go away to the war, you'll need to know how to protect yourselves, if need be. Most days Shamus, Paddymac, and Uncle

Michael will be working in the paddocks while you're busy around the house with the children."

"But the war's not here in Australia, Mark." Mary stepped back as he held the gun out to her.

"No, Mary, it's not. We hope it never will be. But, as Uncle Michael said, there'll be others, besides harmless tramps, humping their blueys hoping for handouts or up to mischief. You may need to defend yourselves." Mark held the gun out again.

"Mam, I'll go first, if you like." Shauna removed the gun from Mark's hands remembering his earlier instructions on safety with guns.

She attempted to kneel near a fallen tree but found the position uncomfortable with her fast swelling abdomen. She moved over to stand beside a tree with a low outreaching branch on which to rest the barrel. Once settled, she peered down the gun barrel to line up her target with the rifle sights. Sunlight glinted on the six cans Mark had lined up near the water's edge.

"Remember, Shauna, ease don't squeeze. And make sure you have the butt pressed tight into your shoulder so it can't kickback." Mark touched her shoulder.

With her one eye closed and her tongue held firmly against her lips by her teeth, Shauna eased the trigger towards herself.

In the distance, one of the cans pinged as it lifted into the air, then fell with a rattle on the stones before splashing into the water.

The thunderous echo of the rifle rang out through the trees. Birds exploded from the branches above them. The glass sheen on the waters shattered as the ducks lifted into the air.

"You hit it, Shauna. That's my clever girl." Mary laughed as she clapped her hands.

"Oh, Shauna, that was so good." A smile lit up Thelma's face as she joined in the applause.

"Well done, Shauna. Beginners luck, no doubt. Now try that again." Mark grinned with pride.

After hitting two cans out of three tries, Shauna checked the barrel was empty then rested the gun butt on the ground.

"Have a go, Thelma. It's not nearly as bad as I thought it might be."

Mark helped Thelma load and prepare the gun against her shoulder. Thelma took a while to overcome her fear of the loud noise it made and the kick of the gun butt. When she only hit one of the cans, Mark suggested she ask Paddymac to take her out for more practice.

Mary came over to have her turn. "You know, Thelma, Lindsay said Uncle Michael told him Paddymac can shoot an eyelash off a lizard. Lindsay spent days chasing lizards to see if they do have eyelashes." The group chuckled.

A warm smile touched Shauna's lips as she watched her husband offering advice. A flutter of butterflies swirled in her tummy. This was the Mark she fell in love with. A sharp voice in her head wanted to know if this sensation was not just the baby moving inside of her. Shauna quashed the errant thought. This was the Mark she married: warm, friendly, kind, considerate, helpful. His choosing to join the army to fight for Australia filled her with pride as well as terror for his safety. Was her baby to lose its father before the new life had taken on meaning? The internal sharp voice once more attempted to interrupt bringing memories of his shortness of temper, examples of selfishness, and domineering tendencies. There was no denying the relief from his dark moods. The recent days had been a pleasure without the guilt filling her mind when she gave time to anyone else but Mark. For over a week now he'd not complained of her teaching the children or offering assistance to the Bobangle and Wong ladies, even her mother, father and Lindsay. His attitude to Paddymac and

Harry's family seemed to have changed. Had he, at last, begun to appreciate how Gabby and Haddi worked just as hard as he did each day? No one put in the hours like Paddymac did and he was not a young man anymore. Mark had been heard talking to the two older Wong boys the day before yesterday instead of deliberately avoiding them. These tumultuous thoughts twisted and twined around themselves like a nest of snakes inside her head. Above it all, she could not deny his attention and loving attitude to her since his decision to go to war. The tingling feeling expanded from her inside to her whole body. Her smile widened. This reminded her of those feelings she enjoyed every day on the ship.

Mary was almost as quick to grasp the practicalities of firing the gun as her daughter had been.

When the last shot resounded through the forest, Mark suggested, "We'd better be going back before you all bruise your shoulders." He took the gun and after checking the barrel wrapped it in the canvas before placing it on the floor of the wagon. "I think we should come out each week to practice."

The mopoke owl hooted its repetitive call from its perch in the Burdekin plum tree outside. Faint screams of the curlews drifted up from the river. Mark lay awake listening to Shauna's regular soft snuffles. His hand rested against her abdomen. At each fluttering wave on the outside surface made by the restless life inside, his own heart fluttered in awe. His mind flowed from one thought to another. Shauna, the woman he loved above all others, carried his child. A frown appeared upon his forehead. Her determination troubled him. He couldn't remember ever knowing a woman like her before. His mother was never heard to question his father. Mary was never heard to question Shamus. Thinking about it, Mary seemed to anticipate all Shamus's needs without his making a request. But then their wishes seemed to fall into line with each other. Were he and Shauna so different in their needs?

A slither of guilt stirred his stomach. Shauna didn't like him to speak ill of her friends. Surely, she knew he was only relieving his frustration at his lack of independence living here with everyone else. He'd be a different man on his own property. She would've discovered that if she'd come with him as he'd hoped. He placated his guilt. On the other hand, with the country at war and his plans to join up, it was reassuring to know she and the baby would be safe here at Emerald Flats.

The frown deepened as he grudgingly admitted his short temper and moods did not help their situation.

Had he been too harsh and overbearing? The recollection of her accusation of lack of respect niggled inside his head. Should he apologize? He'd never heard his father apologize to anyone in his whole life. The man's often repeated reasoning rang in his ears. 'Only weak people apologize.' Was father wrong? The idea almost took Mark's breath away.

Envy of his brother, James, burnt in his belly. James was nothing like their father. He took after their mother but this did nothing to lessen his internal strength. The envy turned to a fire-storm throughout his body. James never fawned or tried to please like William was wont to do. How does James manage to come across as a strong character without saying a word or giving orders? Mark tried but failed to remember ever succeeding in stirring his brother to lose his temper.

The stiffening of his body and the gritting of Mark's teeth appeared to disturb Shauna who groaned and rolled over. With his hand returned to its position feeling the presence of his baby, Mark relaxed again. The mopoke ceased its call. The curlews grew silent down on the river-bank. Sleep drew him deep into her arms.

Chapter Thirteen

Unforeseeable Futures

Sobs echoed off the walls of the room at Leaning Rock Station. Bella Littlewood was sure her heart had broken into pieces. The sodden pieces of paper in her hand were the remains of the letter William had written to say goodbye. He was off to the war. His older brother James had sent a written resignation to her father on behalf of William and himself.

Matthew Littlewood was disappointed at this turn of events. The brothers had proven to be the best pair of workers employed at Leaning Rock Station for quite a while. He did understand their desire to join up when they heard of the declaration of war while on a short break in Townsville.

Mrs. Littlewood sat on the bed holding her distraught daughter's hand.

"Darling, I'm sorry you're so sad. Remember you're only very young yet and will meet lots of eligible young men in the years to come. As a soldier at war, I'm sure William McIvor will appreciate a letter now and then. Nothing silly, mind you; in fact, I'll want to read all the correspondence to ensure it's suitable."

The September elections were over. The Labour Party had been returned with an overwhelming majority. Mr. Andrew Fisher was once again Prime Minister. This did not change things at Emerald

Flats to any great degree. The cane harvest was nearly at an end for them.

Next year we should have twice as much cane to cut, God willing, thought Shamus. Many adjustments to equipment and practices had been made in recent months to improve their system. Everything seemed to run smoothly now. As he guided the horses pulling the dray of cane to the siding, his thoughts drifted to his daughter.

Mary had assured him Shauna's pregnancy was progressing normally but he often found himself worrying about the coming birth which was only a matter of a few weeks away. Never could he forget the difficulty Mary had with the birth of their third child. The doctor, who eventually was able to come to the house, said it was a wonder they had not lost Mary as well as the child. That was the last time Mary was able to fall pregnant. His heart broke, not just for himself but mostly for Mary when he saw the look of desire upon her face when she held another woman's child.

"Please, God, don't wish that on my Shauna," he prayed.

As the loaded cane truck rattled along the tramway in the siding, he pondered further on the article they had read last night about the new War Precautions Act. This included things one would expect relating to punishment for those who may be seen to be communicating with the enemy or sabotaging public works. To secure important secrets and means of communication, the Government had virtually taken over control of the press. Was this a good thing or not? Shamus was undecided. He understood the need but he was a passionate believer in freedom of the press.

The muscles in Mary's arms strained as she stirred the men's work clothes in the boiler heating on the fire at the end of the fallen tree. Steam and smoke added to the perspiration running down her face. The salt stung her eyes. When she paused to wipe her face, she heard the dishes rattling inside the old kitchen where Shauna cleared away the breakfast things. Mary had insisted her daughter take the easier chore this morning. Mary's experienced eye recognized the changes in her daughter and knew the baby's birth was not too far away. As if to confirm her thoughts, she heard Shauna's startled gasp and soft cry.

"Mam, help. My waters have broken."

From the classroom under the big house, Lindsay looked up to see his mother leading Shauna across the compound. He dropped his pencil and rushed outside.

"Mam, is everything alright? What's wrong with Shauna?"

"Her time to have this baby is near. I want you to go to Mabel Bobangle's hut and ask if her daughters can come over to finish the washing and clean up the kitchen for us."

Lindsay's feet bounded away. He stopped in a long skid as his mother called him again.

"If you see the men, tell them to let Mark know."

"Yeah, Mam," drifted back to Mary and Shauna as they moved towards the steps of the big house.

When they reached the landing upstairs, Shauna's face paled.

"Mam, I think this baby's coming now."

Mary smiled indulgently. "Now, Shauna, you've assisted me at several births before. You know the first baby seldom rushes its way into this world. Subsequent ones maybe, but seldom the first; although it does happen on occasion."

Mary helped her daughter manoeuvre herself and the swollen abdomen into a comfortable position on the bed. When Shauna lay settled with her dress drawn up above her raised knees and her upper body covered with the sheet, Mary leant across the bed to make her examination. She froze. The first thing to greet her was a distinctive crowning of the baby's head. She drew in a sharp breath. This speed was unusual. She struggled to breathe steadily and slow her own heart rate.

"What is it, Mam? What's wrong?"

"Nothing, darling. You were right, this young one is in a hurry."

Mary barely made it back into the room with her delivery-basket in her arms when Shauna gasped.

"Something's happened."

Dropping her basket at the end of the bed, Mary took another peep.

"Something surely has happened. The head's out." Disbelief filled her voice. Taking a deep breath to calm her racing heart, Mary slipped her fingers in beside the baby's neck to feel if everything was as it should be. "Don't push just yet if you can help it, Shauna."

In what seemed a record time to Mary, the baby slipped out without any fanfare and flopped onto the bed. It lay unmoving on the end of a bloodied umbilical cord. Mary bit her lip and swallowed hard. Visions came to her of another baby lying flaccid on the bed – her own dead newborn. Fear held her breath. Her heart pounded inside her chest. With trembling hands, she lifted the child and smacked it smartly on the bottom. Silence was her only reward.

"Mam, Mam, what's wrong? What's wrong with my baby? Why won't it cry?" sobbed Shauna.

Mary struggled to maintain her own composure. Shaking fingers reached inside the tiny mouth to clear it of any excess mucus. She blew into the mouth and pumped the little ribcage twice. Outwardly calm but inside quivering like a leaf in a storm, Mary lifted the mottled body and slapped the bare bottom again. Praying desperately as she did so.

After a tentative start, indignant screams filled the room. Through her tears, Mary deftly tied the umbilical cord and snipped it free from the afterbirth. She wrapped the infant in a small rug and lifted it on to Shauna's chest.

"You have a baby girl, Shauna."

Awe filled Shauna's teary face as she nestled her firstborn close to her body.

Both women smiled when Mark's voice trembled from the verandah.

"Is everything alright there?"

Mary went outside to give the father the news he had waited so long to hear. But Mary felt sad also, knowing Mark would soon be off to join the army now the baby was born. He would spend so little time with his daughter.

Shauna dozed. On those occasions when her eyes opened, she observed Mark sitting in the armchair beside the bed holding the quiet baby. His soft voice reached her ears indistinctly as he spoke to the sleeping child.

More tears ran down her face to fall into her hair and upon the still-undried pillow-case. If asked she could not have told why she kept crying. The wonder of her daughter overwhelmed her. The vision of a soft and sensitive Mark filled her heart to overflowing. Her long fingers reached over to touch the back of his hand. Their emotion-filled smiles met. Through her own renewed tears, Shauna was surprised to see the moisture in her husband's eyes.

"Are you alright, my love? Are you in pain? Why are you crying?" He asked.

His concern set her tears off in a greater flood. "No, Mark, I'm just so happy right now. If I were any happier, I'd burst."

The wonderful grin, which she had not seen for a long while, lifted his face. "Me too."

"We'll have to seriously consider a name for this little one, soon. I know you've been too busy in the past few months to even think of anything but the work."

Chapter Fourteen

The War Goes On

When will this ever end? William thought as he numbly plodded along on the back end of the stretcher carrying yet another bleeding and broken body. The deep gullies and steep rises with narrow shale-covered tracks might confound a mountain goat. They made the going difficult and very dangerous. *Rivers of blood, nothing but rivers of blood; if only the noise would stop.*

The continual rattle of small fire interspersed with the loud thump of larger guns was a background din which threatened to deliver death at any time. William could not recall how many days had passed since landing in this hell they call Gallipoli; since he had been able to shut his red and swollen eyes. It was hard to remember if the chap carrying the other end of this blood-soaked canvas was the third or fourth different person with whom he had shared these tragic burdens. The first had been Walter, a friend, a mate. It seemed such a long time ago since they had shared the excitement during their training together with the others of the 3rd Brigade, 9th Battalion at the Mena camp in Egypt during the Christmas of 1914. Now, four months later, Walter was one of the hundreds, maybe thousands, of dead. *This accursed shore.*

He remembered seeing his brother, James, laying the field-telephone lines, a day or two after the landing. Communication was a commodity desperately needed. Chaos infiltrated everything and everyone. Eventually, the Turks relinquished, with reluctance, some land as the allies moved further up these cliffs and hills covered with scrub, small trees, and that ever-present slippery shale. William worried for the safety of James. He knew from his own trips to and from the front line what a hell it was up there. How on earth could anything live with all that death about?

James stood hunched over the meagre fire trying to boil a billy of tea, using the last bit of water and wood they had in their little dugout. He looked out over the Aegean Sea far below, where he could sight the various ships lying at anchor. Had it been only a month since they landed here at Gallipoli on that grey drizzly horrendous day, the 25th April 1915? It all looked so peaceful but he knew that was a farce. This short time of relative quiet was to be treasured because it certainly could not last. The guns would soon recommence their deadly call.

The dugout, along with hundreds of others, clung on to the side of the steep terrain like an eagle's nest; or as one wit described it, "Like shit to a blanket". At first, he had shared the dugout with his mate, Ted, who had helped him shovel out a nice cave between two large rocks. A partial roof was formed by another rock. A few low shrubs camouflaged the burrow quite well. Nowhere was safe in this God-forsaken land but it was the next best thing. After being badly wounded, when the Turks had launched retaliation some days ago, Ted was now somewhere down on the shore at the Casualty Clearing Station. Maybe he has made it to the hospital ship. Hopefully, without receiving further damage from the Turk shells, while waiting for space on one of the transport barges.

James ached with weariness. During a nine-hour truce from Kaba Tepe to the Suvla Point on the 24th May, yesterday, both sides had buried their dead lying in no-mans-land. Some of the bodies had been there since the Gallipoli landing. All the troops were exhausted. The damp grey day had matched the mood of the toilers. It had been a horrendous duty for both sides as they dug shallow graves near where each corpse lay. Many bodies had reached such putrefaction they fell apart emitting a foul stench making even the toughest gag. A thick black fog of flies accompanied the men as they worked. Now, Jock, his new friend in the dugout, snored loudly enough to awaken the enemy.

Today the sun shone. James lifted his hat and wiped his brow. The brim of his hat sagged a bit where a bullet had ripped past his ear within those first few hours of the landing. In the dugout, Jock stirred.

"Want a cuppa tea, mate?" asked James. "If things stay this quiet, we may get to the shore for a swim later. We can try to drown some more lice or teach them to swim too. We'll need to ask the Indian Mule Corps to bring a couple of water drums to this area. If we want to eat and make more tea, we'll need to bring back some wood and tins of bully beef too."

Jock stood at the entrance of the dugout. He scratched at the lice irritating his body. The short, freckled-skinned youth drawled.

"Sounds like a pleasant reprieve. While we're at it, we'd better take these empty tins to the boys making their home-made bombs for our lot to throw at Johnny Turk."

In the Littlewood dining room at Leaning Rock Station, Matthew looked down the table to where his eldest daughter sat picking at her food.

"Bella, do you have to pick at your food like that? There are many starving bodies in the world today who'd kill for a feed of steak and spuds."

"Sorry, Dad, I just don't feel like eating."

"You're not sickening for anything, I hope?" He turned to his wife and slipped her a quick wink. "She's alright, isn't she? I mean too much excitement if one is unwell cannot be good for a person, can it?"

Bella's head lifted sharply. "What excitement, Dad?"

The twins, Maryann and Thomas stared at their father, their eyes and ears alert.

Their father grinned at them both. "Sorry, nothing of interest for either of you curious cats." He turned back to Bella. "I looked for you when I got back from The Towers earlier. Your Ma said you'd gone for a walk."

"What excitement, Dad? No one told me you were going to The Towers today." Her blue eyes began to glow. "Dad, was there mail for me?" Her voice rose.

Matthew Littlewood dug into the pocket of his trousers. "It was here somewhere."

"Come on, Dad, where is it?"

"Would this be what you're waiting for?" He pulled out a dirt-smudged envelope and passed it to his wife.

Bella's radiant eyes never left the epistle. She reached to take the letter.

"Now, Bella, we agreed, we'll read the mail from William together. You're not yet seventeen; far too young to receive unsupervised mail from a beau. Far too young to have a beau, probably."

"But, Ma." The developing woman whined like a small child.

"Come, help me do the dishes? Once they're cleared away, we'll read it together." She turned to her youngest daughter. "You too, Maryann. You can help with the dishes, then I want you to read the next chapter of your book."

"What about Thomas, can't he help with the dishes too?"

"Thomas is doing a man's job out with your father these days. He's excused doing the dishes at night."

Maryann wasn't finished. "Can't I read William's letter too?"

Before Mrs. Littlewood could say a word, Bella jumped up. "Not likely, you're just a kid."

Matthew grinned as he threw his wife another hidden wink.

As the girls tidied the kitchen, Matthew turned to his wife sipping thoughtfully on her tea.

"There was an answer from Michael Doolan in the mail today, as well. He has a young aboriginal lad, Akama Bobangle, who's looking for stockwork. Michael says he's only young but a good worker and an able stockman. He recommends him."

"Oh, Matthew, how wonderful. I've been saying for months you need another couple of stockmen to replace the McIvor lads. We do miss those two." She reached across the table and squeezed his hand. "Will you give this Akama fellow a trial?"

Matthew's smile lit up his tired eyes. He nodded.

On Emerald Flats, ensconced in Mark's armchair positioned at the corner of the verandah, Shauna watched, mesmerized, as her six-month-old baby, Maggie, suckled contentedly. She ran her fingers over the soft hair, a shade darker than Mark's. Occasionally, Shauna lifted her head to observe the excitement down at the Emerald Flats cattle yards. Clouds of dust rose over the trees and sheds along with the sound of bawling calves, bellowing cattle, the cracks of the stock whips, shouting voices, and the bossy barking of the dogs. Her father and Paddymac with the assistance of Lindsay and Haddi mustered the mob of breeders through the house paddock towards the open gates of the cattle yards. Uncle Michael and Gabby stood at the ready to slam the gates behind the animals when all were enclosed.

The noise lifted in volume as the smoke of the branding fire lifted with the dust. On horseback, Paddymac and Gabby selected a beast and cornered it. As a team, they lassoed the front and hind legs of the calf which needed to be branded – plus or minus castrated. The animal collapsed into a heap. Like a flash, Paddymac and Gabby leapt from their horses to throw themselves across the struggling weaner-calf. Haddi and Sabbo joined the wrestling match. Shamus wielded the small bloodied knife used to perform the surgery with an expertise born of years removing the testicles of male calves. Once the operation was completed, Lindsay removed one of the three hot branding irons from the fire. Holding a sugar-bag around the handle to protect his hands from the heat and with his teeth clenched, necessary to keep his hands steady, he slapped the shaped-end of the red-hot iron onto the hip of the grounded beast. Altogether, three hot irons were used; a number, and two separate letters. 6 M D. Each unhappy animal fought to rise. The brand threatened to slip and blur the mark but Lindsay held steady each brand in its turn. Smoke and the smell of burnt flesh filled the operating space on the ground in the side pen of the cattle yards.

Upstairs, Shauna pondered. *Was it twelve months since this process had been last completed? Seems only yesterday. Mark spent weeks talking about his first big muster in Australia. He would have enjoyed it here today. Who knows where, in this troubled world, he now lay his head to rest?* The last news from him reported his section was to be transferred to the Mena camp in Egypt. Now, Easter had long gone and every day dragged, waiting for further news of his well-being.

Her thoughts were interrupted by the soft voices of Thelma and her mother as they made their way around the verandah to her corner.

Shauna's smile greeted her visitors. The grin widened as she looked at the now very-obvious abdomen of her friend, Thelma.

"Oh, Thelma, not too long to wait now. How are you keeping?"

"I do find myself complaining sometimes at this extra weight but at least the nights are becoming cooler which makes sleeping more pleasant."

Heard above all the other din, a yell followed by whistles and raucous laughter erupted from within the yards. Three sets of eyes from the verandah snapped around. Lindsay and his father were hanging from the top rail. Only inches from their feet, an escaped and discontented customer bellowed its threats.

Eventually, the day arrived. Shauna had almost given up. Every evening she watched the track along which the Wong boys travelled to deliver the irregular newspapers or mail collected while in the town selling their vegetables. These were usually for Uncle Michael or her parents. This day, she almost missed the Wong boy's arrival. She and her mother were preparing the evening meal. Since the kitchen of the big house had been completed, the Doolan family, including Uncle Michael, took their meals here. This provided many advantages for the women.

By chance, Shauna looked out of the windows of the vegetable-cleaning room just in time to see one of the Wong boys approaching. The man, Déhuã, the one Paddymac had nicknamed, Curley, could not be called a boy now; grown with a family of his own. This did not stop Uncle Michael from referring to him and his brothers as the Wong boys. Shauna's heart stopped, as it always did when mail was a possibility. She felt the trembling within her belly. Her teeth caught her top lip. Was today the day?

Curley Wong noticed her at the window. With a wide grin, he waved the envelope back and forth. In a most unladylike fashion, Shauna raced through the kitchen and out into the vestibule. Her feet thumped down the stairs as she took them two at a time while holding onto the railing to balance herself.

26/5/15

My Most Treasured Love,

It's been nearly two weeks since we came ashore on the beaches of Gallipoli near where James and William are stationed. Our arrival was greeted with a welcome from the Turks (Abdul or Johnny Turk is what everyone here calls them) situated higher up the cliffs but I think our landing would have been a lot easier than the boys who braved the beaches on the 25th April.

We arrived in time to assist with the repelling of the Turks' attempt to retake the areas they'd lost then. The fighting's been fierce. We've not long finished burying the bodies left in no-mans-land since the first landing. One asks, "Where is God in all this?"

I've intimate companions in the lice and flies. Water's as scarce as hen's teeth. When one gets a break from the fighting it's nice to go to the beach for a swim and a wash. I've been told it's not uncommon to go for weeks without a bath. Open latrines are our near neighbours and again, I have been told, it's not unusual for them to be hit by a shell; the end result is gruesome. Something to look forward to, I guess. Many of the men suffer from dysentery; in fact, all of us can expect it at some time.

Later: I ran into James in the sea this afternoon. He looks very tired; says William is pretty exhausted also. We must all be as mad as hatters swimming around with the odd shell landing not too far away. No wonder the British troops (the Tommies) think we're a bit strange. James explained how the Indian troops used the mules to carry water and supplies to the front trenches. He also told me how to get a supply of the jam-tin bombs the boys are making.

Darling, I miss you and want to write on forever but my eyelids are too heavy. Please give my other best girl a big kiss from her Daddy.

All my love, Mark.

With the lamp turned low, Shauna re-read her letter once more. Tears shone on her cheeks in the dull light. She found it hard to contemplate what it must be like to endure these deprivations Mark talked about. Throwing the sheet back she jumped out of bed to drop a light kiss upon the sleeping Maggie's forehead.

Every night before turning the lamp down, she read the same letter, craving for another to arrive.

It was her brother who next received news from Gallipoli.

Chapter Fifteen

Gallipoli

20/6/15

Dear Lindsay,

It was great to receive your letter. Thank you. Only a day later we received the parcels your mother sent. Will you say "thank you" from us both, for those? The writing paper was especially a boon as it's pretty scarce here. Often the men want to send a note home before going into the front trenches.

Lindsay, when I first came here, the thought of killing "the enemy" was big excitement to me. Now I do it to survive but it's not a nice thing. Those that we're fighting are men, flesh and blood, just like us, with families who'll mourn them. War's not a pleasant thing, believe me. It's certainly not to be glorified.

I've learnt why my mother always made us bathe regularly. As water is in such short supply here, we only get to clean up now and then, in the sea. The lice fill our clothes and make us itch continually. The men place rocks on their uniforms under the water in the hope of drowning the little blighters, but I think they swim home again. That reminds me, thank your Mother for the knitted socks, also. They arrived just in time. The pair that I had been wearing was more hole than sock; even the lice had walked away in disgust.

My job's to help keep the lines of communication open which means running up and down the trenches repairing and splicing the wires the Johnny Turk has blown to smithereens. William's a stretcher-bearer and transports the wounded to the Dressing Stations and then on to the Casualty Clearing Station. He was sent over to the hospital ship for a week recently, to work as an orderly. Those poor devils hadn't rested for over a month. From what we've been told the few doctors repairing the damaged bodies never get to stop. They sleep standing up.

It's shaping up to be a hot, dry summer that has withered what little grass there had been here and the stench is indescribable. We're allocated a pint of water per man per day. I could drink a gallon without any trouble. Dysentery's rife. I think more infantrymen are cut down by the trots rather than by bullets.

It's my turn in the front tonight so I'll close now and send our regards to you and your family,

From James and William McIvor.

"Another allied offensive; how many of those have we had, and to what purpose?" William asked in frustration and exhaustion.

"You're right there, cobber. Here we are in the middle of August. In the past months and after how many offensives, very little has changed. Our side makes a little headway and then Johnny Turk takes most of it back. We'll carry endless bodies to the medicos, bury how many more, yet it all ends up in the same stalemate situation." Tiny's tired reply barely drifted to the other end of the stretcher they carried to collect the last of the bodies from the Lone Pine area.

Things had quietened down a little after the barrage of the last few days. William passed James in the front trench.

"Hi, brother! Glad to see you're not on my stretcher. What's happened to your arm?" asked William when he noticed the blood seeping from under a torn rag bandage.

"Abdul, out there, tried to make one count, but he only managed to nick me a bit. The damn cable had been blown out over the parapet. Luckily, I'd just pulled my head in when he got me. Guess it's not my time yet."

"Yeah, well, keep your head in, from now on," instructed his brother.

"Who's your t'other ender now? Strewth he's a biggun!" James looked in awe at William's tall and broad companion.

"This little fellow?" William laughed as he looked up at his very large companion. "Meet Tiny, from the Atherton Tablelands. His mother stood him in cow-shit every day for years to help him grow like this. He's always happy to take the heavy end of the stretcher so I'm not complaining."

A call came from up the line. "Stretcher-bearer! Where are those damn stretcher-bearers?"

As William and Tiny began to head towards the call, a voice sounded beside James. "McIvor, I told you sometime this morning to go and get that wound stitched. Now follow those stretcher-bearers down to the Dressing Station, for God's sake."

The dawn remained behind the horizon as if determined not to view the carnage of another day. A belligerent haze of smoke and dust hung in the air. In silence, the men stood on the firing step of the front trench waiting for the word to advance. There were as many different last-minute thoughts as there were men waiting for the order to make this dangerous leap over the top and into the firing line. The Allied warships' large guns had stopped pounding the Turks line on The Nek some time ago. Already the enemy had returned to their trenches and their machine guns.

"What's the damn hold up? Is someone daft?" Mark looked up from his contemplations at the sound of the voice nearby. Bayonets glinted on the ends of the rifles which had nothing up the spout as ordered. Sweat moistened the men's palms, hearts raced and prayers were said. Eyes focused inwards as they concentrated on remembering the details of the rough terrain across which they would have to run while the resettled enemy took aim with all they had, including those confounded machine guns. The call eventually came and as one, they lifted up and over the top.

Mark's legs were just clear of the parapet when he was sent barrelling back into the trench. Blood poured from a scalp wound. He lay unmoving in the dirt in the trench. He did not see almost the whole of his regiment shot to ribbons. Hardly a man returned from this blood bath.

It was late in the day before Mark's still unconscious body reached the waiting hospital ship. After removing the rough dressing on his head, the nursing-sister felt the bone under the wound. She was pleased to see the skull did not appear to be fractured. The fact one eye pupil was slightly larger than the other was of some concern but at least both pupils reacted to the light, albeit somewhat sluggishly.

After months of practice, she had the wound sutured and dressed without bothering the few doctors who worked round the clock repairing major body damage to many other infantrymen.

When one of the doctors eventually examined Mark two days later, he was pleased to see the pupils were back to normal even though the soldier remained semi-conscious.

It was nearly two weeks later, in the Lemnos Island Infantry Hospital, when 'the head injury in the corner stretcher' showed more positive signs of stirring. Mark knew he was lying under the mango tree near the kitchen at Emerald Flats. The noise of the ladies in the kitchen penetrated his dream. He could not understand why everything looked hazy, as if through a fog. Was that his beautiful Shauna sitting by his side? Slowly the fog began to lift. The lady had black hair; she could not be his Shauna. He discovered it was not a mango tree overhead; it looked more like the dull green canvas of a tent. When he lifted his aching head a fraction, he realized it had not been kitchen noises he had heard but the groans and rattles coming from an unbroken carpet of wounded and bloodied bodies being cared for by very few nursing-sisters and orderlies.

"So nice of you to join us, Trooper," commented the black-haired nurse with red tired eyes sitting by his side.

30/8/15

Dear Big Brother,

The word has come down the line that you're over at the Lemnos Island Hospital and slowly recovering from Abdul's kiss. How many times have I told you to keep your noggin down?

I can't say things have greatly changed here since our big offensive earlier this month, which is disappointing. So many dead on both sides. Everything seems to have returned to its usual stalemate. Don't rush back. Believe me, you're not missing anything, maybe the lice if you're lucky.

Recently, Tiny and I found a wounded soldier hidden from the sight of the Turks in a hollow protected by a small shrub. One of the blokes in the front trench said he heard someone moaning in the afternoon so as soon as it was dark, we were able to investigate and found a young lad with a smashed leg and a head wound. He was unable to say much but it appears he'd been there for more than two days.

The weather's starting to become a bit chilly at night. You have champion in-laws. Mary and Shauna have sent another parcel in which we found more knitted socks, gloves and a pullover each. They may come in handy with the autumn and winter approaching. We're wondering when we'll ever get the chance to use the bars of soap included. Oh, to feel clean again.

Hope this finds you up and about. Kindest regards from your brothers,

William and James.

The mottled shade from the olive tree danced across Mark's features as he read his brothers' letter. Above his head, the leaves rustled in the light breeze. Mark looked up from his reading when an orderly called on his way across from the office. In his hand, he waved another envelope.

"Mark, another letter to you. It had been sorted incorrectly. We found it on the bottom of the pile."

5/8/15

My Dearest Husband and father of our Margaret,

Darling, I cannot tell you how lonely the nights are without you by my side and how I miss your wonderful smile. When will this ever end? It's almost a year since you had to go to that horrible war and there doesn't appear to be an end in sight.

Baby now sits up on her own and gabbles away to herself all day. As well as the two bottom teeth that I told you about, she now has one tooth through, on the top, with the other not far away. I can feel it with my finger. She's a happy child but does miss her father so. Did I tell you she can say Dada now and does so every time I show her our wedding photo?

My love, I fear for your safety after reading the latest newspapers. Uncle Michael likes to read everything the journalist Ellis Ashmead-Bartlett writes. He thinks this man appears to seek out the real truths. He tells of a fierce battle last month. Please, God, you are safe and of course William and James as well.

The Government has imposed a tax on people's incomes to raise money for the war effort. This will mean more difficulties for many, I should think; but what else can they do?

The Ayr newspaper says that Dr. James is presenting a marble plaque in honour of the 27th North Queensland Light Horse. The Wyandra Hospital, where Thelma and Paddymac's little Patrick Michael was born, has been sold but a nursing home called Tralee has since opened. Thelma is so good with young Pat. She always seems so confident. I feel so uncertain all the time. Have I fed her enough? Have I fed her too much? Is she rugged up enough? Is she too rugged up? Is she crying for food or in pain? So, the questions go on. Thelma says it was caring for her numerous nieces and nephews that brought her down to earth. Mam says I need another half dozen babies to sort me out. The only thing wrong is, I cannot do it all on my own. Please hurry home safely, my darling.

Uncle Michael says to tell you the BHP Iron and Steel Works that opened at Newcastle in the middle of the year seems to be doing well. Pa and Uncle Michael are grateful the sale of the viable cane as fodder has done better than expected. It's such a shame that, due to the drought, the mill did not have enough cane to crush this season. The southern area of Australia appears to be getting some rain but still, it's very dry here. I believe they've had some bad bush fires in the south of Queensland recently.

Lindsay went with Gabby and Paddymac to deliver bullocks to the Home Hill Rail Yards en route to Townsville abattoirs. As you can imagine he was very excited. He would have preferred another three-day droving trip to Bobbawabba, but this was the next best thing. Uncle Michael said we may have problems with cattle ticks this year due to the weather. I hope we don't lose any to the sickness.

Gabby has been able to get a little extra work at the saw-mill. His boy, Akama, has gone out to Leaning Rock Station to help them out for a few months. Uncle Michael and Paddymac don't have a lot of work here now with the cane gone and the excess cattle sold. Paddymac and Pa manage to keep the irrigation going, when needed, on the latest crops. Never a day passes, Uncle Michael doesn't remind everyone it was his idea to invest in the irrigation pump.

The winter will be approaching where you are now so we're all knitting furiously again to ensure you're kept as warm as possible. I knit a ton of love into every stitch I sew for you.

Baby Maggie is now ready for a bath so I'll close. Sending big kisses from us both.

Your loving wife, Shauna.

Thanks to the ever-helpful orderly, Mark acquired a sheet of paper and a pencil to write a letter home while he waited for his transport back to Gallipoli.

6/9/15

My Darling Ladies, Shauna and baby Margaret,

At the moment, I'm skiving off at the Hospital on Lemnos Island about 95 miles from Gallipoli where I've been recovering since receiving a bit of a bump on the head in the August offensive. The parcel you sent last July, with the socks and gloves has even found its way here. Yesterday I received a note from William who says it's becoming chilly at night on Gallipoli so this gift will come in handy when I return sometime in the next week. They've received their parcel also and are very grateful. I do hope they remembered to thank you all.

It's amazing the work the medical people have done here. We see the broken bodies arrive and within no time they're slowly making their way around. Many are sent off to Britain for further care.

The great things about this place are the improved diet (even fruit and vegetables at times) and the lice have deserted me, thankfully. I guess our acquaintance will be rekindled when I arrive back at the filth of Gallipoli and the food will be back to the good old bully beef and hard biscuits.

There's my call. The doctor is checking me out this evening.

Will close, my love, my heart; take good care of yourself and our little girl.

P.S. Regards to the family.

"Bloody hell, Tiny, can you put those feet down a little more quietly? Do you want Abdul to know we're sneaking out the back door?" William begged silence from his mate as they, along with the remaining thousands of others throughout the Anzac and Suvla areas, made their way slowly to the shores of Gallipoli.

It was an amazing feat how little noise was being made by the men as they carefully wound their way through the foggy night with rags and torn strips of blankets tied around their shoes. Squad by squad they crept through the trenches in a prearranged time passage on their way to the beach for embarkation on the barges and other craft.

Last night, the first 20,000 troops left the cursed place right under the Turk's noses. William knew his brother James had left last night but was not too sure about Mark.

Why on earth did they send him back from sick leave if they knew an evacuation was planned to take place within a couple of months, he thought to himself. He felt on edge. His belly rumbled as his bowels struggled with fear and with old bully beef. The chances of a second evacuation being completed with the success of the first had to be pretty small. William was sure if the Turks got wind of this exodus, they'd let fire and annihilate all of those remaining. He wanted so much to be gone but he knew the Medical Corps must be the last to leave. Who else would there be to care for the wounded? Most of their recent work had been caring for the men affected by frostbite. On more than one occasion, a sentry had been found frozen on the spot where he stood.

The past few weeks had been a great effort in subterfuge. Lulling the Turks into believing their opponents may have been planning a large offensive rather than the truth, which was a gradual evacuation. Troops were taken out, unseen, to the waiting ships under the cover of night. Some returned in the daylight, giving the appearance of new reinforcements arriving – over and over for days.

For weeks before the evacuation began, the Anzacs held their guns silent for long periods. Many times, they did not respond to the Turks gunfire; all this to familiarise the enemy with the quiet moments. Little did Abdul know this new practice had a definite purpose. On the two nights when the final evacuation was to take place, on the 18th and 19th December 1915, it was hoped the Turks would not be expecting what was happening on the beaches where the troops made a well-disciplined retreat to the craft removing them from the area.

Even with the cold and frostbite affecting many of the inadequately supplied troops on both sides, Johnny Turk knew not to be complacent against this foe. These soldiers had proved themselves to be a force deserving great respect. Every day the mad bastards could be seen playing their cricket on the beach without apparent heed to the shrapnel shells dropping nearby. They were not so keen on swimming since the wild freezing storms, sleet, and snow in late November had damaged some of their landing piers. Their leaders held numerous parades and marches, pure madness surely, here on Gallipoli, but maybe it warmed them up a bit.

James was so pleased to be away from Gallipoli, even though he had found it hard to say another final goodbye to so many of his friends.

I wish I knew if William and Mark have made it out all right, he thought to himself as he climbed, along with so many others from the barge which had carried them around to the waiting troopship in Suvla Bay. All of the men were emaciated, dirty, unshaven, extremely tired, and cold – oh, so cold. *Maybe we'll have Christmas together at Lemnos Island.* He could not believe this was over at last. James would not let himself think about what may be waiting for them in the future. He did not want to think further than the Mudros Harbour at Lemnos.

He smiled ruefully when he thought about the surprises the Anzacs had left for the enemy. Several timed bombs were left at selective blind trenches and underground short tunnels before their last soldiers left. He had also watched them prepare the rifles rigged to fire without anyone there. A rock was tied with a string to the trigger. The string led from this weight to a tin catching water from a leaky container above. When the water in the receiving tin reached a certain weight, the rock fell pulling the trigger and the gun went off. James did not see them all but according to the men they had set several of these in various areas. The intermittent noise of the rifle fire would, hopefully, make the Turks think the men were still in the trenches.

Mark stood with the thousands of others on the ship's deck watching the glow of the fires which had been lit before the last men left Gallipoli. Anything that was unable to be removed and could be of assistance to the Turks had to be destroyed.

"I wonder if they're a-wake-up yet?" he asked the man beside him.

"I'm sure they will be. Thank God, we made it out with very little trouble and the good weather held. It could have been a lot worse if they'd discovered how few men were in the trenches yesterday. Now they'll find none – only the ghosts."

Chapter Sixteen.

Europe and the Desert.

7/1/16

Darling Dearest Mark,

I have not heard from you since the letter written at the hospital where you were recuperating and expecting to be returned to Gallipoli in September. I guess several letters will come together, shortly. We heard the ANZACS were successfully evacuated from Gallipoli. We pray God you are safely amongst them.

It's hard to believe the war still goes on. Our beautiful Maggie is over one year of age. Another Christmas has passed without you. Home Hill has many sons who went to war and quite a few will not return. Those poor families.

Akama returned from Leaning Rock Station at Christmas time. His family was so pleased to see him. Akama says your brother, William, is sweet on the owner's daughter, Bella. They write to each other. He knows because he had to post and pick up the mail a few times. The cheeky fellow read the names on the envelopes.

Oh, that reminds me. Did I mention there has been a new school opened at Inkerman, just south of Home Hill?

Uncle Michael seems to have slowed down a bit lately but then he is well over sixty now. Harry and Old Mr. Wong, who are both nearly seventy themselves, spend a lot of time yarning in the shed with Uncle Michael. Pa and Gabby mostly run the place now. Paddymac helps when he has the time free at his place. Haddi works with Paddymac.

193

Lindsay and Sabbo are kept very busy before and after their lessons helping with the house animals and chopping the wood. Anguó, Curley Wong's eldest, does the work of a man in the gardens when he is not in class. Lindsay has been keeping up his Chinese lessons with Old Mr. Wong. The Wong family gave him an abacus for Christmas. I was surprised at how quickly he learnt to use it; he is now teaching me.

A few more acres of land have been cleared for the cane on Paddymac's farm. We hope the weather this season will be an improvement on last year.

Did I tell you Coutts opened a new shop in town? We buy quite a lot of our needs from there. Thelma had her sister visit for several days recently. They came over one day for morning tea.

Madam Maggie is just opening her eyes. They are so big and beautiful. Darling, I look forward to your being here with us to enjoy these moments.

All my Love and Kisses from Shauna and a big kiss from Maggie.

A haze of smoke drifted above the battlefields of the Somme like a thin fog. The silence of the guns felt heavy on the soldiers' ears as they waited for the inevitable return of the rattle of death at any moment. The two men were glad to take this opportunity to explore the mail awaiting their attention.

"Goanna Oil! Pull the other one digger." William laughed at his friend Bruiser Mitchell as they sat behind the Dressing Station tent where he was opening another of Mary and Shauna's parcels. "Is that some kind of French joke you've picked up here?"

Bruiser, a solid fellow almost as wide as he was tall replied, "No, cobber it's true. Don't knock the family for sending you a bottle of Goanna Oil or a tin of Goanna Ointment. It's known to cure almost anything. Rub it into tired muscles, lumbago, anything; you name it.

The fellows 'ere 'ave been using it to lubricate their rusting rifles and that's no lie. One chap always carried a tin of Goanna Ointment in his top pocket. It saved 'is life. A sniper's bullet was on its way to smash up his 'eart when it 'it the tin and diverted; only managed to lift a bit of skin around 'is ribs and left 'im with a large bruise. Mind you the bloke was pissed off at the mangled tin that 'e was left with."

"In this game of carrying stretchers, it's the head that usually gets blown off. Maybe I need to make a hatband of tins," laughed William as he visualized the sight.

"You said your name was McIvor, right? Are you any relation to Splicer McIvor, the signaller up the way?"

"James? Yes, he's my brother."

"They say 'e climbed over the parapet and pulled a wounded officer back into the trench during the fighting last evening; saved 'is life most likely. When they tried to praise him 'e said, 'The bloody bloke was lying on my telephone wire and I needed it back.'" Bruiser Mitchell laughed heartily as he retold his tale.

"Silly blighter, I told him to pull his head in." Anxiety roughened William's reply.

"Do you think anyone'll ever find all those bodies out there sinking into the mud? Do you think anyone'll ever care? Everyone who's been up there running in the quagmire 'as 'ad to reach down to get their balance at some stage. It's inevitable when the hand sinks into the mud it uncovers some part of a dead body. The stench is unbelievable." Bruiser looked over to where William sat in deep thought. "I suppose it 'appens to you fellows all the time when you try to carry your stretchers steady. It can't be easy keeping your feet under you," commented Bruiser as he slowly rose to his feet. "Anyway, mate, I'd best get back. They'll be thinking I've cashed in my chips and not just come down for a few stitches. See you later." Bruiser started to make his way back to the frontline.

"Hey!" yelled William to the retreating soldier. "Don't forget your gas mask. You don't want to go anywhere near that mustard gas without your mask, friend."

2/4/16

My Love, my Heart,

Still, we waste time in this hot desert. James and William have been sent with many others to the Somme Valley in France to face the Germans there. Most of our Light Horse fellows around here fretfully sit idle doing little but training horses and ourselves. Our task is to defend the Suez Canal, I guess. That bit may get blotted out by the censors.

I just wish we could be more active and get this war over with. I feel I've missed Maggie's growing up. Am I to miss her second year also? Will she ever get to know her Dad? We have missed two Christmases and I missed your twenty-first birthday last year. Thank heavens, Mr. Chiswell, was able to obtain the special necklace I had planned for that. I can imagine how it will set off the colour of your brilliant eyes and glorious auburn hair. As I go to sleep every night my last thoughts are of you.

It's good to be out of those miserable trenches and on the back of a horse again. They're Australian bred horses called Walers, truly magnificent. They go for days with little water or sustenance – impossible conditions. They are intelligent and brave animals. I do enjoy working with them. These days we do a lot of trips out into the desert learning what to expect and how to recognize possible water sources and oases. Water is just as important as ammunition in this country; a bit like the inland of Australia, I think.

Thank you and the family once again for the parcels. By the sound of it, you, Thelma, and your mother are kept pretty busy with the Red

Cross work.   You can take it from me the effort is very much appreciated.

The call has gone up, we're off again,

Bye my dearest and give my little girl a big kiss as well,

From the one who loves you above all else, Mark.

"Could you pass me the pliers, lad?" James asked the young Londoner who had been standing in the new and already muddy trench watching his every move. Things were a little quieter than they had been recently and James was now working his way along the trench setting up telephone wires connecting the command stations to their newly taken ground around Pozierres. "How long have you been over here, then?"

"Just cummin' up twelve months," the young soldier replied.

James looked quizzically at the lad and then asked kindly, "How old are you, son?" When the boy said he was eighteen, James looked at the smooth face that had not seen a razor and raised an eyebrow. He smiled and pushed his hat back on his head, "Really?"

The boy smiled back, "Not far off," he offered.

"How far, not far?" quizzed James.

"Seventeen next birfday," was the answer. "You won't dob me in will ya?"

"What's your name?" queried James then offered his name, "My name's James McIvor."

"Ralph Watson," was the reply.

"You keep safe, young fellow. Don't listen to all that death and glory rubbish some of them go on with. Remember, it's better to be a live coward than a dead hero. What will your parents say if you return home dead?"

"I doubt if they'd even notice."

The remark silenced James for a moment. "What do you plan on doing when this war's over?" he asked. A slight shrug of the shoulders was the only indication the youngster had heard the question.

James kept working with the willing assistance of Ralph. "You know, you have nimble fingers which are a great help in this job. Have you ever thought of getting in with the Signallers? I know Stripes, that's my sergeant, has the ear of the man running this show. At the moment, signallers are in short supply. If you wish, I could put in a word for you and he may be able to wangle you a transfer."

"Would they teach me how to do what you do?" asked Ralph keenly.

"No trouble at all. Once the war's over there'll be telephone lines to almost every house in England, you mark my words. Telephone linesmen will be in high demand. You'll soon find employment," was James's advice to his new friend.

10/8/16

Dear Lindsay,

It was good to hear from you again. Glad you're doing so well with your schoolwork. You seem to know more about this war than we do over here, as you trace the news reports on the wall-size map you and Shauna have made.

You must have really upset your Pa to wind up having to take the dunny-can out to empty and bury the contents. I've had to do that a few times in my life, I can tell you. Not a pleasant task, but guess what, someone has to do it.

I bet your mother got the shock of her life to find a baby croc enjoying life in the washing tub. Am I to assume you did not get to keep it for very long?

Things here in the Somme Valley have been pretty noisy and deadly lately but now we have all returned to a stalemate it seems. The Germans were dug in first so they have their trenches on higher and more advantageous sites. Our trenches are usually on the lower ground without the height advantage when attacking and these trenches are constantly waterlogged. Many soldiers suffer from trench-foot. We now have duck-boards on the floor of some of the trenches which makes things a little better. When it rains, the mud's so deep in no-man's land it can take up to six stretcher-bearers to bring back a wounded soldier. It takes a lot of effort to lift the weight, without moving the man, thereby putting him through more pain which could bring on shock and kill him. Once that's been accomplished it's a nightmare trying to lift one's limbs buried in the mud.

The scene is like something unimaginable; millions of craters from the bombing, scrambled barbed wire in the mud and not a blade of grass left. Most of the time, I've been working at the Dressing Station behind the lines but we still had a couple of close calls from some of the shell-fire. You know I may go and study medicine when, and if, we make it out of here. The doctors are to be admired for their stamina and the work they do.

James is still a signaller; someone gave him the name of 'Splicer' and it's stuck. Recently he took a young boy from London under his wing and is training him.

Word is we may be moving on to Belgium soon but this world is full of gossip and furphies. I just keep doing what I do and wait until the order comes.

Keep safe and keep away from the crocs. It's always dangerous to get between a mother and her baby, you know. While you're digging holes for the pan contents you can think of us here digging so many trenches. I won't be surprised if one day we go right through the earth and turn up on your front doorstep.

Once again, I ask you to thank your mother and her friends for the parcels they send. They are truly appreciated.

Regards from William and James.

"Shauna, what's the matter, dear?" Mary asked, concerned at the sudden pallor of her daughter's face when she stepped out of the sitting room. Shauna's gaze fixated on the front verandah and Maggie, now almost-two-year-old.

She watched Maggie lean forward offering her biscuit to a friend, out of view – presumably her doll. Maggie then leant backwards. The head of a large brown snake followed the hand still holding the biscuit. Shauna could not speak. A gasp escaped her lips. A trembling arm pointed.

"Oh, dear, God," Mary whispered.

Both women inched towards the open door at the end of the hallway outside of which the hypnotizing pendulum of child and snake swung. Once at the doorway and without further thought, Shauna leapt out onto the verandah to swoop up her child. She dragged Maggie into the protection of her own body. In a single bound, Shauna jumped away from the reptile. In a reflex action, Mary used the broom in her hands to move the snake in the other direction. Maggie screamed at the indignity of it all and the pressure of her mother's hold.

After delivering two strong strikes to the head of the broom, the brown snake slithered through the bars of the child-gate at the top of the stairs. The reptile disappeared to freedom outside.

Shauna sobbed, gulping great breaths of air. "Mam, I can't go on without Mark here to help me. How can I keep my baby safe? Why is he away at that damn war? Who makes these wars?"

Mary threw her arms about her beloved girls and started to sing in her clear soprano voice one of her favourite hymns. Slowly the calming music soothed the child. Shauna's sobs quietened as she now sat on the nearest seat which was an old box full of her father's books. Mary continued singing until Shauna had completely settled and the wee bairn listened happily.

"God forgive me for being so selfish," Shauna spoke normally at last. "How many have lost loved ones in the war with no one around to help them? At least I have my family here. Why am I complaining?"

When peace reigned once more, Shauna wiped her face, then Maggie's tear-stained cheeks, as the child attempted to sing along with her 'Ganma'.

Clouds filled the skies over the desolate landscape of devastation. From further west, the sound of sporadic rifle fire drifted across the plain.

"Hello, brother. Glad to see you still in one piece. I thought they must have sent you to that Belgium show in August? This is an interesting way to see the world, don't you think?" William laughed with relief to find his brother, James, still alive in this godforsaken hell.

"Can't say I'd recommend the accommodation. The mud, cold, rain, dirt floors, and poor sanitation along with the noise, day and night, might turn away the visitors." James joined in the repartee.

"Why should we complain, with free travel and our third Christmas away from home – this one in France?" William laughed again as the brothers threw their arms around each other's shoulders.

With the thousands of dead bodies, it seemed inevitable their time would come. They were both grateful it had not come yet.

The battles they encountered at Fromelles earlier, in July of 1916, were an indication of how most of the battles on the Western Front were fought. Similar to what they had experienced in Gallipoli. Heavy bombardment started the show for the attackers. The purpose of this was to tear apart the barbed wire and, in the process, remove a few of the defenders and their munitions. The big guns were closely followed by the attacking army's advancement over the no-man's land where the defending army usually gave them their marching orders, either to their trenches or to their Maker. Many lives, on both sides, were lost during these continual ongoing skirmishes. A horrendous activity is war.

November 1916

Dear James and William,

It was with regret we watched your ship sail off carrying you all to the Western Front in France. At the time we felt we'd been left out of things. We spent a couple of months doing little but training exercises and patrols.

That all changed in August when the Turks made their second attack on the Suez Canal. As you can imagine we had to keep it open at all costs. The Brits were ready to respond at Romani but the wily Turks (there were many, many more than us) thought they'd sneak around them only to be met with our boys in the Light Horse (thanks to General Chauvel's clever planning). It looked like they were going to outdo us for a while but by the next day, we had them on the run. We lost many good men and many good horses that day. I had to seek new mounts three times.

There are all the appearances of another big offensive to come but we've not been told where or when yet. Keep your heads down, brothers. You'll be lucky if there's anything left of this letter but the censor's black pen.

Must away back to this donnybrook over here.

Your brother, Mark.

P.S. Have you heard from Mother lately? I received a long epistle about a month ago. Our Pa's not been well but seems to be on the mend now.

Dust and the bellow of cattle swirled in the air around the two riders wearing handkerchiefs tied over their noses. Perspiration and dirt trickled into their eyes as the sun beat down upon their shoulders. Sweat foamed on the dark coats of their mounts.

"Those two young blue dogs are working well," commented Shamus riding beside Paddymac as they pushed the cattle up to the yards near the house. "Lindsay teaches them a new trick every day."

"He's done a good job with them in such a short time, Shamus. Do you realize it's only a couple of days until Christmas again? Christmas 1916; where does the time go to?"

"I reckon. Your Pat must be one-year-old already. I guess it won't be too long before you have him on horse-back?"

Paddymac laughed. "Give over, will you. Thelma would skin me alive if I even thought of putting him on a horse before he's three. I have to admit, I'm keeping an eye on the young foals though – you know, looking for a likely candidate."

They moved apart as they directed stray bullocks. Once the gates were closed behind the bawling stock both men stood with their arms on the top rail looking over the animals. Paddymac turned to Shamus.

"Heard any more from Mark, lately? How are he and his brothers doing over there, poor blighters?"

"Not for a while, Paddymac. Shauna's out most nights ready to accost the Wong boys when they've been to town. She keeps hoping for mail. It'll be hard for her not to have Mark, here again, this Christmas."

"Well, we'd better draft out what we want here. At least the butchers will have plenty of meat."

After the cattle drafting was completed and unwanted animals were driven back to the far paddocks, Paddymac joined the family at the big house for lunch.

Uncle Michael sat at the head of the table where Mary ensured he was seated every meal. Paddymac sat on his right and Shamus on his left with Lindsay beside his father. While the males discussed recent political and war news, Mary and Shauna made plans for the gathering of the townswomen for the next Red Cross meeting. Occasional snippets of the men's conversation drifted down to the ladies.

Shamus looked at Michael and asked, "What did you think of Mr. Hughes purchasing those fifteen steamships in July? Now Australia has its merchant fleet. Hopefully, our wheat will get to a hungry Britain sooner. Even our mail may be more regular; many will look forward to that."

Michael nodded as he swallowed the stew in his mouth.

Paddymac lifted his head to talk to the ladies. "I've a message for you from Thelma. She was at Ayr last week. Coutts' store had leaflets about the new book written by C.J. Dennis, 'Songs of a Sentimental Bloke'. She thought you may be interested."

"Thanks, Paddymac. I could do with some new reading material." Mary smiled.

Shamus reached for the salt. "Prime Minister Hughes is back from his six-month trip to Britain and the Western Front. I bet he'll be pushing his compulsory overseas military service idea. That'll put the cat among the pigeons."

Michael grunted a reply.

Paddymac wanted to know how the Home Hill Power House plans were getting along but Shamus couldn't be sure.

"They'll have some news for us at the next Farmer's Meeting after Christmas."

The chairs scraped as the men rose. Farm work called.

4th January 1917

Mark my Dearest,

Another Christmas has passed but I have decided to think differently; another day closer to when you arrive home. The papers today have mentioned the successes of the Australian Light Horsemen in Egypt, Palestine, and a town called Magdhaba. It doesn't go on to say how many of our brave soldiers have been lost. My darling, I do fear for you but pray every minute of every day for your safe return.

Maggie is learning something new daily, now that she is two. Young Pat and her seem to enjoy each other's company very much when they're together. Luckily Pat doesn't mind her bossing him about, which she is wont to do all the time. A bossy britches is our Maggie.

"A schoolmarm," as Pa says.

We spent Christmas day on the river-bank as usual. Pa and Paddymac took the babies swimming with them. Déshi and An Wong showed us their new baby girl.

We've had quite a bit of rain lately and rivers have been up from Cardwell to Bowen. Our Burdekin Bridge was partly washed away. I can't believe how hard the rain falls here; and when it's not raining, the humidity suffocates. There is either no rain or it comes down in buckets. We've two new rainwater tanks which have both been filled to the top.

I think I told you they've begun plans for an Irrigation Power House in Home Hill. I'm not too sure how far along they are with the building though.

Our parliament seems to be in a terrible mess since the rejection of the referendum about the compulsory conscription of overseas recruits. Mr. Hughes has been dismissed from the Labour Party and has now set up the National Labour Party, with the support of Mr. Cook's Liberal Party. It seems as if a new election will be inevitable.

I think the Government has totally lost its mind. They've passed the Daylight Savings Act (in December 1916) whereby from the first day of this year we had to move our clocks forward one hour. This will last until the end of March. You'll not believe the reason. It's to make the most of the daylight hours. Don't they realize there'll still only be the same amount of daylight and if they want to 'make the most of the daylight' perhaps they should arise earlier in the morning and finish work when the sun goes down as the farmers have been doing forever? There's been terrible confusion with postal services and railway schedules etc.

I'll go now and join Mam, Thelma, and Sophie as we knit some more socks to add to the next parcels destined for the Front. Hopefully, I'll get back to this before we send it in the post tomorrow.

All our love from your two best girls, Shauna and Maggie.

Tears streamed from the corner of her eyes down into her ears. A tentative hand reached up to feel the pillow damp under her head. A wispy dream floated on the periphery of her conscious mind but the more she attempted to grasp it and analyse the content, the further away it drifted leaving Mark's blue eyes a hazy memory in her head.

She swung her legs around and sat up on the side of the bed. Maggie stirred in the cot in the corner. The floor felt cold under her feet as Shauna padded over to cover her child. Silently she slipped into the chair beside the sleeping toddler. Her work-rough hand reached in through the railings to hold the soft tiny hand. She wanted so much to recall her dream. There was something important there to discover but nothing revealed itself.

Not for the first time since Mark had gone to war, Shauna found herself examining her feelings for her husband. Those weeks on the ship when they had first met; when Mark filled her every thought. Those moments of ecstasy when they were together; nothing else existed in the world around them. How she had felt depleted when they were apart, even for a short moment. Mark had filled her every waking thought and most of her sleeping ones too.

She struggled to understand how, within a few short weeks, her feelings of absolute adoration and love had turned to resentment and disgust. How could the Mark she married reject her friends and embarrass her in front of the family? The respect she held for him had taken a severe hiding after that first Christmas. Her mind pondered the concepts of respect and love. As far as she could see, without respect, true love cannot exist. Respect is as important to love as oxygen is to the body.

In her favour, she had tried to submerge those black feelings deep into the back of her mind. As far as she was able, she endeavoured to become the person he wanted her to be. A grimace curled her features as she acknowledged, with honesty, her stubborn, independent, natural instincts. In all fairness, she had to admit during those times of her compliance, her husband responded. Things softened between them. The dislike buried deep in her heart faded. Love had almost refilled the spaces when the war took him away. The pain of his going hurt. She felt his absence like a living thing, a blackness in her soul, or was that her guilt? Reluctantly, she admitted her pleasure in making her own decisions about her life again. She enjoyed just being herself and knowing she was appreciated by others for herself. Why could she not completely love the Mark she had discovered him to be, as she had the man who captured her heart on the ship?

Her finger reached out and traced her daughter's face. Mark helped to make this baby, she thought. He is the child's father. Maggie is the image of her father. How can the child grow up proud of herself if she is not proud of the man who is her father? Shauna knew it would be up to her to ensure the child admired Mark. She understood her own wants must take second place. Maggie's needs must come above all others.

She closed her eyes and whispered, "God, if you see fit to return Mark to us, I promise I'll try harder to quell my stubborn streak and work harder to keep him contented, for our child's sake."

30/2/17

My dear Muirnīn and Maggie our little shamrock,

Things have been busy here in recent weeks. I think I've already told you of our success at Magdhaba just before Christmas 1916 and then again in early January, just gone, the success at Rafa. It was touch and go both times with the need for water by men and horses but we took both oases eventually.

The Arabs call us the "Kings of the Feathers" because of the emu feathers we have on our hats. Most are looking a bit bedraggled at the moment.

No doubt we'll be off again shortly as our numbers have been replaced and supplies are coming in by the ships-full.

I guess the men on Emerald Flats will be preparing the paddocks for the planting in the next few months. Has any further clearing been going on? Did I tell you I had a letter from James recently? He mentioned how very cold and wet it is in France. Both he and William are very grateful for the socks and gloves. Many of the men end up with frostbitten feet and fingers.

It's great to hear the Queensland Government will make land available for the Returned Soldiers with an easy repayment scheme.

The men at the front are making a monumental sacrifice for our country. Some of these poor lads are struggling to cope. It's only the love I have for you and little Maggie that keeps me strong.

This desert is amazing. It's so vast – so hot by day and sometimes very cold at night. Heat can be seen shimmering in the distance and the stories that speak of the mirages of the desert are so true. The strong colours are something to behold; the many hues of red, gold and orange by day, and the black and silver of the nights. Only you, my love, could give me greater pleasure than entering a soft, green, fresh oasis after spending a day out on patrol.

Have to dash, all my love, Mark.

None of those present in the classroom noticed the young blue dog lying at Lindsay's feet prick her ears, raise the hairs on the back of her neck, and stare intently at a point behind Shauna's head as she stood leaning against the house post. The children's minds focussed on their work. Lindsay struggled to fathom the trigonometry exercises. The young ones practised writing their letters and the middle group made sentences out of given words. Shauna's mind had wandered thousands of miles away, with her husband on the battlefield. The animal's eyes never blinked as it watched the large snake wind its way around the rafters and stop with its head just above Shauna's auburn locks. The forked tongue flicked in and out, reading the messages on the air. Slowly it began to descend past the side of her head and touched her shoulder. Shauna froze. In one huge bound, the blue dog leapt. The animal's strong jaws grabbed the reptile six inches from its head. The bitch shook the reptile from side to side while falling with the snake to the ground. The head-shaking continued faster than the eye could see until the blue dog broke the snake's back. All eyes followed the action, mesmerized. Not a word was spoken. The snake, when dropped to the ground, wriggled feebly. Once more the dog snatched it up and shook it back and forth. Over and over this was repeated until she was happy her job was done.

"Good, dog." Lindsay patted the snake killer.

Shauna's voice squeaked as the words were forced through her throat. "I think it's time for a break. I'm sure Mrs. Doolan has our milk and biscuits prepared in the kitchen near Uncle Michael's hut. You may pack up your things and go." Struggling to continue, Shauna waved her finger in the direction of the mangled mess on the floor. "Lindsay, will you find the shovel and make sure that horrible thing is completely dead, please?"

A great rush followed as the children tore over to the kitchen, squealing in their excitement. They tried to outdo each other in telling the tale to Mary as she worked at the old stove. Left in the classroom, Shauna sat on the children's bench resting her head in her hands.

In the kitchen, Mary took some moments to make sense of the children's babbling. She rushed across to the classroom.

"Are you all right, dear?" she asked her daughter. "It sounds like you had a bit of a fright."

With a feeble smile, Shauna, replied, "You could say that. These damn snakes are everywhere. The only damage was a dirty paw mark on my pinny but I guess that's a small price to pay for my life."

15th July 1917

Dear William and James,

Wow, did we have some excitement in the classroom yesterday? A snake slid down off the rafters and wound itself around Shauna's neck. Thank heavens for Bluey (she's one of Paddymac's new dogs) who grabbed it in one leap and quickly smashed its back to pieces.

Uncle Michael said it was probably looking for a rat to eat although it's a bit early in the season for a snake to be out and about. Boy, have there been a few of them about this year; rats and mice I mean. Sabbo and I often kill a few in the shed with the help of the dogs. Even the chooks have been seen to eat the mice. It's like a plague.

The cane harvest season is about to start. We'll miss Mark again this year. Gabby and Haddi have been sharpening the cane knives and oiling up the new chop-chop machine. Sabbo and I collect the cane tops after school and put them into the machine and out comes edible chopped up stock feed. Pa gets a drum of molasses from the Inkerman mill and pours a little over the feed and the animals love it. Paddymac showed me how to grease the axles on the drays this morning. He's going to let me help him repair a wheel next time they have to do one.

This place is full of babies at the moment. Shauna has Maggie who is nearly three. Paddymac and Thelma have Pat who they bring over to Emerald Flats when they come about twice a week. He has just turned two. The Wong family has a baby girl who is about a year old. Sabbo and I like to escape to our favourite tree on the riverbank and get away from the howling sometimes.

Last week Pa and Uncle Michael let me watch as they pulled a calf from a cow. That was a sight to see. I think the old girl knew we were trying to help her. The calf's feet had been showing for a while and the rest of the body seemed to be stuck. Pa poured cod liver oil around the tiny body inside the cow then tied a rope to the feet and pulled. It took a lot of pulling before the calf popped out like a cork. We dragged the calf around to the cow's head and she started to lick it straight away. Pa said that, if I want to, he'll let me go to University to be a Doctor or a Veterinarian. I think that would be great. It was better seeing that cod liver oil used on the cow and not having Mam pour it down my neck when she has a mind to.

Shauna said I was to tell you that Mr. Hughes and his new National Party easily won the election in May. Every week Shauna and I read the paper together after Uncle Michael and Pa have finished with it.

I can hear Mam coming to see why I've not turned down my lamp so I'll close. We're a bit low on kerosene at the moment.

God keep you both safe. Regards from Lindsay.

Leaning Rock Station, south of Charters Towers, spread out below where Bella sat in the mottled shade of the chinky-apple tree which clung desperately to the dry, rocky soil on the side of the hill. Her fingers stroked the worn folds of the letter in her hand. The smudged pencilled writing was almost indecipherable after frequent handling. When she noticed her father in the distance approaching the homestead, she shoved the paper into the top pocket of her shirt and jumped to her feet. Her heart broke to see her once young and vibrant father now riding slouched in the saddle. She ran down to open the yard-gate for him. His smile, as he passed through the opening, was almost lost in the weary-lines of his face. After shutting the gate, Bella ran after her father to the stable.

"Wait, Dad, I'll look after Brandy for you. Just drop the wire and pliers, and the fence strainers here, I'll put them away."

Matthew Littlewood reached out and touched his eldest daughter's shoulder. His wan smile touched her heart.

"Mum has your tea on the table for you." Bella looked down at the barb-wire-torn trousers. She noticed the dirt-encrusted hands and dust filling the wrinkles of his face. "Might be an idea if you can muster the strength to clean up first."

His smile widened. His grey eyes sparkled. "You might be right, lass. Is Thomas back from the billabong paddock yet?"

"Yes, Dad. He's out chopping more wood for Ma."

Matthew watched Bella as she removed the saddle and brushed his horse with her strong capable hands. He helped her collect the fencing supplies and secure them on the bench.

"You know, lass, it'll be good to have William back here after the war and of course, James. I miss them both. They were good men to have around."

"It might be a good idea to contact Mr. Doolan on the Burdekin to ask if he has a spare man for several weeks – even months might be good. The young fellow he sent before worked well."

"Akama? Yes, he did do a pretty good job. I'll think about that for a bit."

"I miss William too, Dad, so much it hurts."

He rested his tired arm upon her shoulder and they made their way to the house.

10/8/17

Dear James and William,

It's a while since hearing from the pair of you. Hopefully, this will find you safe even if you are wet, cold, hot, muddy, hungry, exhausted and fed up. Cheer up, you may grow to like feeling this way soon – it's been nearly three years already. They say things grow on you.

I don't know about you two but sometimes I wonder what the great white masters running this show are thinking about. A couple of months ago we attacked and won a Turkish strongpoint at Gaza, after quite a long day. Word comes from the powers-that-be for us to withdraw. No one could believe it. We thought it was an enemy trick. All those men and horses wounded and killed for what???? Many of us were asleep in our saddles as we sadly made the return trip. Now, as if that was not bad enough, a month later they decided we needed to attack Gaza again. The dead and wounded were everywhere. What a damn waste. So now we sit in trenches (where it's possible in this country to dig a trench) from Gaza to Beersheba eyeing the Turks as they eye us from a stone's throw away. This is a hot, God-forsaken country I can tell you. I wonder how much the censor will leave of this???

Can you imagine what our father would say if he heard me complaining like that? I doubt I'd be able to sit down for a week, at least.

Hopefully, things may look up now. We've a new Commander in Chief they call "The Bull". The first thing he did was to move the headquarters much closer to where the action is. Maybe he'll have a better understanding of what's going on. He should do anyway. He's always dropping in unannounced to inspect the different sections. I hear the Signallers send out unofficial warnings to each other, "Bull on the Loose". James, you'll get a laugh out of that.

My turn at the outpost; I must move.

Stay safe. God be with you both. Your brother, Mark.

"Mrs. Doolan I seem to have run out of wool for this last sock," Cabri wiped the sweat from her arms with her skirt. Today she wore green and red ribbons like streamers from her hair. On the verandah of the big house, the women sought any little breeze passing their way. The humidity stifled. Rain must surely be on the way, maybe before this Christmas.

Her fellow knitters, Mary, Thelma, Shauna, Lee Wong, and Sophie Bobangle looked up from their work and smiled.

"You're working like a bandicoot looking for fresh shoots," laughed Sophie as she finished off the hem of a man's dressing gown.

Rosie Bobangle could be heard playing hide-and-seek in the yard with the small children whilst the older children, not yet able to knit and sew, played war games over near the hay shed.

"Cabri, fetch the box the carrier left earlier this week, dear. You'll find it on the front verandah near the sewing machine. The Red Cross sent it out and I think it'll have more materials, cotton, and wool," instructed Mary.

Sophie had turned her attention to cutting out face towels and washers. "I hear Red Cross make plenty money at the races this year. People good to give when have not much themselves." Today it was going to be her turn to use the sewing machine. It was always exciting making the needle go up and down ever so fast.

Mary paused her knitting needles and leant back in the chair.

"We'll be late at the Christmas Picnic this year. Shamus, Shauna, Lindsay and I are going to the church service being held at the Osborne school. Thelma and Paddymac have volunteered to stay here and help set everything up," she told the group.

"You will come, Mrs. Doolan, please?" Sophie begged.

"Yes, my dear I wouldn't miss it for the world."

Thelma smiled as she joined the conversation. "I hear the new hospital in Ayr has been so busy, they're not taking people with a long-term illness or those with an infectious disease including that dreadful new Spanish Flu. These people are to be cared for by their families."

"That'll not be easy for some." Shauna lifted her head from her needlework. "Thelma, your second baby is only a few months away, will you have it at the Tralee Hospital?"

"Yes, Shauna. I'll go over to stay in Ayr with my mother for two weeks before I'm due." Thelma's knitting needles flew so fast the ends could not be seen.

Mary stood up. "I think I'll make a pot of tea for us all. We've made a fine effort here this morning. Can I get a cup for everyone?"

Murmured assents rose from the workers.

"Then you show me to make the sewing machine work, Missus?"

"I'll make the tea, Mrs. Doolan. You help Sophie before she explodes with excitement," Lee Wong laughed as she placed a completed balaclava hat on the table.

"Thanks, Lee." She smiled over at Sophie. "Come along, Sophie, we'll get those face towels and washers hemmed on the machine."

While Lee prepared a tray in the kitchen, next door, the remaining ladies around the work-table discussed the general strike filling the newspapers in recent times.

Shauna held the floor. "It's so good to hear the general strike in New South Wales is finally over. How could they disrupt the war effort like that? It's unbelievable they could do such a thing while our men are overseas fighting for them all," her voice shook with passion.

Thelma reached over and touched her hand. "Yes, Shauna, it wasn't a good thing," her soft smile reached her friend. "Hopefully, 1918 will bring an end to this dreadful war and the tragedies it has brought and our soldiers will come home again."

Later in the afternoon, as Shauna brought in the washing, she noticed Maggie and Little Pat had disappeared. They had been playing under the mango tree near the old kitchen only minutes before. She called out to Thelma who was inside packing her basket to return home.

"Thelma, are the children with you and Mam?" When the reply was negative, she called, "I'm on my way to the big house with these clothes, I'll check if they're playing over there."

Once she had climbed the stairs, Shauna put the basket down on the table near the back door. She heard the children's voices coming from the side verandah. Quietly she approached and stood listening as the two little ones lay on their stomachs side by side staring at Mark's photo. Maggie instructed Little Pat.

"This is a picture of my Daddy. His name is Mark. My Daddy is a sholjur. He's a long way away at war where bad people are trying to come and kill us but my Daddy's going to stop them. See his clothes. They're special fighting clothes. One day I going to see my real Daddy when he beats the bad men and comes home; then I'll have a real Daddy too, just like you have a real Daddy. Daddymac."

Shauna could not stop the tears falling but smiled at Maggie's name for Paddymac. She said quietly to herself, "Yes, my darling, I hope and pray that you do see your Daddy soon, real soon."

Chapter Seventeen

Hope of Peace

Morning class 28th February 1918 had begun. Today's roll call consisted of:

Lindsay who was now thirteen years of age going on fourteen, plus

The Wong children:

Anguó, aged fourteen years, nearly fifteen.

Cai, aged thirteen years, will be fourteen in a month.

Bik aged eight years.

Mali aged six years.

The Bobangle children:

Sabbo, aged thirteen, soon to be fourteen.

'Alya, aged ten years, insists she is eleven.

Mary, aged five years, going on to six.

Cabri, her cousin, just turned fourteen years of age.

Maani aged ten years.

Gabrel aged ten years.

Bia aged eight years.

Akama Bobangle had remained working at Leaning Rock Station.

Shauna gazed out from under the big house thinking about her Mark; worrying if he was safe. Her finger twirled a loose strand of hair dangling near her ear. *Would this war ever end*, she thought; a thought repeated a hundred times a day. At her back, the scratch of slate-pencils on slates confirmed the children worked at their writing exercises. Dust rising in the distance along the track caught her attention. Gradually the shape of someone leading a horse became visible. As they approached, the figures of two small children could be distinguished on the back of the horse. At the house-compound gate, Shauna realized it was a woman leading the horse. An older child walked at her side. In her arms, the woman held a smaller child. Recognition lifted Shauna's head. That was Mrs. MacGregor from a neighbouring farm to the east. The Wong men often dropped off any unsold vegetables at her house on their way home. Shauna had met the lady on the odd occasion when she had been travelling to town. Something must be terribly wrong for the woman to drag those small children over here like this.

Shauna ran out to help, calling for her mother at the same time. She found the woman distraught, exhausted and barely able to talk. Mrs. MacGregor, usually a tidy dresser, today dripped perspiration, blood and mud from a serge black dress as well as from her arms where the sleeves were rolled above the elbows. Shauna eased the baby from her hold and helped her to the house. With the mother sitting on the steps and the baby now back in her arms, the lad, who appeared to be no more than six years of age, moved over to stand by her side. Shauna lifted the two bairns from the horse. She flashed a curious glance Mrs. MacGregor's way. These two infants looked no more than four years and two years of age. How had they managed to stay on the horse – it must have been at least a three-mile journey? Shauna put this from her mind as she poured cool water from the water-bag hanging on a nail in a post of the house. Mrs. MacGregor offered the pannikin of water to her children before drinking herself. The faces of the Emerald Flats school children peered around the schoolroom partition.

"It's rude to stare – eyes back on your lessons," demanded Shauna when she noticed the lack of attention to the school work.

Once the colour returned to Mrs. MacGregor's cheeks, she began to relate her story to Shauna and Mary, who had come down the stairs with a wide-eyed Maggie by her side. Mr. MacGregor had been injured when chopping down a large tree. The wind stirred just as the tree was ready to fall, changing the planned direction. A large branch caught her husband on the head before it landed across his leg. When she left him, he was unconscious and unmoving, his face covered in blood. Mrs. MacGregor could not lift her husband.

Immediately, Mary began to plan. She called to the children in the classroom.

"Anguó, run as fast as you can and get your father, Déhuã. If Old Mr. Wong feels up to it, his help would be appreciated. Sabbo, will you ride a horse over to Paddymac's farm where our men are working and tell them to meet us at the MacGregor farm? Lindsay, harness the two horses in the dray. Bring any big ropes you can find – also, a shovel, an axe, and timber saws. Cabri, come with me to collect blankets, clean rags, the medicine kit, and my sewing tin. When we have those things will you fetch several stout pieces of flat timber for me? Cai, look after Maggie and Mrs. MacGregor's children while Shauna continues with what is left of her class." She turned to Shauna. "Will you stay and look after this lot?"

Shauna nodded.

After half an hour of flurried activity, Mrs. MacGregor, Mary, Lindsay, and Old Mr. Wong with his son and grandson rode in the dray. The MacGregor horse followed on the lead rein behind. Mary's head swirled with all the possible scenarios awaiting them at the accident site.

Mr. MacGregor lay immobile; the pallor of his face broken by the dribbling blood still seeping from a head wound. A large branch of the newly fallen tree pinned his left leg to the ground. His axe lay not far away. Relief flowed through Mary when she saw her husband and the other Emerald Flats men had arrived. The sound of the timber-saw screeched back as forth as Paddymac and Shamus reduced the log into a more manageable size. The other men struggled to reduce the vibrations exacerbating the pain and damage to the man's wounded leg. Mary, with Old Mr. Wong, assessed and discussed the head and leg wounds. The injured man did not open his eyes or move. Once she cleaned the head wound, Mary pulled the edges of the skin together and began to sew. She then tore strips of clean linen. These were used to cover and secure the poultice Old Mr. Wong provided. They turned their attention to Mr. MacGregor's left leg now free of the tree branch. It was surely broken. Mary and Old Mr. Wong agreed it did not appear to be out of alignment and the skin had only an abrasion on the surface. With care, Mary selected two of the most appropriate pieces of timber, padded them with many linen rags and placed one on either side of the affected leg. These reached from the top of the leg to the ankle. With the help of Shamus, Mary began to wind more strips of linen around the leg and timber splints using more padding over the bony protuberances. Mr. MacGregor began to groan. He looked about with dazed eyes. His crying wife fell to the ground beside him, holding him as best she could.

"I think we could lift him onto the dray now. We'll need to take him into Home Hill and try to get him across the river to the doctor in Ayr. The railwaymen may be able to take him over on the railway hand-trolley. But that will only be if they have completed the repairs after the January floods. If not, we could try the dray-crossing further down the river. I doubt if it is passable yet; we may need the barge," suggested Mary.

"No doctors. I don't want any doctors," croaked the wounded man. "My wife'll care for me at my house."

No amount of advice would convince the man otherwise. Mary arranged with Mrs. MacGregor to leave all but her oldest child at Emerald Flats until the father's condition improved. Mary and Old Mr. Wong promised to return the following day.

The men carried the man into his hut where they lay him on a horse-hair mattress dragged from the bed to the floor to provide a firm base.

5/5/18

Dear Mark,

You asked me to look out for a farm nearby that might come up for sale and would be suitable for Shauna and yourself. The chappie next door had the misfortune of receiving a broken leg and head injury earlier this year. When I talked to him last week, he mentioned he may have to sell up if he doesn't improve. Gabby, Haddi, Paddymac and I have been able to get a few acres of cane planted for him to help carry him through next year. We hope to be able to assist him at crushing time with his cane cutting which will give him a small income this year. He promised to let me know first if he feels he has to leave his farm. If this occurs, I'll notify Mr. Chiswell as you requested. I haven't breathed a word of this to Shauna. If it does come about it'll be a lovely surprise for her; she would be so happy to have a place not far from her mother's home.

Innisfail, north of Townsville, had a severe cyclone in March. They're still trying to pull things together. The rivers were flooded right down the coast from Cairns to Mackay, according to the papers.

We're reading our boys on the Western Front are doing us proud. The paper says our forces are under Australian leadership. A good thing, surely. You and your mates in the Light Horse can be proud of your efforts taking Jerusalem, Jericho, and raiding over the Jordon River.

Shauna and Maggie are doing well. That little one of yours is as sharp as a tack. I suppose Shauna has already told you Thelma and Paddymac had their second child a few weeks ago. They called him George Henry McIntyre, I understand.

May God keep you safe.

With kind regards,

Shamus.

Mary enjoyed the trip each week to the MacGregor farm where she gave Bridget MacGregor a helping hand. She had come to admire this quiet hard-working woman who kept a tidy hut, obviously fed her children, and ensured their clothes were clean and mended. Mary could not help but comment on the needlework of the clothes the family wore. It was exceptional.

"My mother was a dressmaker and she taught me the art," was Bridget MacGregor's explanation. "My most prized possession is her old sewing machine."

Lindsay had accompanied Mary today and was out chopping wood with young Robbie, the six-year-old, who had been doing a fair job with an axe made for a man. Mr. MacGregor, with the wooden home-made crutch by his side, sat on a seat in the sun outside the back door offering advice.

"How's Mr. MacGregor been keeping?" Mary asked Bridget as they pummelled dough for the bread making.

"Jimmy's been improving every day but he does get bad headaches quite often," was the concerned reply. "I wish he'd go see the Doctor, but he won't. He says 'twas the doctors killed his father. Mind you, the man had been smashed up very badly by a charging bull. He was all but dead before they were able to fetch the doctor to him."

The four-year-old, Ian, came in carrying several small logs the older boys had chopped for the stove while the two girls, Anna at two years and Margaret, just able to walk, played in the corner with some wooden pegs.

"Mary, I've appreciated all the help you and your family have given us. I wish there was something we could do in return," Bridget spoke with concern.

"Bridget, we never know what may be in front of us and who knows, one day we could be calling on you for assistance," reassured her new friend.

27/6/18

Dear Lindsay,

I think I may have died and come back as a pig wallowing around in these wet muddy trenches in the Somme Valley. The German offensive started about two or three months ago and we've seen some torrid fighting. Our lads are to be commended on holding the Huns at Dernacourt and Hurbertene. They saved the day by taking the Villers Bretonneux and have put a spoke in the wheel of the Hun's advance. Many prisoners were taken.

We saw one of those newer tanks they've been talking about, with the swivel turret. Those things are so large. Hopefully, we'll see them in action here soon, on our side, of course.

The weather's warmer these days, except when it rains which makes everything miserable again. You can tell your family neither William nor I had frostbite problems during the winter thanks to the warm socks, balaclavas, gloves, and flannelette singlets they've been sending.

It must be terrible for the family on the neighbouring farm who has the man of the place incapacitated after a tree fall. He'll be very grateful, I'd think, for the help your family has given him. I'd a good laugh at your telling of the busters from the horses you've been learning to break in. We've all had a few of those in our time.

Did I tell you William's mate Bruiser took some shrapnel in the chest? I'm not sure how he's doing at the moment.

Keep the letters coming, they're most welcome.

With kind regards from James and William.

The pounding of the horses' hooves was nothing to the pounding in Mark's skull. Blood ran down the side of his face and his neck. An umbrella of thick, red blood fanned out around his shoulders with every thrust of his body as he swayed in the saddle. Grit filled his eyes with the sand, dust, and sweat of those riders galloping ahead and beside him. The brim of his hat flapped constantly against his shoulder; torn when the bullet cleaved a path along the side of his skull removing an ear in the process. Hands and knees unconsciously gripped the reins and belly of the brave horse. When the animal lifted over the enemy trench, Mark's legs clenched the saddle more tightly. A bullet tore through the Waler's heart and guts. The horse was dead before he fell. Mark went with him to the ground to land curled up within the protection of the body of his horse, the reins still firmly clasped in dirty, bloodied hands.

5/11/18

My Dearest Husband, Mark,

We are so excited here as we read the news of the war. At last, things are going our way. On the Western Front, the Huns are on the run and so it would seem are the Turks in the Middle Eastern Front.

Since Australia received its first official wireless message from the English Prime Minister this September just gone, Lindsay has been seeking all the information on the subject of the wireless. He is fascinated by it all and never stops talking about Mr. Fleming and Mr. Marconi who both had great input to the invention. It's amazing we can get news from so far away in such a short time.

Our House of Representatives has passed a Bill to introduce preferential voting which will be similar to that in Victoria and Western Australia.

Pa has just called out to tell us that the Turks have sued for peace. Mark, my darling Mark, I can hardly believe it; surely, they'll be sending you all home soon.

Maggie will be so excited. She cannot understand how young Pat has his Daddy living with him and she has not. At bedtime, her doll takes second place, it's your photo she holds to go to sleep. I'm afraid your mother wouldn't approve of our girl who is not a good example of a little lady. She runs around in shorts, a shirt, and a large floppy felt hat on her head.

"Pat can wear them, why can't I?" is her morning argument. It's a major war right here as we do insist, she wears a dress when going to town. One thing's for sure, she'll grow out of her shoes before wearing them out. She runs around all day barefoot; in spite of the bindii-eye burrs. Pa says they don't make leather as good as the soles of her feet.

A terrible thing happened to the MacGregor family last week. It was so sad. Mr. MacGregor had been having worsening headaches since he had the tree fall on him earlier this year. His broken leg had mended although he hobbled around with a limp. One morning he arose and went outside to cut some cane when Bridget, his wife who had been milking the cow, heard a terrible loud cry of anguish. Looking up she noticed her husband holding his head as he fell to the ground. He was dead. She sent young Robbie over to ask for our help. Mr. MacGregor has been buried in the Home Hill Cemetery. Poor Bridget is devastated although she remains stoic. As she said, she has to be strong for the children's sake. One wonders what will become of them, although Bridget is an excellent dressmaker so she may be able to obtain enough work to feed her family. It'll be sad for the older boy if they lose the farm.

Maggie is looking forward to her birthday. Pa has promised her a horse of her own. Paddymac has been showing Lindsay how to break in the young horses this year and they've picked out a gentle-natured one for her. She rides big old Bess with such confidence; she must be going to be a horse rider like her father. Here's the little miss stomping up the stairs now. I wonder what mischief she has got herself into this time. Yesterday she managed to break most of the day's eggs, looking for the chickens inside. Curiosity is not a bad thing, I guess.

Bye for now my love, my life, God keep you safe until your return. All our love from Shauna and Maggie.

Shauna's hand paused with the pen-nib held over the ink bottle. Should she mention they have not had any mail from him in nearly five months? Maybe it was only the mail service held up somewhere. Mark might not appreciate her nagging if they were under pressure on the battlefield. She lay the pen down.

"Dear God, keep him safe," she begged.

Chapter Eighteen

Repatriation

Thelma's scream brought everyone at the Emerald Flats homestead rushing to the old kitchen where they found her jumping up and down with glee. A smile split Paddymac's face as he held the horse's head. The baby, George, slept undisturbed in his basket in the dray. Young Pat and Maggie stood nearby, wide-eyed.

"The war is over. We heard in town this morning. It's over, over, over. May we never see such a thing like that again?"

Tears poured down Shauna's cheeks as she held tightly to her mother.

"Thank God. Thank God," she kept repeating over and over.

Uncle Michael and Shamus clasped each other's hands. They shook them up and down again and again. The older children exploded from the classroom. They jigged about slapping each other on the back. It was not long before the Wong family was over to join in the celebration.

"We heard news at sugar-mill today. In town, everyone out in the streets, laughing and crying. People hugged complete strangers. It's something special to celebrate. I sent Anguó over to tell Harry and his family," reported Curley.

"I'll put the billy on for a cuppa," said Mary. "Maybe we could add a little something stronger for the men, purely for medicinal purposes," she added with a grin. "All this excitement may make them ill."

Jordon Valley.

With great trepidation, Mark opened the one eye not covered with the dirty linen bandage. His body shuddered in agony. He snapped the eye shut. He lay still; spread out across his bed-roll, too fearful to stir his constant companion of many days. Pain. Vaguely he remembered the doctor telling him the armistice had been signed. He remembered hearing men celebrating during the night but the orderly's painkillers thickened his senses as well as dulled the ache in his head.

"You awake, McIvor?"

Mark recognized the voice of Snowy Lawson, his close chum of the past weeks. He lay doggo – too lethargic to respond. The heat in the tent was becoming uncomfortable. He figured the sun must be high in the sky. His one and a half ears picked up the sound of the horses snorting and stamping outside. Before the last battle-charge which had laid him low, he would have enjoyed this usually gentle, pleasant sound but in recent days the Walers seemed to snort and stamp with unnecessary gusto.

That dammed whistling. The next irritation to reverberate like a ricocheting bullet around and around inside his skull. He knew this sound put Snowy Lawson outside boiling a billy of tea. Snowy's constitution baffled all the men. Snowy could drink any man under the table at night and be up first light each morning serenading, with his tuneless whistle, those who would prefer to catch the last few seconds of sleep. Once again Mark tried to open one eye. His blurred vision picked out the lads nearest him who were draped half on and half off their bedrolls in a disorganized mess. Mark dragged himself into the sitting position and held his head as it threatened to lift off his shoulders. He envied his mates scattered about the tent. The pain of their hangovers would be forgotten by lunchtime but Mark knew the pain from his wounds was to be with him for weeks, maybe months or longer, according to the last report from his doctor.

Not unlike the hungover drunks beside him, he managed to coerce his legs up to his chest before he draped his armpits over his knees leaving his hands dangling down at his feet, still secured in their boots. His throbbing head sagged from the neck. Determination prodded him to make his way upright and out of the tent where he attempted to pour himself a pannikin of tea.

"Here, mate, I'll get that for you. Go sit on the log over there. I'll bring it to you."

"I can do it myself," snapped Mark to his friend Snowy. Mark remembered the words from the Major; was that yesterday or the day before? *If you can look out for yourself, we can get you on an early demobilization back to Australia. If not, you'll remain in a military hospital for who knows how long.*

Snowy did not take offence. He knew the pressure on his friend to get home to Australia as soon as possible.

Ben Parch was the next to brave the glare of the sun. He shook his head in disbelief at the sight of Snowy, squatting on his haunches, sipping hot tea from a dirty pannikin.

"How on earth do you do it?" Ben asked.

"Och, now lad. Where I come from, last night was just a little warm-up for the real thing," laughed the white-haired partly dressed trooper.

"Don't ever let me participate in the real thing then," requested Ben as he also squatted down to drink his first cup of the day. "I see you've stewed this tea as usual. I need a knife and fork to cut it."

"Grumbling about my cooking now, are you? They provide us with such poor-quality tea leaves I have to stew them up to give the tea a touch of flavour," grinned Snowy. "Do you think we should start nudging the lads awake soon? Full parade's at midday. They promised to tell us what the plans are for our return to Australia. No-one'll want to miss that, I'm sure." He looked over at Mark but there was no acknowledgment from that direction. "They'll probably tell us more of the fate of our horses."

Another body stumbled out through the tent flap. A gravelly voice joined the conversation.

"My cousin swears it's true. They're planning to kill off all those animals in poor condition and sell the better-quality ones to the locals. He overheard the Brass talking about it at a meeting. They, in their arrogance, think he, being a minion, is too stupid to understand anything."

Mark groaned as his head lifted upon hearing this news of their beloved Walers.

"They wouldn't dare. How could they?" He mumbled.

Snowy interrupted. "God alone knows what would happen to our brave Walers if sold here. Human life's held dirt cheap so I fear for that of an animal. A poor reward for all they gave us. Some of the horses may get to go home but not many. Apparently, we can't afford their fare back to Australia. Some of the lads are planning to take their mounts for a trip out to the desert and give them a quick and painless end there, rather than put them through what may happen if left behind."

Nearly three months later, with the North Queensland sun beating down upon a dusty track, tears blurred his vision as Mark eased his body off the back of the dray to open the gate leading into Emerald Flats. The pain was partially to blame but that had become a constant companion these days. It was the feeling of coming home which flooded his heart. A groan escaped his lips as he returned to his seat on the dray.

He had been lucky to catch a lift with Sam the carrier who had a load to deliver to Uncle Michael today. Mark remained silent as they followed the track. He felt himself choke up as the familiar sights came into view. Sam never said a word. He had delivered a few boys to their homes in recent weeks and appreciated the emotional turmoil churning inside them.

From the front verandah of the big house, Shauna first noticed the rising dust before Sam's dray emerged, approaching via the front track.

I wonder who that is he has with him, she thought. Never, for a moment, did she expect it to be Mark. Not having heard from her husband for over six months, she had reluctantly assumed he was either killed in action or missing in action and it was just a case of wait for the black-trimmed government letter. She had stopped chasing the mail from the Wong boys when they returned from their trips to town. She now avoided their arrival, rather than face another disappointment.

When the stranger climbed down from the dray at the homestead gate, Shauna recognized Mark despite his uniform sagging from a withered frame. She stared; disbelieving. A groan rolled up her throat from deep inside her. The pounding in her chest stole her breath. The mats, which she had been shaking out over the verandah rail, dropped from her nerveless fingers. Tentatively, her feet moved down the first three steps until her mind caught up with what her eyes were telling her. At the moment of acknowledgement, Shauna flew down the remaining steps and raced across the yard. Just as she was about to throw her arms around him, her feet skidded to a stop. Her eyes opened wide. Her face turned white. An involuntary gasp burst through her lips when the sight of the horrific scars on the right side of his head, partially hidden by his hat, came into view.

"Sorry, my dear, about the scars. Not the man you packed off to war, I'm afraid." Mark shrugged.

"Oh, Mark, I'm so sorry. You must have been through hell. Why didn't you tell me? I've been so worried. Does it still hurt? You've lost so much weight," she stuttered as a million questions flooded her mind.

Tears streamed down her face as Mark pulled her gently into his side with his left arm. He struggled to maintain his composure.

"I think I'd like to forgo all the homecoming and go upstairs and lie down if you don't mind."

A cold chill swept over his hot body as he lay still; his eyes shut but not quite awake. Mark sensed the eyes watching him. He felt the Turk lining up the gunsights to take the shot. He was surprised at how intense small sensations became when one's life was about to end: the heat pressing on his skin, the rivulets of sweat running from his armpits, the weight of his clothes touching his body, and the hard ground. *Wait, something's not right. This isn't hard ground I'm lying on.* Slowly he opened his eyes. Mark started a little, in shock, as he gazed into a set of big blue eyes peeping above the mattress. Right beside the first set of big blue solemn eyes was another set of big blue solemn eyes both in freckled faces under identical droopy felt hats. Both heads were supported by pairs of not-so-clean little hands which in turn rested on their forearms lying on the side of the bed.

"We didn't wake you, Daddy," said Maggie, "we were very quiet. Mummy said you didn't have to get up early today. Why do you think that is? We all get up early because Ganma says it's a waste of

God's day to laze in bed," went on the first child. "Mummy said I wasn't to wake you but I snuck Pat up the front steps to show him my real Daddy was still here and not gone off again to that wicked war. We showed Uncle Michael how to feed the goats and Lindsay milked the cranky one with the baby. Aunty Thelma will take some over to her place today. Mummy said she may get me a sister one day but we had to wait for you to come home. Can I have a sister now? I think I'd rather a brother. Why did we have to wait for you to come home? When can I have a brother?"

With each spoken word the throbbing in his head intensified. He clamped his hands on either side of his skull attempting to subdue the agony. He swallowed.

"Bugger off," Mark growled. As soon as the words left his mouth, he regretted them. They did nothing to relieve his headache. Instead, his discomfort was twofold, as guilt bored its way into his heart. Like a hot poker.

Shauna found Pat playing in the dirt under the house, building miniature irrigation ditches that he filled with water from an old jam tin.

"Where's Maggie?" It was unusual to find the two separated on those days when Thelma or Paddymac brought the boy to visit.

"She crying. She told me to bugger off."

Shauna gasped. Where had the child heard such a word? Thelma would never tolerate such language.

"Where's she crying, Pat?" Shauna struggled to bite her tongue and investigate the swear word another time. She wanted to discover what had Maggie so upset.

"In the henhouse."

Anxiety niggled at Shauna's mind as she made her way to find her daughter. Something about this situation felt odd; could Mark be responsible in any way? When she found Maggie and learnt how Mark had dismissed her in such a manner, Shauna's temper stirred from deep within her. The flush of her face almost matched the colour of her hair. She bit her tongue and breathed slowly as she held her daughter close. Her mind swirled as she struggled with how she should respond. *How dare he,* flashed like lightning strikes in front of her eyes over and over again.

"Maggie, remember I told you how your daddy had been wounded at the war. The bullet hurt things inside his head and makes him say things he doesn't really mean. I'm sure he didn't mean to use a swear word." Shauna wanted to cry when she watched the expression in the tear-filled eyes of the child. "Perhaps it might be best if you only visit him when I'm with you. What do you think? We just have to remember he is unwell."

The dark pigtails bounced on her shoulders as Maggie nodded her head.

"Come with me, we'll go and explain this to Pat." Shauna and Maggie crawled out from inside the hen-house and into the sunshine. Shauna wrapped her arm around her daughter's shoulders.

A Camp in France.

"Once we get back to Australia, I'll never go anywhere near snow or ice again," James promised his brother, William, as they warmed their hands on a billy of tea.

"Has anyone heard for sure when it'll be – us going back to Australia, I mean? The rumours fly as thick and fast around here as the bullets did only a couple of weeks ago," answered William.

"Can't be too soon for me; I hate this cold," stated James. "I suppose you'll be counting the days until you get back to your little lady at Leaning Rock," he teased.

The blush filled William's face. "You bet. I just posted her a letter yesterday. When we get back, I'm going to ask her to marry me. What about you, what are your plans? I'll expect you to be my Best Man if she accepts."

A vision of the beautiful Shauna filled his head but James shook it away and said gruffly, "Oh, I don't know, probably go search for that fortune we used to talk about."

William gave his brother a long and searching stare. He had a fair idea of how James felt about their older brother Mark's, wife. He had hoped after four years, James would have found someone new but then the trenches of war were not exactly the places for romance. There had been a nurse they met last year, who had taken a shine to James, but his brother remained unaffected by her attentions.

"You'll stay at Leaning Rock for a while though, won't you? That's if they'll have us, of course."

"Yeah, I guess it'll be a place to start," was James's reply.

"Have we decided yet if we should go over to Ireland and visit Mum and Dad, while we're so close? The Major reckons it'll be some weeks before we get a berth out of here – maybe even months." William deferred to his brother.

"Should be better than sitting around in this camp waiting to catch the Spanish Flu – count me in. Don't want that Flu to do what the Huns couldn't do before I ever get back to Australia."

Four months passed before James and William arrived on the Australian shores. Soldiers, some with bandages still around unhealed wounds, some leaning on crutches, canes or mates but all carrying their kitbags slung around their shoulders, shuffled down the ship's plank.

"The war's over. Who can believe it? It seems a lifetime since we left these shores." The awe in the man's voice hung over all who heard him speak. James looked out over the cheering crowd spread across the wharf from where they tossed streamers, flowers, and confetti.

At the bottom of the gangplank, James turned back and saluted the ship and its crew before joining the river of uniforms. Having spent four years waiting for someone to give orders, the men hung about with little complaint waiting for their last orders to be given. James sat with a few mates in the shade of the shed awning. They discussed their future. The conversation sparkled with laughter and jokes. As usual, it was a hot day. Whether summer or winter, every day is a hot day in Townsville, James remembered.

Fifty yards away, along the jetty near a large pile of cargo crates, a group of men including William, cheered and laughed around the circle where a two-up game was in full swing. Above their heads swayed a large netted load of cargo being craned from a ship to the jetty. A loud crack like a heavy weapon-fire echoed along the waterfront. All eyes lifted. Some saw the incident unfold, others did not. A chain snapped on the crane's load. Heavy machinery smashed into the cargo crates. These crashed to the ground on top of the group of soldiers. Yells erupted. Men circled the scene.

The noise attracted James's attention. He jumped up and ran to the edge of the building where he was able to see out onto the open wharf. He took in the situation immediately. With dread in his heart, he raced over to where the cargo was scattered about like huge toys tossed out of a baby giant's cot. Three soldiers were seen crawling out of the heap with the help of mates. They appeared to have only minor wounds. James's eyes searched for William's familiar figure.

He was not among those standing. Frantically James, with the help of many others began to remove some of the lighter crates, endeavouring not to do more injury to anyone trapped underneath. Orders, issued by a newly arrived officer, rang out above the hullabaloo. The crane was directed to assist with the removal of the heavier crates. The replacement chains creaked, the pulleys screeched, the timbers groaned as the last crate began to lift from the accident site. Bloodied legs first appeared protruding from the broken wooden edges of the crate. As the load rose into the air, a shattered body was revealed, in increments.

"Jesus, God, he's unrecognizable."

"He's smashed up like minced meat."

James forced his way through the crowd of men. With shaking hands, he dug into the bloodied top pocket and removed the dead soldier's papers. Amongst them, he found the miniature leather envelope identical to the one he carried in his own pocket. The writing on the front was in his mother's hand. He did not have to look any further; he knew what he would find inside. It was the ring of his mother's hair which she had plaited with so much patience, one for each of the three brothers going to Australia years before.

"This is my brother, William McIvor," he told the Commanding Officer who arrived shortly after. The words spilled out without meaning. James did not comprehend. It felt like he was watching this horror happening to someone else.

Two days later, he buried his brother at the Townsville cemetery. His only thought was to catch a train to anywhere, he didn't care, just anywhere. Duty demanded three chores to be completed before he could escape. He must write to his parents and visit Mark at Emerald Flats; that's if his brother was home yet. The last thing to do was deliver the news, along with William's ring, purchased in Belfast, to the young lass at Leaning Rock Station. Once his obligations had been completed he just wanted this big country to swallow him up.

It was Shamus who arrived at the house-compound gate at the same time as James hauled on the reins of the horse which he had on loan from the Home Hill blacksmith.

"I'll get it for you," Shamus called. He eyed off the stranger. There was something familiar about the man. And then it came to him; this was one of Mark's brothers. The changes made in a man over four years of war made it difficult to identify someone he'd only met a few times before.

"Thanks, Mr. Doolan," James rode through the open gate before jumping to the ground.

The men reached out to shake hands. "Tell me now, which one are you. James or William?" Shamus thought it best to find out which brother he was talking to.

"James, Sir." James drew a deep breath and for the first time acknowledged out loud, "William was killed in an accident on the Townsville wharf the day we arrived back." His throat tightened with each word. In barely a whisper he asked, "Is Mark back yet?"

Shamus lifted his hat and scratched his head. "James, how terrible for you. Having spent all those years in the thick of it, thinking you're both through it all, then to have William die at the final hurdle must be hard to take in. I'm so sorry."

James nodded. The voice of Lindsay running over from the house brought his head back up. His lips struggled with a smile.

"Hello, Lindsay, it's good to see you again. Thanks for all your letters and parcels. I hope you said thanks to your Mum and her friends for us."

Lindsay grinned. He looked about him, he looked down the track. "Where's William?"

James struggled to speak. Shamus answered in his stead.

"William was in an accident on the Townsville wharf. He has been killed."

"Oh ... I'm sorry, James; that is terrible. I ..."

Shamus again spoke up. "Now, Lindsay, how about you go and give Uncle Michael a hand with those new horses?" When Lindsay looked like he might argue the point, Shamus frowned. "Now; and take James's horse and settle it in the stable, lad." He was thinking it might be best if only he took James up to tell Mark the bad news. With Mark's unpredictable moods of late, one could never be sure how the man might react. It could be something as small as Lindsay's presence which could set him off in a totally irrational manner.

"I'll see you later, James. There's so much to show you here." Lindsay called over his shoulder.

James lifted his hand in acknowledgment.

"Right, lad, I'll take you to Mark but you need to know a few things first. I don't know if you knew he was wounded bad in the last charges the Light Horse made." Shamus paused. "We hadn't heard from him in the last six or more months."

"After the armistice, we heard he had been wounded but they didn't say how bad; only that he was to be shipped home." James found his voice again.

"Well, it was pretty bad, James. A bullet nearly took his head off. The right side of his head has some horrific scarring. It's the damage inside his head causing constant agonizing pain which gives him the greatest trouble. He spends most days in his bed on the verandah. His nightmares and mood swings can be very frightening for the women."

"Good heavens; no one mentioned Mark was going through anything like this."

"I thought it best to tell you face to face when you got home. James, I'm sorry, I don't know how Mark will react to this news of William."

James stood in deep thought for some moments. He sighed. "I'd better go up and face the music. He'll most likely blame me. The last thing he said as we parted ways was, 'Look out for our little brother'. Seems I haven't done that very well."

Shamus rested his hand on James's shoulder. "William came through the war safely. You cannot be held responsible for an accident on the wharf. Remember, after four years of fighting in terrible conditions, William, like yourself, became a man. A man's fate is his own."

The two men made their way over to the big house. James knew the churning in his belly was not only for his concern at Mark's reactions to the loss of William. A part of him wanted so much to see the beautiful face of Shauna but he was terrified of what it might do to him when he did. On the other hand, he may have built everything out of proportion and her presence won't affect him at all.

Shamus led James out onto the verandah where Mark had set up residence on the corner near the room where Shauna and Maggie slept. At his first sight of his brother, James was glad Shamus had warned him as to the changes in Mark. Clothes hung from the shrunken frame. The usual brilliant blue eyes were dulled. The unshaven face carried remnants of foodstuffs. He sagged from his position on the side of the bed. Bare feet rested on a woven mat.

"Shamus, where's Shauna? She should be back home by now. I don't know why she has to go visiting at Paddymac's house all the time. She should be here looking after me." He never even mentioned the presence of the man at Shamus's side.

Shamus never responded to Mark's outburst. He'd heard it all before, repeatedly.

"Mark, I've your brother, James, here to see you."

Mark's head slowly moved towards the newcomer. "You've changed. You look okay though. Lucky you. Where's William? Why isn't he with you? I told you to look after him." He grabbed his head in both hands and groaned.

Shamus retreated with the words, "I'll stick the kettle on."

James made every effort not to reveal his shock at the sight and sound of his brother. Thoughts swirled in his head. How was he going to handle this? He'd known things would be bad but it looked like it might be a lot worse than he'd anticipated. Maybe it's best to just say everything outright and stand by for the crossfire. And that is what he did.

He told Mark about the visit they had made to see their parents. James reported how everyone in Ireland sent him their best regards. He told of their ship journey back to the Townsville wharf. At this point, he began to stutter. He stopped speaking and drew a breath.

"Well, come on then, hurry up, I've got a flaming headache. You always did take forever to tell a story. I just want to know where's William."

James felt the resentment burn his guts. He swallowed the first words threatening to explode from his mouth.

"Mark, there was an accident on the Townsville wharf. Our brother was killed when the crane dropped its load on top of him."

Mark's body stopped its impatient twitching; not a muscle moved. He raised his head and hatred filled the blue eyes as they bored into James's eyes.

"I told you to look after him. That's all you had to do. You couldn't even do that simple task properly."

James turned on his heel and retreated along the verandah.

"Get out of here, you cur; and don't bother to come back."

James was all for leaving down the back stairs but Shamus took his arm and led him into the kitchen. "A strong cup of tea and a scone is always good after a dose of Mark's bad mood. Don't take anything personally. He can't help himself. It's just the brain damage talking."

James was in two minds about whether to stop for tea. He could sink a pannikin of tea for sure, he may be lucky enough to catch a glimpse of Shauna too.

"Shauna has taken Maggie over to a friend's place. Thelma and Paddymac have a boy not much younger than Maggie. Maggie and Pat are a pair of rogues when together but good kids really; Shauna sees to that. Shauna teaches classes here on Emerald Flats. Besides her brother Lindsay, her pupils come from a Chinese family, the Wongs who farm vegetables here and a native family, the Bobangles who work with Uncle Michael." He passed the plate of scones to his guest. "More tea?"

James gave his first real smile for a long time. "My stomach has shrivelled after years of bully beef. I don't think I can eat anything else. It sounds like a community you have living here."

At that moment, they heard the footsteps on the stairs and the small voice complaining. "Mum why did we have to come back home so soon. Pat and I were busy building bridges over Paddymac's drains."

"I don't think he wanted bridges over his drains, Maggie. You have to learn to ask before you go off half-cocked."

"What's that mean, Mum?"

Shauna was relieved of the duty of answering when she stepped into the kitchen to see her father sitting at the table with the man whom she visited in her dreams, more than she knew was healthy. He had grown taller and grey hairs were visible but she knew how those eyes could trip her pulses. Or was she only thinking so much of him because she was lonely for a man to love? She lowered her eyes when he stood to greet her.

"Hello, Shauna." James' voice struggled through the spasm in his throat.

When James told them, he was planning on exploring the country as soon as he had been out to Leaning Rock Station to deliver the news to Bella, William's intended, Shamus wanted to know how he planned to travel.

"I thought I might see if the blacksmith in Home Hill has a horse to sell me." He snorted with laughter. "Definitely, not the one I'm on now. I swear it has one leg three inches shorter than all the other legs."

"You're family, James. We can't let you take your chances on a dodgy horse from a seller you don't know. We've a few horses just arrived from out Charters Towers way. A good-looking lot too, if I say so myself. A couple of them are of the Waler breed; the same horses they used in the Light Horse divisions. We'll give you a fair price, too. You can bed down here overnight; there's plenty of room in Uncle Michael's hut. I'd invite you to stay in the big house but who knows what Mark may make of that after his earlier attitude. It'll give you time this afternoon to examine the animals."

Shauna jumped up from her seat. "I'd better go and see if Mark wants anything."

When she came to the verandah corner, Mark had moved to the canvas squatter's chair at the end of his bed. He sat staring into space with tears running unchecked down his face. She stood still, not wanting to disturb him. He looked so unhappy. Her heart felt as though it was breaking. It all seemed impossible to believe Mark had come to this.

The apricot glow of the pending dawn filled the eastern sky. Standing at the compound gate, Michael and James waved to

Shamus, Gabby and Haddi as they left with the cane dray on their way to Paddymac's farm.

"The cane harvest's in full swing. They'll be at it until dark tonight. Mary and I'll take the small dray into town to collect supplies later. We'll drop that horse off to the blacksmith on our way, James."

"Thanks, for everything, Mr. Doolan. I'd best be on my way, too." James's glance when he swung up into the saddle did not miss the pale face, fanned by its auburn halo, of the slim figure standing at the top of the front steps. The thump in his chest caught his breath as he lifted his hand in a salute. He patted the lump in his shirt. "And thanks for the pup, Mr. Doolan. There'll be many strangers camped out along the tracks, I should imagine. Most of them will be harmless but one can never tell. A guard dog may be useful."

Michael watched the lone figure cantering along the front track. As much as he would have liked the man to stay with them, he recognized the look of heartache deep in James's eyes. There was the pain for the loss of his brothers, but the look Michael recognized was a different ache. Michael knew the look well. He'd seen it in the barber's mirror, on those occasions when he chose to have his hair and beard trimmed, for nigh on fifty years. His love for Jessica never faded over all those years, just as he knew James's love for Shauna would never fade also.

Shauna lifted her hand when she saw James glance up and wave as he mounted his new horse. The weight of her heart held her arm back. Guilt, love, pity, regret all added to her despondency. The voice from the other end of the verandah sawed at the air like a blunt knife.

"He's gone then. Good. Why he should get off scot-free, I don't know."

Shauna wiped the moisture at her eyes. "Can I get you some breakfast, Mark?"

"Some fella's comin', boss," called Ding. "His horse belonga Old Ned by the looks, hey." Work at the Leaning Rock yards paused while the group of men watched the approaching rider. "Ya know, he sits a horse bit like that James fella, hey." Ding had the eyes of a hawk.

"It's not likely to be James without William by his side," commented Matthew Littlewood.

When the rider pulled the horse to a standstill, they were surprised to see it was James McIvor without his brother. It was the hollowed, shadowed eyes with the unfathomable stare Matthew noticed first. Those eyes had seen more than their fair share of devastation, sorrow and tragedy. As James dismounted, Matthew also noticed the loss of physical condition of the lad; who was not a lad anymore, but a man.

Once greetings were over, Matthew led James to where a billy of tea sat near the hot coals of a scant fire. Over a pannikin of brew, James explained to Matthew he had come to give them the news of William's death. He related the tragedy on the Townsville wharf shortly after he and William had disembarked. James knew William would want Bella to be told by her family, those who loved her, not just words on a cold piece of paper.

Matthew shook his head in disbelief. His heart filled with anguish for his daughter who had been dancing and singing around the place for days anticipating the arrival of her beau. He agreed willingly and with understanding, to take on the task.

"Will you please give her this parcel?" James asked as he pulled the leather envelope from his top pocket. "William carried this with him throughout the war and gave me particular instructions to ensure Bella received it if anything happened to him." He delved into his hip pocket and retrieved the little box with the emerald ring. "William bought this in Ireland when we visited our parents before coming home. He bought it especially for Bella."

As James prepared to remount, Matthew asked, "Are you leaving already?" When James nodded, Matthew went on, "Where are you heading, now? You know you'll always have a job here?"

With a shrug of his shoulders, James replied, "Thanks, Mr. Littlewood, but at the moment I don't know what I want. I may head out west. Apparently, there's a large muster beginning out that way. The mind-numbing tailing of thousands of beasts for thousands of miles with thousands of flies may be just what I need right now."

"What about your brother on Emerald Flats?"

"Yes, his name's Mark."

"I have a young lad working here, Akama Bobangle, comes from there. Would you like me to send him down with word of your plans?" asked Matthew.

"Thanks, but I've already delivered the news on my way here." The men shook hands.

Only one thing left he must do and that was to write to his mother. A daunting task.

While Bella helped her mother bake the bread, the lamentation wails drifted up from the blacks' camp down near the creek. Mrs. Littlewood went to find Biddy the Aboriginal helper at the house.

"What's happened, Biddy? What's all the noise about?"

"Old pella man tells someone nearby has died, hey. No pella know who. Just death, hey."

As Bella overheard the conversation, the hairs on the back of her neck rose. A ghastly white infused her face. She knew. She did not know why or how but she knew her William was dead. Maybe the ship he was coming home on was sunk. Maybe he caught the Spanish Flu they were all talking about and he died. She knew in her heart and soul he was dead. Without a word, she washed her hands and walked out of the room. At her bedroom window, she stood and stared outside with unseeing eyes. Her ears followed the Aboriginal lament.

Mrs. Littlewood finished what she was doing before she walked down the hallway to talk with her eldest daughter. The girl's pallor had not gone unnoticed. She felt a sense of foreboding herself.

It's just that continual infernal wailing, she thought and shook her shoulders. She lifted her head. *Now, put a smile on your face; a look of gloom will hardly brighten Bella.* It had been so wonderful to see the happy smiles and hear the joyous singing that had been part of her daughter's days since receiving word of William's impending arrival. *Please, God, give us strength.*

When she walked into the room, Mrs. Littlewood found Bella standing looking through the window out towards the camp from which the wailing floated on the air.

"Bella, what's the matter, dear? You're quite pale and where's that beautiful smile?"

"Oh, Mother, those black fellows are right, you know. Something has happened to William. I just feel it. I know."

Mrs. Littlewood had spent all her life on bush properties. She'd seen many strange aboriginal premonitions proved correct but she didn't want to give any credence to this latest sign. She stood quietly by her daughter's side silently praying until they heard her husband and the workers returning from the cattle yards.

"Your father's home, ready for his tea. Brighten yourself up dear and join us."

"Yes, Mother," replied Bella but she went and lay on her bed instead. She gazed at the ceiling and listened to the dirge of the aboriginal people.

When her husband walked through the kitchen doorway, Mrs. Littlewood knew something was dreadfully wrong. He walked up to her and held her tightly for such a long time. At first, she thought something had happened to the twins but he reassured her they were still safe at his parents' house nearby, learning how to plait whips.

"My dear, I have some dreadful news for our Bella. Her young man, William, has been killed on the Townsville docks. He went through the whole war without a scratch and an accident on home soil has taken his life. His brother dropped in to tell us."

The tears welled in her eyes and almost stole her voice. "Matthew, that's terrible. Matthew …" but Mrs. Littlewood could not go on.

Her husband continued. "James is pretty lost; devastated, I think. I invited him to stay but he wanted to get away; he doesn't know where to. I think he just wants to be alone for a while. Will you come with me to tell Bella?" He lifted his head and asked, "What's that blasted wailing coming from the blacks' camp?" Matthew was usually a man of few words. A long speech such as this was certainly out of character.

Mrs. Littlewood swallowed hard and held her husband's hands. "Matthew, there's something I need to tell you before we see Bella. The wailing is the old people's lamentation of death. It's been going on for hours. As soon as she heard it, Bella went pale and disappeared into her room. She's not been out since. She believed it foretold of bad news relating to her William. Oh, God, and now it has. I'll never understand how the aboriginals know."

"But how did she know?" Matthew's brow furrowed.

Mrs. Littlewood shrugged.

When her parents entered the room, they found their elder daughter recumbent on the bed, gazing at the ceiling, dry-eyed. She did not move or change her expression on hearing her father's news.

She could not even cry. She just felt numb. Her father drew the leather envelope from his pocket and gave it to her.

"William carried this with him all through the war. He gave James strict instructions to see you received it in the event of his death." He reached into his other pocket and held out the little box. "This, William bought in Belfast to give to you."

She did not notice her mother and father as they quietly left the room. Bella idly ran her thumb back and forth over the dark stains on the oilskin wrap. Slowly she began to unwrap the folds. One small envelope had BELLA'S LOCKS written in capital letters; another had MOTHER'S PLAITED HAIR. Bella had never seen the ring made of plaited hair before. She gazed in amazement at the painstaking handiwork. Her shaking fingers opened the little box where she found a felt sachet containing a gold ring holding a brilliant green emerald stone. *Bella with Love* was inscribed inside the band. At last, the tears began to flow for the loss of a wonderful man, a great friend and a future husband who would have made a perfect father for half a dozen perfect children. A third envelope held a letter addressed to her.

My Dearest Bella,

If you are reading this note then I guess I have not made it home.

I thank you for the constant friendship and love that you have given to me throughout these past years. Your friendship has carried me through some horrendous times. Not a minute goes by, no matter how exhausted I may be when your vision is not in my mind.

Now I am gone. I guess this will make you sad. Remember though my darling girl, there will be a time for mourning but then it will be time to get on with your life.

Please do so with my blessing.

I wish you a fulfilling and happy future.

All my love William.

Huge suffocating sobs engulfed Bella and that was how her mother found her when she brought in tea and toast. Mrs. Littlewood knew there was nothing she could do to make things better; only time would ease the pain. She did the only thing left to her. She hugged her daughter tightly and cried along with her.

Chapter Nineteen

Desolation

Mary walked up the neat pathway. This was her first visit to the new home of Bridgett MacGregor since the death of her husband and the sale of her farm. A worm of guilt wound through her head but it was the men's secret to keep from Shauna, not hers. Mark hardly took any interest these days. She couldn't remember him even going to visit the place he now owned just a stone's throw from Emerald Flats. Hardly had her hand dropped to her side than Bridget herself answered the knock on the door.

Bridgett served tea and biscuits on the landing where she could watch the young ones playing in the thick shade of the fig tree.

"How's the dressmaking going; have you had any customers?" asked Mary.

"Things are a little slow, but three ladies have commissioned dresses and several gentlemen have asked me to repair trousers and coats, so it's a beginning. I have small samples of several materials to show the ladies and pictures of dress patterns I'll make." Bridget was very happy at how things had started and was grateful to Mary whom she knew had encouraged friends from the Red Cross to seek her out.

Their conversation meandered on to the Pneumonic Influenza. Bridget's frown accompanied her relating the concerns she harboured for her children's safety. Since being introduced to Australia by the returning soldiers and other European immigrants after the war, it was still responsible for killing people or at the least making them very ill. Bridget told of how she heard the Ayr hospital had converted the verandahs into isolation wards for those cases too ill to be cared for at home. She offered Mary two newly made cotton masks. It was compulsory to wear masks when in public, she explained. Not many of the country folk had even heard of the new law but in Townsville city, many complied.

Bridget warned Mary the shops were still low in foodstuffs even though the war had been over for more than eight months. They spoke of the ways to make do without a regular supply of the necessities such as flour. The women did not have the added worry of a meat supply because they killed their own on Emerald Flats and Mary ensured Bridget did not go without.

They discussed the issues relating to prices still being so high and the wages being so low. How one could understand but not condone the workers on strike in the transport and the meatworks industries. The terrible riots of last month by the Townsville meatworkers and the resulting response of the police with rifle fire leaving many wounded, were events unheard of until these dramatic days. They both sighed and shook their heads.

A sparkle of satisfaction lit up both the ladies' faces when the subject of the signing of the Treaty of Versailles on the twenty-eighth of June was brought up. Bridget explained where to buy some of the Official Peace Buttons which were introduced to raise money for the Returned Soldiers Appeal. They talked of how Mr. Hughes, the Prime Minister, had gained mandated control of New Guinea and surrounding islands. These had been previously owned by the Germans.

"Oh, Mary, will you give this knitting pattern for a child's jumper to Shauna? I copied it from the People's Friend magazine." Bridget went inside and lifted the sheet of paper from the end of her table.

Before she left, Mary examined the samples and dress patterns Bridget had spoken of. She also commissioned a new dress for herself and another for a maternity frock for Shauna. Her daughter's shape was changing now, with her second pregnancy. Mary removed the piece of paper from her handbag listing Shauna's measurements. Bridget slipped this into a large book sitting beside the old sewing machine. Bridget carefully took Mary's dress measurements before writing the results neatly in her book.

"I see you haven't bought your new treadle machine yet," commented Mary.

Bridget took the pins out of her mouth. "No, I was a little concerned with the economy at the moment so I've put that luxury off until I'm sure my venture will be a success."

Mary was about to put her gloves and hat back on when Bridget asked if she could examine Mary's hat. She smiled as she told Mary the hat had caught her attention on the day when she had first seen Mary dressed in her best clothes.

"My mother used to do a little millinery work and I was thinking I may like to try my hand at some."

While Bridget examined the hat, Mary studied the exquisite stitching on several pairs of gloves the dressmaker had completed.

The October midday sun was hot. Streams of perspiration trickled down Shauna's face. The heat from the oven sent her back and forth seeking the cool water in the waterbag hanging on the post near the kitchen door. The family sat down to their Sunday meal of roast and vegetables with plum duff and custard for dessert. Before sitting to eat, Shauna picked up Mark's tray and delivered it to where he sat on the chair near his bed. Anxiety swallowed her appetite as she watched him pick at his meal.

"Mark, can I help you with that?"

"Just bugger off, woman; I'm not an invalid. You'd like me to drop dead, wouldn't you? Well, I'll not give you that pleasure just yet."

Shauna sighed and bit her tongue before returning to the kitchen table with the others. It was Shauna's turn to pick at her food. What was she to do with Mark? It was obvious the pain in his head was becoming worse; the nightmares certainly were and the pacing of the verandah at night. Shauna knew if she mentioned anything to a doctor, Mark would be extremely displeased.

While Mary and Maggie cleared away the dishes, Shamus spoke to Shauna where she stood at the sink.

"Remember our discussion the other day about the need to send Lindsay somewhere for higher education? Mr. Featherston told me of a new boys' boarding school the church has started in Charters Towers. "Thornburgh" is the name of the college. It opened in June; although the official opening is not until next year. Mr. Ward's the Principal. I have the address to write away for a prospectus. What do you think?"

"That would be a good idea. Lindsay's fourteen now and will need to include more advanced science and mathematics studies if he wishes to make it to University. I'll write a letter for you to send tomorrow, Pa."

Lindsay listened in to their conversation with mixed emotions. It would be exciting to go to a boarding school but a bit daunting also. At least Charters Towers was only a couple of days horse ride away. Travelling on the train would be an adventure in itself.

After contemplating these thoughts for a while, Lindsay remembered the question he wanted to ask Uncle Michael. It was a question he thought wasted on his father. Uncle Michael was always curious about new inventions.

"How would you like to buy a wireless radio, Uncle Michael – when they come to Townsville?"

Lindsay explained what he knew of the wireless experimenter, Mr. Fisk and his work with radio entertainment. Mr. Fiske had been radio broadcasting in Sydney since August.

Michael's white whiskers jiggled up and down as he laughed. "Not silly enough to ask your father then, Boyo? I'm not so sure about the idea myself. There'd be no peace and quiet around here with a stranger's voice going on and on all day."

"You can always turn the switch to shut him up though, Uncle Michael." Lindsay grinned.

The November days were heating up. Clouds filled the skies each afternoon but no rain had fallen for some weeks. From where she worked in the kitchen, Shauna's gaze flew up from some half-prepared pastries. The terror in Maggies' squeal chilled her heart. The pastry roller was tossed aside on the table, left to roll onto the floor with a thud. She raced out through the kitchen doorway shaking her hands to remove the remnants of flour as she did so.

The child barrelled into her mother's arms in the vestibule. Before Shauna could ask, the near five-year-old stuttered out her tale.

"Daddy's sitting on your bed and pointing a gun at his head." She paused as she demonstrated. Maggie swallowed and gulped her tears. "Mummy, you're holding too tight."

Horror exploded across Shauna's face. The fumes of shock and fear infiltrated every corner of the room. Shauna found it difficult to release her arms paralysed with fear.

Mary appeared at the top of the steps. She ran inside and eased the child from her mother's arms. "Go, Shauna, go. Be careful, my darling," she called to her daughter.

Before approaching the bedroom door, Shauna paused; loath to move into the room and discover what awaited her. The final three steps felt more like three miles. She found Mark sitting on the side of the bed. Amidst all her panicked thoughts, Shauna could not help but notice how her husband's clothes hung from his bony body. Tears trickled from his sunken eyes and down his face. The gun now held on his lap in hands white with the force of their grip.

With her mind in turmoil, Shauna wanted to yell the question, "What do you think you're doing, frightening our daughter like this?" But the sight of the pain etched in every furrow of his drawn face brought tears to her own eyes. Looking at him from this angle, she only saw the handsome man he had once been but she knew with only one more step into the room, the twisted mess of thick scars and damaged ear on the other side of his head would become visible. She sat on the bed beside Mark. Tentatively her arm slipped across his shoulder. Having experienced his erratic behaviour since his return from the war, her heart pounded in fear. Was he going to take offence at her approach?

In a voice she hardly recognized, he whispered. "I can't go on, Shauna. I cannot stand the pain or the dreams a moment longer." His deep gulping sobs filled the silence. "I cannot bear to see what I'm doing to you and Maggie."

At a loss on how to help the man she had once loved so much, a man now gone forever it seemed, Shauna's thoughts thrashed around seeking suitable comforting words.

"Mark, I'm so sorry this has happened. I can't hope to understand what you're going through but please can I beg you not to do this again; and certainly, never where Maggie might find you."

On Saturday afternoon, the following week, thunder rumbled continually in the skies around them. The heat and humidity frayed everyone's tempers. Maggie whined at her mother's skirts continuously. Even Mary was heard to swear when the sewing machine broke two needles and knotted her thread three times within a half hour. Dark circles ringed Shauna's eyes. Her tongue felt as if it had been through the cane-tops chop-chop machine. She had bitten it so much in an attempt not to say more than she should to a disgruntled Mark. The raised voices of Shamus and Uncle Michael drifted up from the shed where they were repairing the broken axle on the dray. Occasionally Lindsay's breaking voice was heard making his opinions known. Prickly heat irritated everyone like a singlet-full of cobbler-peg-seeds.

With a tremendous crack of thunder, the heavens released their burden. Sheets of rain fell across the house gardens, pounded on the tin roof, and sent the fowls scurrying for cover. The men stood at the edge of the shed with grins upon their faces. Shauna and Maggie joined Mary near the sewing machine where smiles dissipated all sour humour.

Only Mark did not move where he lay upon his bed. He could not move. The noise of the storm pummelled his head. It prodded every nerve ending into a screaming frenzy. In blessed relief, the pain dragged his mind into oblivion.

When he again returned to consciousness the storm had paused. Mark lifted his eyelids but snapped them shut immediately. Even the dim moonlight was enough to set the bubbling molten lava of pain stirring within his head. Had he been asleep? Whispers drifted out from the room beside him. Were Shauna and Maggie still awake? Or was he only hearing the shuffling leaves in the trees outside? He wanted to call out but the boiling lava lapped at the insides of his skull, it trickled down into his mouth, his nose, his throat, cutting off all sound. Only his thoughts remained to torment his soul.

God, what did I do to deserve this ending? Why could the bullet not have been a fraction to the left? Did I not deserve an honourable death? Mark McIvor, a brave and decent man, a man to be respected, a man of integrity. Was I so bad to merit torture like this? A sickening, cowardly, bitter, man to be hated, despised, or worse, pitied by those I love most.

His Shauna's beautiful eyes never sparkled with love for him anymore. They overflowed with clouds of pity and disappointment. Fear filled the eyes of their beautiful daughter whenever she came near him. How will she remember this stranger; her father?

Had he really sent his brother off as he did? James was never a cur. Why didn't I tell him how much I loved him? Yes, envy was always present but alongside it, love bound us together; ever since we were young bairns foraging for mischief in the neighbourhood.

Pain now drags me down into a sea of regrets. Can I not have that last charge one more time? Let the bullet take me out clean? Don't leave me in this cesspit of pain and misery – a half-life, half-death.

The night felt heavy upon Mark as he forced his feet to the floor. Only his stubborn determination controlled the swirling in his head when he stood upright. Avoiding the squeaky boards, he moved around the verandah to the back door. The movement to bend and pick up his shoes from the floor sent an involuntary groan into the night. Leaning heavily on the railing of the steps he made his way downstairs. At the bottom, he dragged his feet, without socks, into the boots. He wanted so much to sit and give up on his plan, but no; he knew it would be his last chance. He must go on.

At the stables, he found the horses huddling under the awning. All but one animal stamped nervous feet and tossed restless heads. Mark ran his hands lightly down the steady horse's back and over its limbs. The animal snickered. Fumbling hands managed to slip the bridle over the head and settle the saddle in place. Hands that could, not so long ago, prepare a horse for action in a matter of seconds, now took nearly thirty minutes. Using the shoulders of the horse as a prop, Mark led the animal out into the darkening night. Once through the gate, he fought the dark waves of oblivion and lifted into the saddle. Intermittent lightning streaks lit their way west.

Heavy rain and thunder joined the lightning, to add to a filthy night out in the open. The water ran over his body unnoticed. His horse snickered questions to the rider but never failed to obey the orders relayed through Mark's hands and knees. They picked up the pace down a track laced with low branches. Faster and faster, rider and horse thrashed their way through the wet leaves. A loud groan from Mark as he stood upright in the stirrups was swallowed by the noise of the night about them.

"Go, Celtic. Go!" He yelled. "The last charge, Celtic. The last charge!"

Pounding hooves, pounding head, thundering skies, streaks of lightning, and sheets of water crashed in upon Mark as he encouraged the horse to more and more speed. With one arm and knees guiding the animal and the other arm outstretched as if holding a weapon, he rode until the sturdy tree limb removed all pain. His body spun over the back of the horse leaving his right foot in the stirrup. On and on the horse galloped.

Eventually, the horse came to an exhausted stop. It sagged, splay-legged. Its rib cage heaved in an attempt to drag in some oxygen. Despite the earlier rain, blood and debris of the shattered man's skull and its contents lay splattered across the horse's hide and the saddle. The animal trembled with exhaustion and fear.

In the clear skies of the morning, it was here Shamus and Lindsay discovered the gruesome spectacle. Shamus tried to shelter his son from the worst but when Lindsay insisted, he did not push him away. This lad had worked as a man for the past five years. This boy was now a man.

"We can't take Mark back like this, Pa."

"No, you're right, son. Neither your mother nor your sister, particularly so close to her delivery time, needs to see this. I suggest you go back for the dray and a tarpaulin. If you get the chance let Uncle Michael know but try not to let the women or Maggie see you."

Chapter Twenty

Looking Forward

Standing with her back against the sink, Shauna felt detached, even numb. Mary had warned her several times, shock may be delayed. Her mother believed it was nature's way of protecting people; in her case, keeping her strong for Maggie and the baby only two months away. But here it was five days since they had brought what remained of Mark in from the paddock, three days since he was buried in a hurried affair at the Home Hill cemetery, and twenty-four hours since the solicitor had arrived to read the will. At least the death certificate listed the cause of death to be accidental and not suicide which Shauna firmly believed it was. At least this will be one blessing for his parents, to know their son's death was accidental and not suicidal; that's if there is any blessing in losing a son. The writing of such news for her mother-in-law was something she had avoided in the past few days. Her thoughts turned to James. Not even Lindsay had heard from him since his departure. She had no idea of where or how to inform him of the death of his second brother.

From his seat at the kitchen table, Mr. Chiswell looked up. His grey eyes were kind as he asked, "Shauna, why don't you sit down here at the table? Mark's Last Will and Testament mostly concerns you and there will be papers to sign after it has been read."

"Thank you, Mr. Chiswell, but I don't think I can bear to sit still at the moment. I can hear quite well from here."

Shauna marvelled at how this man could change his appearance. When they first met on their arrival at the Townsville docks over six years ago, the man was in his business suit and didn't give the appearance of knowing what a farm looked like. On the few occasions he'd visited Uncle Michael at Emerald Flats, he always turned up in clothes, not unlike those Uncle Michael wore, with a worn pair of boots and a sagging grey hat to match. When Uncle Michael and Mr. Chiswell were not yarning on the front verandah of the hut, they were out wandering around the sheds or riding out to check the cattle. One might easily believe they were brothers or at least best mates, rather than a solicitor and his client.

With the breakfast dishes cleared away and her mother and Maggie gone in the buggy with Lindsay to visit Paddymac and his family, Uncle Michael, Shamus, and Shauna prepared themselves to hear the reading of the will. Her uncle and father were executors of the will; Mr. Chiswell had explained to Shauna. Mark made the will before joining up. At that time, Mark's brothers had already left for the war. No one knew who'd return from the front and who would not.

All told, the reading was brief and to the point. Everything Mark owned was left to his wife, Shauna. This included a sum of money received annually under the will of his grandfather. A similar bequest from the grandfather went to all the brothers, explained the solicitor. The second item was the bank account in Townsville in which the above bequest and Mark's army pay had been deposited. At this point, Shauna learned Mark owned the farm which the MacGregors had previously owned.

"But when did that happen? How did that happen? Mark was still in the Middle East?" She was at a loss to understand.

Shamus stood up and walked to her side. He rested his roughened hand on her shoulder.

"Shauna, before Mark went away to war, he gave me instructions to keep an eye out for a block of land for him to buy. He desperately wanted to make a go of farming himself. He insisted it must be somewhere nearby so you and your children would be close to your family. When Mr. MacGregor had the tree fall on him, it was not hard to see he would never be able to manage a developed farm let alone have the physical capabilities required to start from scratch. I wrote and let Mark know of the situation. He told me to contact Mr. Chiswell. He had Mark's instruction to purchase land on his behalf if a suitable property came on the market. We were all sworn to secrecy. He wanted to tell you himself but when he returned in such a terrible state, we did not know quite what to do."

Guilt slithered in her belly. So, Mark hadn't been trying to separate her from her family as she had suspected. She'd been wrong. He wanted to be an independent man – a man's man. How had she wronged him so badly? Tears swam in her eyes. She stood biting her bottom lip.

"Oh," was all she could manage at first. The men remained silent as she absorbed what she had just learnt. "What am I to do with it now?"

Mr. Chiswell gave a soft cough. "I think, Shauna, it might be prudent not to make any decisions for the next few months. The land has been there a long time it will still be there in six months or longer if need be."

Uncle Michael was the next with a suggestion. "Shauna, as you know, we planted the small area Mr. MacGregor had managed to clear before his accident in an attempt to provide an income for his family. In the meantime, until you decide what you want to do, we can continue to incorporate that area into our cane farming businesses under Paddymac's supervision, if you wish. Any profits received will go into your funds for Maggie and the little one to come."

The red curls bounced as she gave a silent nod of her head.

Shauna sat at the small table on the verandah where Mark had taken his meals after his return from the war. A writing tablet lay in front of her along with the ink and a pen with a new nib. Her supple fingers rolled a pencil back and forth as she sat in thought. How was she going to write this letter to her mother-in-law whom she had never met? Previous letters had never proven so difficult as there were always farm activities to fill the pages. How do you tell a mother, her son is dead? How does a mother cope with losing not one but two sons within a year? Sons, whom she thought had made it safely home from the war.

She took up the cloth beside her and wiped the perspiration running down her face and neck. The humid summer weather was a particular challenge to a pregnant woman in North Queensland. Silence sat heavily upon the house. Her mother had taken Maggie to visit the Wong family at the market gardens. Old Mrs. Wong had been poorly of late. They went to deliver a pot of beef broth for the invalid. Maggie had carried a picture of her horse tucked under her arm. Uncle Michael and her father were attending farm business over at Paddymac's place. Even the stock in the house paddock were unusually quiet as if respecting the difficult task in front of her.

Shauna wrote a few words in pencil and as the frown appeared on her brow, she scratched out her first attempt. Her mind shifted. Maybe if she had a photo of Mrs. McIvor in front of her, she might find it easier to write to the woman. Awkwardly, Shauna stood up holding her swollen tummy. She walked over to lift the small wooden box off the shelf near Mark's bed; a bed stripped of its coverings with only the mattress ticking in place. She sat on the bed and opened the lid. Inside were the few photos he had of his family. The clearest one was a group portrait. The two girls sat on either side of the parents with the five boys, tall behind them. Mark, William and James side by side as usual. They looked so young; the war changed that. Amongst the photos, Shauna found a sealed envelope with JAMES McIVOR printed on the front in Mark's unsteady handwriting of his last months. She lifted it to her face. The smell of sour sweat still lay in the paper. Her finger traced the letters of the name.

"How am I supposed to deliver this?" She asked herself. "Not even the solicitor knows his address." She tucked the envelope back with the photos before she was tempted to read the contents.

Shauna's fingers sifted through Mark's other documents which had lived in the box since he had returned home. She stopped. A look of puzzlement darkened her eyes. Where was the small leather sachet with the fine plaited hair-ring his mother had made for him? Shauna had worn it when she married Mark on the ship. They did not have a gold band until they were able to purchase one in Townsville. Where could the hair-ring be? Mark had carried it in his top pocket for the duration of the war. She had assumed it would have been kept with his other important trinkets. Where else would he have kept it? For a moment she contemplated the thought it may have been with him when he was killed but she tossed that idea aside. Uncle Michael said Mark had nothing with him except the shirt, trousers and boots he went out in. The frown returned. Supporting her back she again rose to walk into her bedroom. From the top drawer of her bedside table, she took out her jewellery box. The one given to her by her grandmother when she was ten years of age. Sitting at the very top of her treasures sat the leather sachet holding the hair-ring. Mark must have left it there for her to find and treasure for Maggie.

The tears began to fall. They threatened never to stop falling. Shauna stumbled back onto her bed and sat heavily. Sobs wracked her body. She lay on her side curling her legs up as if to protect herself and the unborn child. The flutter of the baby's kick rippled her fingers as she stroked her abdomen with one hand while the other held the sachet close to her heart. Choking sobs deepened; her sides ached. The pillow under her head became saturated. Gradually sleep suffocated the tears and sweet darkness swept over her. A deep sleep; something she had not experienced in a long time.

It was the following day before she once again sat to write the letter. It flowed from her heart with ease.

There was only one more official thing she had left to do, but it could not be done. She really should write to James and notify him of his brother's death, but as Mr. Chiswell, the solicitor explained, even he had no mailing address for Mark's brother. Any mail for James was addressed care-of Mr. Chiswell. In her innermost heart, Shauna knew she felt relief at being excused from this task which could have proven to be more difficult than writing to Mrs. McIvor. James McIvor's face had a way of sneaking into her head when she least expected it. The vision raised her heartrate until her hands trembled. As much as she wanted to see James or hear his voice or see his sparkling eyes, she knew she could not. It would not be right.

Shauna was determined that today, twelve months and ten days after Mark's death, Maggie was going to have a wonderful sixth birthday. His passing was not going to dictate the flavour of her birthdays for the remainder of her life. Instead, today's celebration was going to do that.

With Shamus's help, she harnessed Old Master into the dray. Shamus loaded the three large baskets of treats Mary had packed ready for them to go.

"How many people are you expecting, woman? There's enough here to feed an army. How long will it be before Lindsay gets home from College? We need his muscles here."

For his troubles, Mary slapped another folded tablecloth on the top of the last basket. She wore a grin. "Come on, old man. A party's what you need."

Maggie, with her grandfather's help, guided Old Master's reins while Mary sat on a cushion in the back with her ten-month-old grandson, Little Mark, in his basket beside her. Shauna and Uncle Michael rode two black horses on either side of the procession.

"Don't forget to stop at Paddymac's place, Granpa," Maggie's eyes never left the reins and the horse's ears as she delivered instructions to Shamus. "They're coming to my birthday party too." She leant in close to her grandfather. "I hope the two babies don't keep bawling. Pat and I hate bawling babies. We're not having any babies when we grow old."

Surprise filled Shamus's face. He turned to his wife. "Did you hear that, woman?" His eyes twinkled. "Pat and Maggie aren't having babies when they grow old. Babies bawl too much."

"A wise pair." Mary winked at her husband.

Shauna took a pull on the reins as the group approached the lagoon on the farmland she now owned. Some land was under cane crops and much still to be cleared of its timber.

"Uncle Michael, you mentioned we've two farmhands staying in the hut now."

"Yes, Shauna, a couple of Englishmen looking to buy a place of their own. They're glad to have the work here while they search."

Paddymac spoke up. "They seem fine fellows, Shauna, good workers."

"Thanks, Paddymac." She opened the gate into the area in which several steers grazed. "I hope these are quiet steers, Paddymac. They won't bother the children, will they?"

"Like lambs, girl," Shamus answered the question. "Now, come on everyone, we've instructions to party here this afternoon."

Shauna and Michael laughed and moved their horses forward looking for a suitable picnic spot.

Twenty-One

Slaying the Demons

Dust exploded in clouds from under the pounding hooves. The crack of low branches and crunch of dry leaves foreshadowed the direction of the runaway beast as it forged a path through the trees. The bay horse, with the rider lying low along its neck, was never far behind the bullock's heels. The bullock, they called "The Runner." This was James's third cattle run from the Kimberley district to the Wyndham meatworks. On every trip, there was at least one "Runner" in the mob that took it into its head to break-away and run as far and as fast as it could. The stockmen usually took delight in egging on their peers as they brought the errant beast or beasts to heel. By the last days of each journey, the cattle, the horses and the riders were happy to just amble along without rebellion.

Every time James was the rider hell-bent on turning the latest beast, he silently thanked Michael Doolan for this brilliant stock horse, he had named Mick and for the intelligent blue dog now called Billy. Both animals appeared to read his mind obeying commands not consciously yet given.

On this day, when he coaxed the steer back to the herd, James's thoughts broke free themselves. His mind hooked into the recent conversation between himself and old Mrs. Rogers at the boarding house, where he stayed when in the town. He liked Mrs. Rogers.

She was a good old stick who kept a clean establishment and provided edible food, which could not be said for every eating house in town. Her conversations never failed to hold his attention. She could speak on any subject with insight. They had sat on the verandah listening to the cicadas and frogs filling the air with their chorus. She told him he was running. Mrs. Rogers had said it was time to stop and face his demons. Nothing good ever come out of running.

Was he running? Maybe he was not unlike the runners found in every herd. She told of her husband who fought in the Crimea war. He wanted to run away from himself. His wounds outside healed but it was years before the wounds inside began to heal and that didn't happen until he talked them out. He was the reason she ended up at Wyndham. This was as far as he got when he died of the fevers.

With his neckerchief pulled up over his nose and his eyes almost shut against the choking dust, James pondered their conversation once more. She was probably right. He was a runner too; running away as fast and as far as he could go. Once he had completed the necessary family duties after his brother William's death, he had turned his head west. He barely stopped until he hit Broome. Along the way, he found casual work where he could to provide for himself and his loyal companions, Mick the horse and Billy the dog.

Christmas 1919 he spent three months shepherding sheep around the Julia Creek area before moving on to Cloncurry. Short-term work as a stock-hand helping with the muster and branding of calves, brought in a few pounds before the haul on to Katherine in the Northern Territory. He was tempted to avoid Darwin, having heard of the union trouble going on up there at the time but it seemed a shame not to have a look at the place. Where did he have to be anyway? Who would have thought working as a deckhand on a fishing boat could have been so exciting? When they weren't fighting the nets or the contents of the nets including several very large sharks and an angry crocodile, they were fighting the rough seas and tides.

A shiver ran down his body as he recalled his attempt at fossicking for gold at Halls Creek. He nearly buried himself out there when he slipped into a partially collapsed mine.

James relived those mixed feelings of accomplishment at reaching the west coast of Australia which had been something William, Mark, and he had talked about before leaving the old country.

In sorrow at their absence, his eyes teared up mixing with the dust. He rubbed them away with his neckerchief.

Broome, a cosmopolitan town of shanty dwellings, numerous languages, heat, humidity, and flies, alongside blue seas and a flotilla of pearling boats, had captured his imagination. A town with an intriguing and frightening underbelly of human contradictions. The suffocating humidity sent him on his way to explore the signpost he'd bypassed earlier. TO WYNDHAM, it said.

James felt unsure of what exactly his demons were. Or if, in fact, he was running. He struggled to analyse what was hidden deep inside his mind, just as Mrs. Rogers had instructed. Regret at the parting of ways with Mark tore at his soul. That was October 1919 and here it was February 1923 and still, the hurt festered. Mark, William, and himself had been inseparable when growing up. They'd argued then too. A twisted smile broke his dusty face as the vision of his mother, with her straw broom, shuffling them outside to have their squabbles, played inside his head. But always, by nightfall, peace reigned once more. Now, here he was bearing a grudge for over three years. To be fair, Mark had a lot going against him at the time with the horrendous physical wounds and mental trauma gifted to him from the war. His brother was unwell at the time. Guilt filled James's body along with the thirst for water after a long day in the saddle. No doubt, by now Mark will have healed physically and maybe healed mentally as well.

His brother would have no idea how to contact him to let him know the latest news. Nobody knew where he was. James reached over and patted the horse's neck.

"What do you think, Mick? Time to head back east?"

The horse lifted its sagging head, twitched his ears and snickered. Not to be left out of the discussion, Billy yapped excitedly like a young pup.

Again, James looked inwards, which is an easy thing to do when rocking in a saddle. He knew full well what or who the other demon was. She tortured his every night's sleep. The demon of knowing the only woman he had ever loved was married to his brother, Mark. The only woman he could ever love. His thoughts were of her sea-green eyes, flaming hair and the smile which lit her face up like a ray of spring sunshine. Inside his grubby shirt, his heart pounded not only with love but fear. His greatest fear was not knowing if he could hide his feelings from her and the world.

The Wyndham meatworks appeared through the dust of the bellowing stock. The end of another trip. Perhaps his last cattle drive through the Kimberley.

With the slam of the gates behind the last beast, James slid from the saddle and rested his head against the horse's mane. It was up to him to be the bigger man. He must go and make peace with his brother, Mark. Billy sat at his heels dripping with water from the waterhole. Faithful eyes watched his master's every move as his ribcage dragged in the air. A lolling tongue drooled saliva into the dust. Mick tossed his head impatient to be rid of the saddle so he might roll in the water also.

The light breeze tempered the heat of the sun caressing the familiar lands of the Lower Burdekin district. The man's relaxed body as it swayed with the gait of the horse did little to reveal the turmoil within. With only thirty yards left before he arrived at the house-compound-gate on Emerald Flats, he needed to decide whether he really wanted another confrontation with his brother or should he turn around and leave.

Guilt drove him onwards. He was as much to blame as Mark for the disastrous outcome of their last meeting. He should have been more understanding of the wounded man, a man in constant pain, a man like so many who had seen too much of things no man should have to see. How did he expect Mark to react when told of William's death; a death for which James blamed himself anyway. If only they had chosen not to dawdle about on that wharf. If only they hadn't been there at that time. If only … He hoped he might feel better if he, at least, made an effort at reconciliation. Maybe this might help Mark also.

Dust from the horse's hooves drifted off to the west as he came to a halt at the gate. James looked up in surprise to see a young bairn standing watching him in silence. The dusty face of the red-haired child held a solemn expression reserved for a court judge.

"Hello, young fellow. What's your name?"

"I's Mark McIvor. Are you my Dad?"

It was James's turn to stare in silence. Having no experience with children and certainly not with any just out of nappies, James fished around inside his head for an answer.

"How old are you, Mark?"

"I's nearly three. You're big. How old are you?"

"I don't know. I can't count that far."

"I'll count for you. I can count all the chooks."

When Billy, the blue dog, approached the child, James gave a soft warning.

"Easy, Billy."

Without fear, the child reached over to pat the dog. "I got dogs like you, too." He looked up at James. "Is that its name, Mister, Billy?"

A smile teased James's lip as he nodded the affirmative. "So, Mark. Where's your Dad, then?"

"He's dead. Mum said he went to Heaven. I say my prayers every night and ask God to send him back here."

The earlier hint of a smile disappeared in a face of shock and anguish. Dead; that can't be right. James looked over towards the big house. His heart stopped. He recognized her even from this distance – her flaming hair and swinging stride unusual in one so short. He swung his leg over the horse's rump and dismounted. The churning of his stomach and trembling of his hands threatened to betray him as she approached. His heart performed somersaults when a smile lit up her face.

"James? James McIvor?"

"Hello, Shauna, you're looking well."

"Oh, James, has your mother been able to contact you, then? I'd no idea where you'd gone. I wrote to your mother with the news of Mark's passing, hoping she could get word to you."

"No, Shauna, I've only just learnt. I'm so sorry. I hope I'm not intruding. I came in the hope of a reconciliation with Mark after that last encounter we had."

James felt unable to draw a breath. His mouth felt as dry as a cup of desert sand.

Shauna walked over and opened the gate.

"Come on in, James. It's lovely to see you but I'm sorry to be the bearer of such sad news." She swung the gate back while James led his horse into the house compound. "Will you join us for afternoon tea?"

With Shauna standing so close as he unsaddled his horse in the shed, James's hands fumbled. He nearly choked on the stricture in his throat. His voice was hoarse when he spoke.

"Where's your daughter; Maggie, wasn't it? She looked the spitting image of my sister when we were kids."

"She's with her grandmother visiting friends next door. Maggie has found her father's death very hard to come to terms with. They say children forget easily but Maggie has it in her head it must be her fault Mark died. It breaks my heart sometimes."

James so much wanted to hold her close and take her pain away. "Shauna, please, can I help?"

Her watery smile broke his heart. "Come, James, I think a cup of tea is what we need."

The plate held the last scone. The dregs were cold at the bottom of the pannikin. The tale of his adventures had come to an end. They looked directly into each other's eyes for the first time since sitting at the table. James struggled to breathe. Shauna's pink lips were partially open as if straining to breathe herself. Murmurs and rustling from Little Mark and the dog, Billy, making friends outside the kitchen door were only a whisper in the background.

James started when Shauna jumped up, nearly dragging the table cloth with her. Her trembling hands fussed with the material for a moment. She stuttered when she tried to explain.

"J-J-James, I-I just remembered. There's a letter here amongst Mark's things. I found it sealed in an envelope with your name on the front. I'd no idea where I should send it." Her feet almost ran through the doorway. A cursory glance ensured her son was not up to mischief.

Both their hands trembled as the message was delivered to its owner. James turned the envelope over and over in his fingers as if afraid of its contents. Mrs. Roger's voice sounded in his head. *James, you have to face your demons.* He removed the penknife from its holder on his belt before unsealing the letter with a single swipe. Again, he paused, unsure if he wanted to know the contents. With a firm hand, he removed the letter and unfolded the pages.

November 1ˢᵗ. 1919

My dear brother, James,

Not for the first time in our lives, I owe you an apology for my short temper and my runaway mouth. This time the regret I feel is deeper than ever. My words were cruel and unnecessary. I know I'm not too long for this world. I feel it every day as my body fails me bit by bit. You've no idea how much I wish I'd been killed outright rather than rotting away inside my head.

The incessant pain is driving me insane. I find this every day when I'm doing things, I don't even know I'm doing. My greatest fear is how I'm hurting those I love the most. I include you in that number, Brother. I must take control of my life before I'm too far gone to do so. Forgive me.

When I'm gone and the mourning is over there's another thing I must mention. I'm not blind and I know how you felt about Shauna when we first met her on the ship. I don't hold this against you, James. How could I not understand how easy she is to love. I admire the fact you didn't intrude in our relationship and thank you for not doing so. I'm not sure I would've won her heart if you had made your feelings known to her. I saw the occasional looks she cast your way. But she's an honourable woman. Since the day we made our vows I know she's never betrayed me in any way. I so much want to ensure you and Shauna and my babies have a good life after I'm gone. If the opportunity does arise please don't feel you can't make your feelings known to Shauna. Your union if it should occur would be blessed by me.

Send my love to our parents. Thank you for being a brother to be proud of.

Have a good life.

Mark.

James sat in silence. The dishes in the sink stilled. Shauna turned to face her brother-in-law. His eyes watched her intently. Curiosity filled her every pore.

"Come and sit down, Shauna. I think you need to read this letter too."

Her heart rolled over. What further bad news was awaiting her?

As if reading her mind, James rose and took her hand. "Please, sit down, Shauna. You really should read this."

EPILOGUE

A rare day indeed; they were completely alone at last. He took her hand and led her to the bedroom. At the doorway, he pulled her close. The kisses began as soft as a butterflies' touch before deepening, lengthening. Their bodies melted together. They shuffled into the room.

"Shauna, are you sure about this?"

"James, I've never been more sure of anything." She reached up to undo the buttons on his shirt. Slowly she eased it over his arms and shoulders. He leaned in closer.

In return, James turned her gently to reach the three buttons behind her neck. She pirouetted back, lifting her arms as she did so. The blouse fell to the floor. His waiting hands cupped her breasts. He kissed each one before returning to those lips he had dreamt about for all those years. It was Shauna who removed her skirt before reaching to undo the buttons on James's trousers. His garments joined hers on the floor. Her lace-edged panties drifted silently on to the heap.

James gasped. Shauna's lips curved in a soft smile. He lifted her in his arms and lay her on the bed. He rested alongside her with his head propped up on one elbow. He swam in the depths of her eyes. She opened her mouth to speak but he kissed his forefinger and lay it softly over her full lips.

"Hush, my darling."

The finger traced a line down to her left breast. As it moved in a slow circle around her dark nipple Shauna's sharp intake of breath induced a soft moan from deep inside him. His finger moved on to tease her second nipple. Shauna's moan joined that of James. The finger edged gently towards her navel while his lips caressed her nipples.

Shauna went to speak, but his lips on hers begged silence. Pent up emotion and desire threatened his control. He groaned as his lips swept downwards again.

"James, please, please, take me; take me now."

"Hush, my darling; good things come to those who wait."

Shauna giggled. "Oh, James, I cannot wait a moment longer for you."

He paused.

"Oh, please, don't stop."

THE END